KARRANA

Anne Skyvington

Aerus Publishing
Sydney
2019

Cover Design by Kate Onslow

The vast green canopy in the Valley of
Karrana propagates its lushness forwards
towards the far off
horizon of
resolution

Part One

Chapter 1

Bridie slid into her wine red satin dress with the rose pink sash. She pushed her toes into shoes, which added three inches to the five foot four nature had given her. Posing as she'd seen the stars at the movies do, she looked at her figure from all angles. Perfect. She sat at the dressing table and painted her lips bright red. Pursing her mouth for full effect, she fluttered her long curled eyelashes at her image in the mirror. The eyebrows needed reshaping one more time. She fiddled with the bobby pins that fastened the roll at the crown. Lovely.

Half closing her eyes to capture what someone else would see, she stood up, pulled her tummy in and poked out her sharp pointed breasts. She tossed her dark brown hair, watching it cascade around her shoulders, like Vivien Leigh or one of the other Hollywood stars.

Johnny will say that I look like a million dollars. This was the opposite message that her mother, Eliza O'Toole, plump and pot-bellied in middle age, had tried to plant in her mind: 'He wouldn't want you, too good for us,' she'd said of one of the town's well-to-do bachelors.

Bridie knew better. She couldn't properly put it into words. She'd heard the saying 'uncouth'. Maybe, a *couth* man … someone with manners *and* good looks. Someone to take her away from all this. She intended to use her own advantages to the fullest.

'Mumma, how do I look?' Bridie did a twirl for her mother, sweating at the wood stove in the kitchen.

'Not bad, though I say so myself,' Mumma said, looking up and wiping her forehead, 'seeing as I ran it up on the old Singer.'

'Yeah, thanks Mumma, don't stay up for us, will you?'

'Just you make sure an' come straight home with Ned and Johnny. Don't want any goings-on in back lanes afterwards.'

'You know, Mumma, I'm not a child anymore.'

'You'll do as I say while you're under my roof,' her mother, red-faced from the heat in the kitchen, sighed, 'and have a bite to eat with your brothers, before you go out.'

'I'm not hungry, Mumma,' Bridie called out as she turned toward the verandah. Voices and static assailed her senses through the thin walls of the house. 'I'll have some bread-and-butter, when I get back.'

The noise was coming from the dining room, a dark interior space where the brothers listened to the races, leaning on the mantelpiece ledge. Johnny and Billy who were a bit deaf glued themselves to the Bakelite wireless to hear the caller chanting like a maniac at the race meeting.

Bridie perched herself prettily on the back verandah railing and watched the sun dipping, a voluptuous ball, into the mountains. *Please don't let it rain tonight, not tonight of all nights*.

The War had ended and she was determined to enjoy herself at the victory dance tonight.

She glanced back at the grey clouds looming up from the north and spreading their menace over the tin roof. Was bad weather brewing out west? High up on the peaks large dark birds circled. Swifts, a sign of real crook weather to come.

Storms sometimes shook the old farmhouse, sending Bridie screaming along the unsealed track to the neighbours' more solid dwelling on the banks of the Karrana River.

Returning her thoughtful gaze towards the far horizon, she whispered *infinity*, that the nuns at the convent had talked about, as the hills gobbled up the last rays of the sun.

One part of her loved the farm and nature with a passion. She'd always carry the country with her. It was in her veins.

Her other side was a headstrong filly that wanted to get away. Always two sides. *Was everyone like that? Two sides to them?*

Now she had to endure the outside lavatory before it turned pitch black. She shuddered as she tiptoed along the grassy path, recoiling at the thought of the black widow spiders called *red backs* that hid in the wood heap out the back. Huge green tree frogs, throbbing in high up crevices of the lavatory, blinked down at her with yellow eyes.

Back on the safe hub of the verandah, she picked up snippets from Chifley's speech about the war ending: Soldiers, many wounded, and prisoners of war coming home. Who were these Jewish camp survivors she heard so much about? If only she'd been allowed to stay at the convent longer, maybe then she'd understand things better. The future looked brighter, though, that was for sure, the war taking a bit longer to peter out down here in the Pacific.

She wondered if her two missing brothers would be amongst the returning soldiers.

Irresistibly, the image of young men vying for her attention intervened. American soldiers and sailors with their snappy uniforms and polite manners.

'You're a good-looker, Princess Bridie,' Cyclone Johnny said back in the kitchen.

In spite of herself, the syllables that slid from her brother's tongue sent waves of pleasure throughout her body. He'd been saying this to her since she was an infant, the first girl born after five sons. She hardly understood the words at first, until one day her mother caught her looking into a mirror, saying, *Yes, I have a pretty face.* This became part of family folklore. Humour, inherited in the family, was often at the expense of the target.

Johnny had an announcement to make.

'I won the race again today, this time pitched against Will Featherstone. He's pretty fast too. From the north side. Old man's loaded.'

'You're a real champ, Johnny,' Bridie said, smiling at him, 'All the girls'll be throwing themselves at you, I bet.'

'Sure thing, Bride, wouldn't miss it for the world.'

Johnny, with his star status as a champion cyclist, fancied himself as a bit of a ladies' man with his playboy looks. He was wiry and handsome, his brown hair sculpted into waves with the aid of Brylcream.

He took Bridie into the men's dressing room and showed her earrings from one of his recent flings. He kept them as trophies on the mantelpiece of the darkened room the brothers shared.

'Johnny, that's awful,' shrilled Bridie, 'I'd hate a man to do that to me.'

Her eyes flashed as she faced him now. 'You're disgusting when it comes to women. Dadda used to call you *black sheep* and *loafer*, said you didn't know the meaning of a hard day's work. I stuck up for you then, but now I think I agree with him.'

Her voice, rising in anger, dropped, as Johnny hung his head. 'Trouble is, you're nothing when you're not behind the bars of a racing bike.'

'Don't worry, we'll take you along to the dance, Bridie. Introduce you to some of the lads.'

'Mumma will only let me go if I'm with you and Ned. She's so old fashioned. I'm nearly eighteen, for God's sake.'

She'd managed, when she'd stayed over at Stella's house, to go out with town boys. The good-looking ones were often vain and boring show-offs. She'd found it easy to slap fumbling hands from straying into unwanted territory in the dark.

Town boys, they're only after one thing, Bridie. You be careful, Mumma's voice would ring in her ears.

'We'll look after you, Bridie. What's the word? Chaperones, isn't it?'

Johnny grinned at her.

Ned tooted the horn out the front and they ran out together. Bridie jumped in the back seat and let Johnny sit next to his brother at the wheel of the navy Pontiac. Mumma's parents' legacy had provided the family with this shiny dark car, but that's as far as the money stretched.

Like a needle stuck in the groove of a record, Bridie's mind went now to the dreariness of the dairy farm. It went there often, especially since Dadda's passing. The shabby farmhouse signalled the rut her family was stuck in. If only one of the five brothers could have used his head to do something more with the hundred acres.

Mumma, with Ned's help, was only just making ends meet, spending every penny they earned from the small herd of milkers.

She looked over at poor Johnny, and thought of him amid the blood and guts at the local abattoirs each week day.

The car bumped over the potholed dirt track that led to the sealed road towards the township of Karrana. She'd like to belong to the well-heeled northern side that she glimpsed as they passed by, driving north out of town.

She thought of Billy and his shyness that kept him away from dances. When he talked, the words jostled over one another in a jumbled mess, as if in a race to get out.

'Pity Billy's not here,' she murmured. 'He's good-looking enough to attract some nice girl when he gets dressed up.'

'Argh, Billy's better off at home,' growled Ned, 'no girl will have him, the way he can't get his words out. Embarrassing, is what it is.'

'Don't be too hard on him, Ned,' shouted Johnny, 'you've got a bit of a stammer yourself when you get worked up. Yeah, Bridie's right, he should'ev come.'

'Wonder who will want to take me home this time,' said Bridie.

'You're comin' home with us,' said Ned, pulling up on the grass below the dance hall. 'I've promised Mumma, and that's the end of it.'

'I know, I know... all I'm saying is Paddy Maloney wanted to, last time, that's all I'm saying,' said Bridie, screwing up her face at the thought of those calloused hands on her waist and his cocky, stuck-up looks.

They'd pulled up as the rousing strains of *We'll Meet Again* reverberated down the slope. Bridie felt tears prickling her eyes as she walked in. Everyone stood stock still on the dance floor, patriotic mouths putting words to the music played by the home grown band at the front. Dressed in royal blue and white with khaki pants and slouch hats, the popular *SkyLights* were intent on warming the crowd up with nostalgic songs first. A funny mixture, Bridie thought, noting their uniform.

The dance hall was done up with allied flags and tricoloured rosettes. Blue irises and hydrangeas symbolised victory alongside red gladioli. Was blood included in the symbol? There was a large sign hanging above the doorway with 'Victory in the Pacific' splashed across it in black letters. Stars-n-Stripes, Union Jacks and Australian flags stood bunched up in vases like tricoloured flowers. Streamers in red, white and blue hung from the ceiling.

A few men stood erect in uniform, proudly displaying wings or other insignia on their shoulders. The band was now playing *Bless Em All*. People clapped and cheered, as partners entered the dance floor.

Johnny danced with her first. A bit jerky, but fun nevertheless. Then Ned, in grey striped trousers and a white shirt, waltzed her around the hall. He looked good when he dressed up. No one would guess he was a farmer.

She'd seen the big man, towering over most of the other men at the dance, as she'd entered the hall. He'd spotted her coming in too. It was hard not to notice him. Different from most of the cow cockies around the place. He'd watched her partnering Johnny, followed them with his gaze as they danced the first waltz together.

Don't Sit Under the Apple Tree was up next. Not exactly easy to jitterbug to, but fitting, a real tearjerker.

She had no time to accept or to refuse the next invitation. The tall stranger swept her up in strong arms and guided her around the dance floor with confident strides.

In the red calf length dress, tight belted at the waist, and raised up on stiletto heels, she knew she was the belle of the ball, her dark hair twirling, as she danced around the hall with this stranger. He made her feel oddly like Cinderella before the fairy godmother got to her. It wasn't shyness, so much as a sudden dread, that made her withdraw a little from this upright man.

Bridie stole a glimpse at his shiny face. He was good-looking. Sculpted features. A russet tinge to thick dark hair. His eyes shone.

Was it his heart she could feel beating against her breast. Or was it her own? She looked up into warm hazel eyes that were looking down at hers. *Lit up with a tiny spark and ... those lips....* She couldn't take her eyes off his mouth.

Boys had tried to kiss her before, down behind the stables at pony camps. Freckled face sons of dairy farmers.

She was proud that she'd resisted their clumsy attempts. He was different. So different from her loudmouthed brothers, too.

She felt that she had seen him somewhere, had known him.

He wheeled her around the farthest edges of the floor towards the door. 'Let's go outside,' he whispered into her ear.

'I can't,' she whispered back, 'no, please, I want to dance.'

Gently he pulled her out through the door into the darkness at the back of the hall. Once outside, on the verandah overlooking the river, he grabbed her in a fierce embrace and crushed his lips against her wet ones.

'My brothers,' she stammered, savouring the touch of his mouth, dry and salty, and secretly wanting more. She pulled away from him, 'my brothers will be after me. I don't even know your name.'

'It's Will Featherstone, Bridie O'Toole. I know you.'

'H-how?' she stammered. 'Where from?'

There was something about the intelligent bearing of the man. Something manly and gentle all at the same time. And yet, he had no right....

Johnny came out and joined them.

'This is my ... brother, Johnny,' Bridie shook a little as she tried to say names. 'Will Feather....'

'I know, Bridie, Will's my cycling mate,' laughed Johnny.

'Cyclone Johnny,' said Will, shaking his hand with vigour. As if he and Bridie had not, a few minutes earlier, been locked together like one.

9

Bridie blushed as she turned her wide pools of eyes, fringed with dark lashes, towards Will.

'Is that how you knew who I was?'

'I've seen you for a long time, Bridie. I think … as if… always. You went to the convent, didn't you?'

'Yes, that's right. How did you know?' Bridie exclaimed.

'I go to the cycling tracks near there.' He seemed to be drawing up a memory from somewhere deep. 'Saw you once wearing a navy beret. Just outside the convent. You had a fringe.'

'Gee,' Bridie gasped, 'I must have been in third grade! H-how could you remember?'

'You were wearing a pleated tunic, white blouse, and a beret perched on your head.'

'That sounds like me,' she said. 'How could you remember, after seeing me just that once?'

'Couldn't take my eyes off you, even then. A teenager, you must have been, same as me.'

She blushed with pleasure.

'Where did you go to school, Will?'

'Karrana Public. Then to the high school.'

'You're from the north side, then?'

'Yes, I live in Riverdale,' indicating with his hand, 'directly opposite your farm.'

'Lucky you, Will Featherstone … that's where I'd like to live.'

Will smiled a private smile and pulled her close, once again. 'I've heard a lot about Hilltop.'

'Another dance?' She relaxed as he swept her up in his muscly arms, an imperceptible scent infusing their bodies like that from a perfumed flowering vine.

No man managed to come between Bridie and Will, as they danced every number together. While they danced, and in between dances, they spoke about the war and how it had affected their families.

How on the dairy farm, she'd felt safe from the conflict. How she'd known that the war would never come to Hilltop. How she just knew certain things in her heart, a bit like how the cows knew when it was time to come back for milking. It had touched them, sure, like her favourite brother Charles, wounded and lingering in a military hospital somewhere. The other one Shaun, lost in action.

'Mumma's made Ned take over the role of father,' she said, 'watches me like a hawk. Dadda was a lot easier, let me do whatever I wanted.'

Will had the look of a horse wanting to bolt when he talked about his family. He'd been exempt from the war, working for his father.

She liked listening to his voice, to the way he spoke.

'Do you realise,' he said, pointing down through the gum trees, 'that this is the same deep river that runs between our two places?'

Fragrant eucalyptus smells wafted through the cool night air. Bridie looked at his strong features, prominent forehead and mane like hair. He seemed to be bursting with an uncontrollable energy.

She nodded, 'Yes, I love the river, my friend Stella and I swim the horses in the shallows, when they get hot and sweaty after a long gallop.'

'You must be a good rider,' he said, 'living on a farm.'

She nodded. After all, it was all there was to do for fun, if you lived in the bush.

'Can I drive you home tonight and we'll talk some more?'

'I can't,' she said, 'they're strict with me at home. Won't be allowed out again, you know.'

'Well, I want to see you again,' Will said, his voice urgent.

Bridie blushed with pleasure.

Her feet, tapping in time with the lilting melodies of *Over the Rainbow*, she took Will by both hands. She pulled him towards the middle of the hall.

Her heart was already dancing, her mind soaring with the high notes, following where the ballad led.

She wanted time to stop right there and then, the moment to go on forever. Up, up, and up into the ether.

'See you at the race track, Will,' Johnny said as he came up and winked.

Ned followed and bawled out, 'Time to go home, Bridie.'

He grabbed her by the arm, yanking her out of Will's gentle hold, and pulled her across the hall to the front door.

She tried to push Ned away, her face turning as red as the hydrangeas in the vases.

Caught up in the dancing throng, Ned shoved her out the door.

'Stop it, Ned,' she screamed. 'I haven't said goodbye....'

'Gotta get up early for the milking,' he grumbled.

She hated her brother at that moment.

Will followed, keeping his eyes on Bridie's back.

She looked behind her, fearful of losing sight of him.

Outside, they stood facing one another in the dark.

'Can you give me your phone number?' he asked.

She sensed a river of distance between them.

'Yes. Don't be surprised if Mumma is rude on the phone.'

Ned revved the car engine.

Will put the paper with her telephone number scribbled on it in his pocket. He stepped closer to her and pulled her towards him. He gave her a peck on the cheek that was so sweet she longed for more. He opened the door for her to get in the back seat alone.

Will stood like a granite statue, as she looked through the window. He'd raised his hand like a soldier saluting.

The car sped off into the darkness.

Chapter 2

She woke up early the next morning from a luminous dream. Lilting bird sounds rose and fell just outside the window. It was nearly *darling springtime*, after all. Seasons, with their humid gifts of abundance, were premature here on the north coast. The 'trumpet vine', already wrapping the barn outside, shocked visitors with its fiery orange boldness.

Sitting up, she parted the muslin curtains to let in the first shy rays of sun from the north. Was it the same light shining through the windows that would beckon him to life?

She lay back, yawning and luxuriating in the warmth, half awake, trying to remember the forgotten dream.

She sensed him, in those first, half-dazed moments between sleep and waking, coming to her. They were locked in an embrace and a kiss so full of passion, it blotted out everything that had gone before. Was it real, or was she asleep and dreaming? She wasn't sure. She only knew that her being was opening up like an oyster shell, revealing a perfect pearl shining within, inviting her to savour it.

You just know, someone had said about love.

She imagined him still slumbering deeply in his parents' cottage. His barrelled chest rose and fell in time with a dream. He breathed in the fragrant air, coming on a breeze from the Karrana River that flowed between their two places.

Perhaps he'd already be thinking about how he could ask her out. But what would his mother say? Mr and Mrs Featherstone wouldn't approve, that she knew. She imagined his mother's nose sniffing the air. A farm girl with no education. And Catholic too.

Will had told Bridie how they'd named him Winston after their war hero, Sir Winston Churchill, with the ancestors' surname 'Rolands' thrown in for good measure.

The doctor in the outback hospital where he was born had laughed, and bandied the name 'Winston' about in the wards. The Aboriginal nurse who'd delivered him, had taken pity on the baby and said: 'He better be Will-ee, much more simple and better for young boy.'

His mother, weakened after the long labour, had dreamed of a church baptism for her son. It would be accomplished when the time was ripe. Once in a more suitable setting, he would be baptised in the Anglican church; the right name bestowed upon him.

But the simple name stuck in the end and he became Will for life.

She'd remembered every story, every sentence, word for word, that Will Featherstone had said to her last night.

She thought how well the name suited him, his proud bearing and sense of self. Willpower, that's what it was. And yet, he'd not been able to restrain himself from kissing her straight off. She was shocked when it happened. The thought of it now sent warm surges throughout her body. Pleasure, pure and simple. And the way he spoke, the manly syllables rolling so easily from his tongue.

He'd said he was going to ride out to his friends' place for a spot of fishing today. She couldn't expect him to get back to her straight away. Not today, at least.

These Finns were family friends on a cattle station. She couldn't remember the name of it. Something like drum rolls, she thought. Will's parents had sent him there to get better when he was four or so, after a nasty bout of bronchitis. His love of country life had been born then and there.

She could see him in her imagination, riding off now towards the west on his racing bike. He was going to cycle all the way there.

Maybe Will's mother would be asking him about his night. *What did you do last night, dear?* A milk maid, Bridie thought, shame flooding her at the thought of the differences between them.

Images were still floating in and out about last night's dance, every little part of it, each word and sentence spoken between them. And that kiss, before her brothers had come out and spoilt it. After that, she'd had to watch her behaviour, in case she was being spied on.

How would Will have seen her, compared to the other girls he'd met on the north side? Stella always said how classy she looked, as if born and bred in the city. Like a model, really.

Dreamily, she wandered out into the kitchen, and came face to face with her mother. Eliza O'Toole, hair haloing out around a plump face, had been at the fuel stove, preparing breakfast. Bridie tried to appear normal.

'Morning Mumma,' she whispered, still dazed from sleeping so deeply.

'Everything all right? Last night?' her mother intoned in her thin worried voice, as she put plates and cutlery on the table. 'At the dance?'

'Yes, Mumma, no need to worry. The boys looked after me.'

Ned came up from the dairy at that moment, and his mother placed thick slices of buttery toast and jam on a plate for him.

'Don't you worry about that Will Featherstone,' Ned growled. 'Won't let him take advantage of the girl.'

'Ned, shut up,' snapped Bridie, her cheeks red, 'he's … too good for you, that's the trouble, and you're just … jealous.'

'Who's that?' Eliza asked. 'Who's in trouble?'

'I danced with Will Featherstone, Mumma. His father's a manager, in car sales or something. He's a perfect gentleman. Don't listen to Ned.'

'I kept an eye on her all right, Mumma. Don't you worry 'bout that!'

'Good, Ned. Don't want her getting notions in her head about some young lair, sweeps her off her feet and gets her into trouble.'

'It was just a dance, not a blooming date. Probably won't see him ever again in this god forsaken place.'

'Just as well,' her mother said, 'best stick with your own kind.'

Bridie wasn't hungry. She pushed the chair back, shook her head at the plate and cup her mother had placed in front of her, and scowled at Ned. She fled from the kitchen back to her room. She needed to get dressed and get her head together.

Stella tooted the horn out the front to announce her arrival. They'd arranged to attend Mass together, and Bridie couldn't wait to tell her friend about Will. Stella had been one of the smart girls who'd stayed on at the convent, then gone to secretarial college afterwards. She now had a well-paid desk job in town.

Bridie had been clever at school too. She could write stories better than any of the other girls. If only Mumma and Ned had agreed, she knew she could have continued on and gained a certificate. But they'd pulled her out after Dadda died. The nuns at the convent had been encouraging. 'She has the brains,' they'd told Mumma.

Only arithmetic had left her bewildered, numbers making no sense in her world, where she searched for what the eyes and the heart could see.

'What's the use of education for a girl?' Ned had said. And Mumma had been pleased to have the extra help at home.

She remembered the fuss she'd made, shouting at Ned: 'Dadda, if he was still alive would let me go on. You're just a bully, Ned. Always have been.'

And Mumma, in thrall to Ned since her own man's death, had given in, citing money and health worries on her part.

'I've met someone, Stella,' she said, as her friend drove along the bumpy track towards Karrana.

'I want to hear all about it,' the other said.

She told Stella what she knew about Will. That he was the son of Anglican parents who lived in town, his father a manager of sorts.

'Sounds like a good catch, Bridie,' Stella said.

Bridie continued to whisper in church as they knelt down to pray.

'I might need you to be my alibi, some time, Stella. He wants to take me out, and you know what Mum's like.'

'Maybe we can go on a double date, or something. Does he have any friends?'

'That's the problem. His best friends are cattle people, miles away on a property.'

'I'm sure we can arrange something,' Stella said. 'You can stay with us any time.'

'That's if he rings me up like he said he would,' Bridie whispered, 'maybe he's changed his mind.'

'Don't be silly, he probably had something planned for today, he couldn't get out of.'

'Another date, you mean?' She began to giggle.

Heads were turning around. The priest seemed to be looking in their direction, seeking out the culprits of the whisperings. Stella put her head down, as if to pray.

Bridie's suppression of her giggles turned into shakes. She felt like she might lose control of her bladder. Pull yourself together, girl, if it's meant to happen it will, she told herself.

She bowed her head and prayed, still wondering if Will was thinking about her, as she was about him. Perhaps she had come to him in one of those luminous dreams she'd been having: the image of herself as Sleeping Beauty, carried off by the Prince. It was in a classy convertible sports car, with tan leather seats, not on some sweaty horse that snorted and pigrooted about the place.

Bridie prayed that she could keep this new man interested in her. She searched for the proper words to employ, but her thoughts were fuddled by a cloud as thick as the smoke hanging around the farm during bushfire season.

She remained dreamy, as if something had changed inside her head while she slept.

She put on rubber boots and ran outside to collect eggs and feed the chooks. It was the least she could do for Mumma. She walked out the back and looked up at the sky, wondering if the end of winter weather was about to change into spring soon. She ducked her head to enter the hen roost and felt in the straw for the still warm brown and white eggs.

Passing the wash house on her way back, she was singing *Over the Rainbow* at the top of her lungs, sending her soprano voice out over the building and the fields. Her mother, wringing out sheets at the copper tub, called, 'I know you're still thinking about that Featherstone lad...just you be careful.' And shook a wet pillow slip in Bridie's direction.

Eliza always seemed to know what she, Bridie, was thinking. It was like being in a glass bowl, really.

'Rich boys are only interested in one thing. I don't want you getting into no trouble.'

Like you an' Dadda, Bridie thought. The image of her mother, pregnant with Ned, buffeted about by waves, as she eloped with her lover to Sydney sprang to mind. *That will never happen to me. I'm too smart for that. Better educated than Mumma, at least.*

'I know, Mumma. I'll be careful, but he's gunna take me out on a date one of these days.'

'Is that so, well Ned will go along with you. An' there'll be no drinking afterwards. That's the thing that sends the men out of control.'

'Please, Mumma, I'm old enough to look after myself now.'

'While you're under my roof, you'll do as I say.'

Eliza had often told her daughter about her own youth. Covering up, perhaps, some of the worst bits, the ones wrapped in layers of guilt, like the blanket the doctor had placed over the body of her dead husband. They'd all been so shocked by the patriarch's sudden death that they hadn't been able to shed a tear for days.

Losing her husband to *Old Man Death*, was the source of her mother's over-protectiveness, Bridie knew. She felt spasms of shame from the fact of her own reproof. She had been spoilt, yes, by her mother *and* father. But the brothers had made up for it by teasing her.

She pushed the guilty feelings away. The last thing she wanted was to end up like Eliza, too much hard work and too many babies, leaving her flabby, and suffering from 'nerves'.

Billy helped Eliza with the washing and the chooks when she, Bridie, wasn't able to. He shared all the hard work on the farm with Ned, too, planting the crops and baling the hay.

She often heard her mother sighing and saying in her breathless voice to her favourite son: 'You're worth your weight in gold, Billy. If I can't reward you in this life, the good Lord surely will in the next.'

Eliza's God was Anglican, but she'd married a Catholic in Charlie O'Toole, which had brought shame on both sides of the family. Bridie knew that her mother had suffered the most from it.

Life had been so much simpler before Dadda died. He'd been immune to the gossip. And he'd loved her, his first daughter after five boys, giving her confidence in herself, no matter what. She sometimes felt bereft without him.

Now she worried about her country drawl. She said 'dairnse' whereas Will had said 'darnse'. She realised that he sounded better … schooled … perhaps taught by his parents to speak well, English sounding rather than like the country bumpkins around the place.

Yes, she'd have to smarten up her speech if she wanted to keep Will Featherstone interested.

Chapter 3

It was over a week since the dance. Bridie lay on a blanket in the green clover and looked up at the clear blue sky. Concealed from the house by the grape vine trellis, she drank in the warmth of the sun's rays through every pore in her body. She'd slipped into shorts and a matching top, so as to tan her legs and arms, with the first signs of spring weather issuing forth like a promise.

Was it a bad sign that his rugged features had started to fade around the edges? She was mixing it in with one of the Hollywood stars, Cary Grant or Clark Gable.

She longed to hear the well-formed shape and rhythm of his words. She hungered to be near Will once more, to smell his earthy presence. Just to touch him on the skin of his hand, his bare arm, and to flirt with him.... It probably mattered little if her older brother was in tow or not.

An emptiness within came when her thoughts turned to how Will had held her in his arms. And that kiss…. The memory and the feeling from it both shamed and pleased her.

She turned over onto her stomach and breathed in the sweet perfume from the clover. Magpies and larks were already warbling, sending out their mating calls. She was rolling off the blanket onto her back now, finding herself encircled by the soft green and white cover of clover. Bees hovered ready to claim their cut. She stretched out her arms and stroked with her fingers the downy mat. Deep into her chest, she imbibed its fragrance, before rolling over and finding herself safely back on the blanket once more.

Was she right for Will? He'd talked of nothing else but country life. Might be better-off with someone like Stella, a horsey type, but attractive. Perhaps he'd already decided to call on an old flame. Had he started to think better about his choices? Was it the daughter of one of his parents' cattle station friends that he was obsessing over now?

Still, he'd seemed truly attracted to her, little Bridie O'Toole, at the dance.

Her desire for Will's lips had not been satiated. It was like her cravings for her mother's home-killed rooster, when she was ravenous. Served with baked potatoes, peas and pumpkin grown on the farm, there was nothing like it. The smell of it, the scrumptious taste, every bit of the fowl devoured, including the parson's nose, often fought over by the siblings.

Bridie was shocked at the savagery of her thoughts. If she were a spider, she would be ready to pounce and devour his beauty whole.

Johnny had smirked once when telling about a redback somersaulting over the female, to position itself on the mouth.

Her feelings frightened her now. Her feelings towards this man she hardly knew. She would have to take care.

Her mother's imagined voice, shrilling down her ear waves, conjured up nightmarish images within her. *You'll be pushing a pram around the streets if you're not careful, my girl.*

Added to all of it, was the childish sense of modesty the nuns in their black habits had tried to instil in the girls at school: *Do not ever wear patent leather shoes beneath your hemline, lest they reflect your underclothes for men to see.*

Dadda had taught her not to be afraid of hell, even though he remained a Catholic all of his life. Hell was really what you experienced here on earth, sometimes, not after you die, he'd told her. She wondered where he'd got that idea from. She liked it and took it to heart like you'd take a magic totem.

Will'd talked about a night out at the pictures. But why oh why was he taking so long to ask her out on the date?

She thought again about her missed schooling.

How could you make up for something that had passed out of reach, like the last rays of sunny days in winter?

Would he be turned off by her lack of education and her dairy farm background?

She had to do something about it, even if it was just to catch a glimpse of him, a peek from afar.

In her mind she was hatching a plan.

At the cycling track, all the good-looking girls from the town clustered around Cyclone Johnny. If only they knew what he's like, thought Bridie. They'd do better to search elsewhere.

She'd dropped Ned off at the track, his racing bike in the boot of the car. 'See you back home, Ned,' she'd said, waving goodbye.

She'd picked Stella up soon afterwards and returned to the track.

Bridie spotted Will among the crowd, towering over everyone. He was dressed in black racing tights that showed off flexed thigh muscles to good effect. She turned away, red-faced.

'Don't look now, Stella. But that's him over there. With Johnny.'

'Oh Bridie, he's a dish,' Stella said, after whirling around to have a look, and gasping. 'A real dish.'

Bridie throbbed, with urges both pleasurable and threatening.

'I think so too,' she sighed, grabbing Stella by the arms and pulling her into the car.

'Ouch! What's the matter?'

'We've got to get away, Stella, away from here. Don't want him to see me, or he'll think I'm running after him.'

'Oh, well you are, aren't you?'

'Yes, but….'

'You mustn't let that one get away, you know?' said Stella, as they drove the short distance to Stella's family house. 'Are there any brothers in the family?'

'Afraid not, just sisters,' Bridie said, prickling her nose up as she had a habit of doing. 'And I get the feeling he'd like to get away from the whole family. Not much love lost there.'

'Oh well, that's too bad, then,' said Stella, shaking her auburn curls that shone red gold in the sunlight. 'I'll just have to keep on looking.'

'Let's play records. And dance,' Bridie said.

Stella's house was near the river, south side.

'He's lovely, Bridie,' said Stella again, as she turned on the gramophone, allowing the romantic melodies drifting out to blend in with their talk.

'We'd form a nice couple, wouldn't we, Stella?' Bridie giggled, before adding, 'And imagine the gorgeous babies we'd make together.'

'Yes, that's for sure, but what about things in common? You say he's a country type. And his friends live out in the wilds. Would you be able to live in the bush? Happily ever after … and all that?'

'I'd like to live in a modern house with appliances. His parents, they live well, in the better part of town, it seems. Not in a dump like Hilltop. Hayseeds, my family, but I can't help loving them, all the same. Even Johnny, with his goofy smile.'

'Well, his parents have money, you say, and his folks are friends with these people on a cattle station, aren't they?'

'Yes, graziers, a step-up from us lowly dairy farmers.'

'Well, I'm sure Will would love riding horses at Hilltop.'

'I don't want to think about it. I'm afraid he'll tire of me, you know? With his education and all….'

'You're smart, Bridie. And he'll see that if he's clever.'

They danced and played *A Fine Romance* over and over, again and again for the umpteenth time.

'Any dates on the horizon, Stella?' Bridie asked at last. Both puffing now.

'No, no sign of anyone. The types I meet are either taken or coarse hicks, if you know what I mean?'

'Yes, I sure do,' sighed Bridie.

She liked listening to Stella talk. She came from town people, better educated than her family. She tried to imitate her friend's more rounded vowels.

Stella told her about her latest dream, in which a fair-haired lover entered her life, as if he'd been to war and was injured in some way. A soldier, perhaps?

'You're a bit of a witch, Stella,' said Bridie, 'Still, I'd like to see you paired off with a handsome Adonis.'

'You've always liked dark men. Could it be our love of self, talking?' Stella mused, 'The image when we look in the mirror, sort of thing?'

'Like Narcissus staring into the pool and seeing his own reflection there? Will's not as dark as me. Anyway, he might have turned off me by now.'

'Don't be silly, Bridie, how could anyone not like you? Mum and Dad think you're the ant's pants, the way you dress, your style.'

'Mumma thinks you're a tom boy, and a bit wild, but it's only because you're from the town. She wants me to settle down with a cow cocky like her Charlie was.'

'Ugh,' said Stella, 'I know what you mean. Red-faced farmers with beefy hands.'

'Now, how am I going to meet up with Will Featherstone again if he doesn't call?'

'Ask your brothers to bring him home to Hilltop for a visit. He's their friend as well, isn't he?'

'Of course, why didn't I think of it? I know why, because I'm ashamed of our house and home. Oh, Stella, what if he turns off me, and finds a girl from his own social group?'

'You know what you need to do? Impress Will with your equestrian skills'

'I'm sure he can ride better than me.'

'Let's go to the stables. Bert can loan us one of his spare mounts.'

Bridie felt a surge of confidence as they set off.

As they cantered together towards the riverbank, she felt suddenly invincible. On Stella's bay mare, she moved in rhythm with the strides of her mount. Keeping her seat on the saddle, her thighs gently squeezing the mare's girth, she felt one with the breeze blowing in her face. She could hold her own with the best of them, for sure.

'Look at you, Bridie,' Stella shouted, 'you're a pro the way you never shifted in your seat.' They'd halted for a moment beneath the gum trees on the riverbank. 'Nothing wrong with that.'

'I think it's your horse,' she said. 'I love her. So gentle. Not like the wild things they put me on at home sometimes.'

'Yes, she knows what I expect of her by now,' said Stella. 'Like any mating, you have to get to know one another before anything good can come of the coupling.'

'You're wise, Stella, where did you learn it all from?'

'I had a strict, no-nonsense upbringing,' she said, 'and then the nuns drilled more of it into me.'

'Not like me, spoilt, Mumma always says.'

'But you've got style, Bridie. Anyone can see that.'

'Don't know where it comes from, though. Opposite of Mumma, that's for sure.'

'We'll have to give these two a good rubbing down before we put them away for the night,' said Stella, turning her mount's head for home. 'There's a lot of work involved in looking after horses.'

She'd stopped singing about love, as she went about helping her mother, pushing the wet sheets and clothes through the wringer next to the copper, and hanging them out on the stick line behind the grape trellis. She had sung through a moony haze draped around her, the same cloud that'd swept her mother and Charlie O'Toole up in its wake. When they'd got back after Ned's birth, their families'd had to accept the inevitable. And farming was all they knew about. On the hillside farm his father had passed on to him, Dadda had run a herd of Jersey and Guernsey dairy cows. Bridie pictured the red bull stamping on the other side of the barbed wire fence, impatient to mount the pale yellow cows with their splashes of white.

She heard the metallic ring from the wash house and bounded up the back steps two at a time. Hoping. Praying. She tried to reach it before her mother. Too late. Eliza had already picked up the shiny black earpiece and was listening to the deep voice on the end of the line.

Her face showed that she knew, even before he'd introduced himself and asked for Bridie by name, that it was her daughter's young man.

'Bridie, Will Featherstone for you on the telephone,' Eliza said with care, as she handed the receiver to her daughter.

Bridie, too, was careful to guard her speech, the way she had heard the better off girls at school enunciate their words. If nothing else, she was good at imitation. She was only too aware of Will's polished vowels, and the way her own were liable to slip into shoddiness if she allowed it to happen.

'How are you, Will?' she asked.

'Good for hearing your voice, Bridie. How would you like to go out with me to the Palace on Saturday night?'

'Yes, that would be nice. What's showing at the moment, Will?' She didn't want to sound over the moon, but she was almost stammering from the excitement of hearing his voice once again, and from the tension of speaking properly.

'*Wuthering Heights*. It's set on the moors in England. About a young woman, a country girl. Think you'll like it.'

'Can I meet you there at seven o'clock, Will?'

'No, no need for that. I shall pick you up from your place at six-thirty.'

It flashed into Bridie's mind that she would have her brother in tow, and that it would be embarrassing, but she didn't know what to do about it. Her thoughts were jumbled and she could only murmur: 'Yes, six-thirty. Thank you, Will. Bye.' And she replaced the phone on its holder promptly, a little too hastily.

She knew it was an abrupt ending, but she was confused and couldn't help it.

'Mum, does Ned have to come along? Will is picking me up in his father's car? Can't you trust me just this once?'

'Ned's going with you and that's that!'

Bridie was already thinking about how she could get Ned to meet them at the picture theatre. He would surely agree to that. And Will would come in and charm her mother to bits. It would work out in the end. Mumma would just have to give in and accept things, or embarrass herself in front of Will Featherstone.

Mumma'd obviously been impressed by the polite sounding young man's voice, the way he'd pronounced her name. He'd have said, 'Mrs O'Toole? Looking forward to meeting you', with a steady, manly tone, before asking for permission to speak to her daughter. Manners and good breeding, part of his makeup, her mother would have thought.

Was Mumma secretly pleased that this young man from the better side of the tracks was interested in her daughter?

Chapter 4

By the time Saturday night came around, Bridie was trembling, both inside and out. As she got dressed, she thought about her plans for the night. She'd told Ned that she was going to the movies and that Mumma wanted him to pick her up afterwards. He'd agreed, not knowing the full story. Bridie's timing was superb, informing her brother, just as he was leaving to go to the races early on, and he was running late.

'Don't worry, Mumma. Ned knows about it.' Just then there was a knock on the door and she ran to open it.

'Mum, this is Will Featherstone.' Eliza came up behind her, straightening out her apron and wisps of grey-white hair with a floury hand.

Will held out his hand. She did the same.

'I'm delighted to meet you, Mrs O'Toole.'

'Good evenin,' Mr Featherstone.'

'Please call me Will.'

Eliza blushed on meeting the young man's steady gaze and tried to hide a frown. She had had no time to think about the arrangements. Bridie kissed her mother on the cheeks and almost ran down the steps and outside to the shiny Ford waiting on the grass. 'We won't be late back. Don't worry, Mumma!'

'I will look after her, Mrs O'Toole.' And he doffed his hat as a parting gesture.

The picture theatre reminded Bridie of Hollywood. Bright posters displayed the movies and stars and starlets behind glass out the front. Inside were bright ceiling lights, columns and plush red carpets, velvet curtains and padded seats.

Ned was nowhere to be seen. 'He might be inside already,' Bridie said. 'He'll meet us after the show in any case. Let's go in.'

The usherette's torch flashed around the hall, as they pushed along in front of knees to their seats, but they could see no sign of Ned. He'd probably decided not to attend the picture, but to hang out with his mates after the races in a pub nearby.

Bridie felt like a queen as she slipped into the seat next to Will and looked around her at the crowd. Will put his arm around her shoulders as soon as they were seated. It thrilled her to the core.

'I've missed you,' he whispered into her ear. She didn't need to reply. He drew her to him, she playing a bit the coquette, wanting but not wanting. Fearing, yet willing him on.

'Will, no! Please. Don't!'

He drew back, displaying a certain shyness alongside an urge so great that it seemed to take over his whole being. He slid his arm around her again and pulled her body towards him, inhaling her scent as he did so. He was breathing into her ear.

'Your lips,' he sighed. She was melting in to him now. Offering her full moist lips to his urgent dry ones. Oblivious to Heathcliff and Catherine on screen. Oblivious to others sitting next to them in the theatre. They both were.

The usherette's torch flashed, illuminating their row. They separated like guilty children.

'Let's go outside,' he whispered.

'Yes, I want some fresh air,' she said and shivered.

'It's you I want,' he said.

He led her by the hand past peoples' knees, down rows of steps, and out into the foyer.

Once outside, he found a bench in the darkened park opposite the cinema. He fell onto the seat, pulling her a little roughly towards him.

He was fumbling a bit, now. Bridie disengaged his fingers from her breast, and allowed his lips on hers for a brief moment.

When Will's fingers slid down to her knee, drawing back her skirt, she took hold of them.

'No,' resisting his touch, 'too fast.'

He pulled back, his hand trembling.

'Why didn't you call me earlier?' she mumbled. 'I thought you'd lost interest in me.'

'No, no, no,' his voice was raised, urgent. 'It's a long story, the phone wires have been buzzing since I rode out to Tumbarumbar. My mother, Mavis Finn, you know…?'

'I thought it was another girl.'

'Well, that's another story, everyone thinking the same…, but it's all over between her and me. It was my birthday last weekend, a dinner I couldn't get out of.'

'Oh.' A shiver went up and down Bridie's spine. 'Happy birthday,' she murmured, pulling herself up, 'let's go back … inside, Ned might see us out here.'

It was interval when they got back inside. Will bought ice cream and soda for them at the snack bar. They stood up at one of the raised tables there. He kept staring at Bridie, as if drinking her in through the eyes. She was doing the same. Had she dreamt about this moment, it all seemed so natural, so familiar?

'I hope Ned gets here before the end,' she said. 'Mum will never let me out again, if not.'

'Don't fret. I'll get you home safe and sound.'

'Not so sure about that,' she giggled.

'Come on,' he murmured, pulling her to him in spite of glances from the people standing around. 'You like it, I know.'

'You're moving things a bit too fast, Will Featherstone,' she said.

Bridie's eyes shone. This man from the better side of the bank was attracted to her, after all. Her future was laid out before her, a road leading skywards, paved with gold.

'Let's go in,' she said, a little too excited about his caresses.

It was hard knowing how far to let him go with it. He didn't seem in control at times.

And, after all, was she?

Wuthering Heights with Heathcliff calling out for his Catherine on the moors passed fleetingly. After the movie, Bridie went into the powder room before the theatre lights came back on. She needed to fix up her makeup and tidy her hair, to try and conceal the signs of their petting in the darkened theatre.

Oh dear, they'd missed out on a great deal of the movie.

Out on the street afterwards, Ned was waiting in the car.

'How did'jer like it?' he asked.

'Very good,' Will said for both of them.

The two young lovers then gave each other a modest peck on the cheek before saying goodbye.

'I'll see you at the bike races tomorrow, Ned?' asked Will.

'Not sure, Will, but Johnny will be there fer certain.'

On the way home in the car, she tried to straighten out her dress and to refresh her lipstick, in case she had to face her mother when the lights were turned on.

'A bit of snogging in the dark, eh?' Ned smirked. 'It's okay, Mumma's already in bed by now.'

She wondered again what Will's mother would think of this affair with her, Bridie O'Toole? Perhaps he was afraid to even broach the subject with her, let alone bring her home to meet them.

She felt, for the moment, satiated, but she knew at the bottom of her soul that she would be fretting for her young man before the next day was out.

Bridie was excited, over the moon, really. Ned had invited Will home for afternoon tea after the bike races. He was cycling there right now. It'd be good to test the waters, before the meal invite. She knew he'd be nervous about fitting in. Ned had told him how she'd run off to Stella's place after the cycling park that time. *Poor little shy bird.* If only he knew....

She put on rubber boots and was already walking down through the tall grasses in the back paddock, towards the milking sheds.

Horses grazed in the fields. The blackish bull stamped and snorted in the far paddock.

The early hint of spring in the air made her light-headed. Loquat and mulberry trees were bearing fruits dressed in yellow and ruby jackets.

Sunshine caressed her skin like a lover and life was bountiful.

Butterflies, bees and other insects drew nectar from clover and wildflowers that had burst into bloom with abundance.

Magpies carolled and warbled, and crows cawed from the tops of gum trees, as if to usher in the season. She knew that her feelings had been usurped by a kind of madness, but she could neither resist nor even question it.

She went down to the bales to watch her brothers pulling the creamy liquid in noisy squirts from the cows' ripe udders.

The noise was amplified as the stream of milk gushed into the sides of the tin buckets.

'Here, have a go, Bridie,' Billy always called out to her. This time she did, taking the soft teat between her thumb and her other fingers, pulling in a rhythmical motion, downwards, until the milk started pouring out. *Phtt phtt.* Sensual, like breastfeeding, she imagined. You had to squeeze on the teats quite hard to start the milk pouring. A delicious sound as the frothy milk hit the tin bucket. A dairy maid, after all, she thought.

'Good, Bridie, I reckon you've got it now,' Billy said, as he sat back on the stool at the cow's side.

He pushed his head into the soft flanks. 'Went to Mass today, didja?'

'Yeah, Billy. You've got to come one time, you really have to.'

'Ah, we'll see, Bridie, we'll see.'

'And to the dance next time. Meet a girl or two.'

She knew, sadly, that it would probably never happen that way, if at all. He was just too shy. There was his nervous disposition and severe stutter.

She ran up and hugged Will before he could announce himself to the others. Then she climbed up on a railing and watched as Will and her brothers herded the rest of the cows through the dirt and mud, and into the sealed milking area.

Rough voices bellowed above the mooing of the cows. *'Hup! Git in there! Hup!'*

Perched up there like Vivien Leigh, dressed in smart jodhpurs and a checked shirt, her dark hair swept up and back, Bridie felt safe.

Now, she watched, entranced, as this town boy sat on a stool, and roped the cow's leg so it couldn't kick outwards. He squeezed the milk out from the jersey cow's udder, pushing his head against her flanks, using one hand after the other, in unison. She watched and listened to the familiar *phtt phtt*, as the white jets hit the bucket, and the smell of the creamy substance flowing from between his fingers, like she was watching a farmer born and bred.

After the milking, the three men sprawled on the grass under the trellis, and she brought them afternoon tea with buttery scones and jam.

'I'd like to have a block of land one day,' he said. 'I'd give the world to be part of country life.'

Bridie wrinkled her nose, as if smelling something unpleasant.

'Beef cattle, that's what I really want in the end,' Will continued.

'A great place to bring up kids,' Ned roared, butting in in his brutal way.

Will looked at Bridie. She knew he was wondering how she coped with her brothers, hides as tough as the beasts on the farm.

He might need to toughen up, she thought, if he's to fit in with my rough and rowdy family.

'Bridie's a princess, Will,' Ned guffawed, '*Million dollar baby*, they call her!'

'Shut up, Ned!' she whispered, as her elder brother got up and turned back towards the dairy to finish up there.

'Yeah, Will, take no notice of Ned,' Billy drawled as he followed after his brother.

'I love the bush, especially riding horses,' said Will.

'I'm fond of nature, too,' said Bridie, 'and animals, as long as they're on the outside.'

'Well, I'm a bit of a bushie, in spite of my parents' background. Or perhaps, because of it....'

'You know, I really thought you didn't want to see me anymore,' she said, looking around to make sure they were alone.

'I've had trouble getting away from work, from home,' he said. 'Mum and Dad don't understand....'

'They don't like you seeing me?'

'It's not that, it's just … they're always asking questions, wanting to know who I'm with, what I'm doing.'

'They think we're not good enough for them,' her voice trembled as she spoke, 'cow cockies, coming from the other side of the river and all....'

'Don't talk nonsense, my dear,' Will kissed her hair as he spoke, 'anyway, Dad and I don't always see eye to eye. He expects me to do exactly as he wants. Study, get a job in town, follow in his footsteps.'

'What about your mother?' Bridie asked, secret tears pricking her eyes.

'She can't … do … anything. It's the *Old English* way. I was supposed to become a pharmacist in town. Now I'm to be a car mechanic in *his* garage.'

'What will happen if you go against him?'

'He might cut me off without a penny. And he's signed me up to do a Tech course in Sydney now.'

Bridie stiffened inside. 'Oh,' she stammered, feeling her lips tremble.

'Dad's got me working for him in his office…behind the counter. He tries at every turn to show me neither fear nor favour. Some of the staff take great delight in lording it over me.'

'That's awful,' Bridie sympathised. 'Can't your father stop them?'

'He thinks it's good for my character. When I was three, he put me on his back and dived into the river.'

'Why did he do that?' Bridie's voice was high.

'To teach me to swim,' Will said flatly.

She imagined the mother, anxious, running to take the petrified infant from her husband's back.

'That must have really scared you?'

'I thought he wanted to drown me … but it toughened me up, I can tell you. When I was fifteen, I used to dive from the footbridge into the river, a twenty foot drop into deep nothingness.'

'What about sisters and brothers?' Bridie asked.

'There's two younger sisters, that's all.'

'I had five older brothers, two, Charlie and Shaun, lost in action,' Bridie said.

'Sorry about that, your brothers … you know….'

'Yes, and childhood was out-and-out utter chaos, with all of us in an old hovel, but … the love … was always there.'

'This place is great,' Will said.

'Ugh,' Bridie exhaled. 'True, it's better than the old one, further down the hill, no electricity, mosquitoes … the lot.'

She sighed, screwing up her face in a familiar gesture. *A bit like a pug, with her slightly turned-up nose,* she sometimes thought.

'Dad was an orphan,' he said, 'had to strike out on his own when he came to Australia. A self-made man, expects me to do the same.'

'Maybe he didn't learn how to be a real good … father … to a son?' Bridie chose her words carefully.

'Mum's always telling me how tough things were for Dad,' he said, 'and they stick together, *Old English* habits, hard to break, you know?'

She didn't, but she was beginning to learn about it.

Chapter 5

The first fifteen miles had been a breeze, the road climbing gently westwards towards the Great Dividing Range. The last part over an unsealed road would be harder, but he didn't care. It was a joy this day to ride his racing bike the whole way, his heart and muscles up to the task.

It was heaven, head bent down over the handles, flying like the wind.

Cycling along the first few miles were pure ecstasy. The midday sun with relentless light and heat, even in late winter, poured down, filtered by the army of green gum trees. *My protectors*, he thought, *from assault*. With the gorse like smell of eucalypt and the feel of iron in his blood, Will was fearless. He got into a rhythm in which man and machine were one; he felt as if nothing on earth could trip the élan on which his life was set.

He was the only one on the road, king of the road, of the world. Thoughts of the dance floated in and out of his mind. How he and Bridie O'Toole had danced and talked the night away. Until she'd been dragged away too soon, that is. He thought of his mother's questioning, trying to find out all about it.

Ma had noted the shine to his face and eyes that morning: 'You look happy this morning, Will,' she'd said. 'What did you do last night?' He hadn't been able to tell her the truth; just out with some friends from cycling.

He realised now, out on the road, that he was trapped, as surely as a prisoner of war, caught like a butterfly on a pin, or a bee in the heady scent of a rose.

It was a prison where he would go voluntarily, and no one, not even his parents, would force him away from this lovely fate.

He'd liked the farm maid look of Bridie O'Toole behind the makeup, her fresh lips and lovely eyes wide as pools. He'd wanted to crush her to his chest, hold her there forever.

He'd like that right now, too.

What would he tell the Finns? That he'd found the love of his life? They'd laugh at him for sure. Think he was starkers.

Ever since that first stay, when his parents had sent him off to the Finns' as a tiny boy, he'd known in his heart that this was the life he wanted. His convalescence from a chest infection had worked quickly and he'd spent two wonder-filled weeks that had turned into a month, so little was he homesick at Tumbarumbar. He'd accompanied the Finns around the place in their jeep or on foot, later on, he'd learned to ride horseback, climb trees, milk the cows, pick fruit and deal with all the creatures, even poisonous snakes, that lived in the wilds.

Maybe they'd think he was talking about Reenie, his old school sweetheart, if he told them about his feelings.

Passing Reenie's run down cottage, he thought about all the prize unbroken colts and fillies he'd tamed in her breaking in yards. Young horses, only too ready to obey with gentle handling and guidance. And once they trusted you, they were yours forever, such was the bond established between man and horse down through the centuries.

He wondered if it was like this with love and marriage. He couldn't believe he was already thinking of this. What would his mother say, Ma and Pa wouldn't approve, that's for sure He could imagine his mother's nose sniffing the air. *A farm girl with no education. And Catholic to boot.*

But he wasn't really thinking at all. His thoughts were taken over by the scent of her. The idea of *head over heels* became clear to him at that moment. These feelings were different from anything he'd experienced before. Nothing, not his steady home life with his two sisters, his steady going parents, had in any way opened him up to this possibility.

She'd felt good in his arms that night; she'd felt right. It was the sense of touch and that of scent that had spoken to him. Like the feelings he got when he was out in the bush, quiet all around him and the wattle and eucalypt brushing his skin, teasing his mount to go onwards with a gentle touch of the reins and the heels. The soft warm feel of the horse against his thighs. It just felt right. Like how, in a church, it feels right to some folks; the bush was like his cathedral.

He'd stopped at Halfway Creek and taken a breather. The sweat was pouring down his forehead now. His long athletic frame lowered itself onto the creek bank; he stretched out on his stomach, washed his face and took a long drink from the running water.

Some bush animal, probably a wallaby or a rabbit, scuttled away on the other side.

The whole Finn family was there having an early tea on the verandah.

'Come and join us!' Stan shouted. 'Pull up a chair and let's celebrate with a drink. You realise it's d-day today?'

'Yeah, a drink to glory and to victory, eh, guys?' said Will, making the victory sign.

'Think you're bloody Churchill, do yer, mate?' said Stanley junior.

It was always like this. They treated him like one of the boys. There were no sisters in the Finn family. Only the mother, father, three boys, and an elderly grandmother who kept to her room.

'I was just telling my lads about wartime service,' droned Stan. 'Didn't have to see fire coz I was part of the food production corps.'

The boys rolled their eyes as their father repeated stories they'd heard before:

'Did mer bit, though, trained with the light horse brigade.'

Will tried to show an interest by asking polite questions of his host: 'What was it like? In the light horse brigade?'

'The best thing happened to me, lad. Set me up fer life as a fighter.'

'Fightin' bushfires, eh Dad?' asked Leon, pursing his big lips, a flicker of a smile in his calf like eyes.

'Yeah son, that's about it. I hope none of you boys ever have to go to war. Forget the bravery thing. Who wants to go killing other people, eh?'

Will wondered how he would have gone if he'd been called up to fight.

'Let's go for a walk,' said young Stanley, dragging Will and his brothers away from the table.

Will'd mentioned the dance and they'd noticed his lifted mood.

'Come on, mate,' said Carl, 'tell us *orl* about it.'

Like the rest of the family, he spoke in a slow drawl that seemed to imitate the pace of life and the sun filled dome of the sky.

'Any good sorts?' asked Leon, grinning.

'Yeah, and a few crook sorts too,' laughed Will.

'Come on, who is she?' said Leon, pumping his friend on the shoulder, determined to get an answer out of him before he had to leave.

Will allowed his mate a furtive smile.

'It's that old flame from high school, Reenie, isn't it? Thought she got married, though.'

'Ah, that's for you to find out, mate.'

They sat on the grass next to the creek and skipped stones across the slippery surface.

They talked some more about the war and how they'd all been spared because of their youthfulness and farm work. Will thought about how he would not shirk from his duty if called on to protect his country from attack. He knew it, deep in his breast, he already had the fighting spirit. He would kill if he had to.

The three Finn boys all wanted to make their homes right here on the family property; soil and its yield, the stock and farm animals were in their blood.

Will was the cuckoo in the nest, but he felt like one with them.

'Okay, boys, time to get supper over,' Mavis said as they returned to the house, 'and off to bed for an early rise.'

The sun was dipping into the western ranges.

'And as for you, young Will,' said Stan, 'a lift home early in the morning, eh, lad?'

'Thanks, Mr Finn, but I don't mind riding home in the dark, and I need the training.'

'Be a pleasure, lad, to give you a lift. Only glad to have you stay on.'

Will nodded with gratitude at Mr Finn, the slow drawl and broad accent of this rough-hewed man, a positive stamp in his books. That was the thing about country folks. Nothing was too much trouble for them.

'Thanks, Mr Finn, but Mum is expecting me back tonight, and I've got to push off now,' he said.

'Well, if you're sure, young fellow….'

'Yes, thanks.'

'You can count on Mabel to give your Mum a call along the old wire to fill her in on your visit, Son.'

Part of the story of that Sunday evening, he couldn't tell anyone, not his parents, not the Finn boys, and especially not his newfound love, Bridie O'Toole.

Cycling back along the unsealed part of the road had been hard, but Will was able to keep the rhythm going and prayed that he would not have to fix a puncture in the dark. He'd felt the cool air on his face and concentrated on the way ahead, shown by the light of his bicycle lamp. He caught the flash of fireflies, and the sparkling canopy of stars above, when he could afford a glance.

His thoughts returned to last night's dance, and the wonder of Bridie O'Toole's face and body. It had been hard to pull himself away from her at the end of the night. Now he gave himself up completely to thoughts of her, of the way she'd been unable to resist his touch.

She had trembled and fluttered like a beautiful butterfly. A dark winged butterfly. He pictured velvety wings. She would be his, he knew it. He would just have to think of his next step, not to frighten her. She was a delicate flower, a red red rose. Easily crushed.

When he'd got to Halfway Creek, he'd stopped to catch his breath.

It was pitch black now with the stars blotted out by the height of the trees and the lay of the land. Some bush creatures, probably a wallaby or a rabbit, scuttled away on the other side of the bridge.

A *powerful owl* made an eerie sound like a warning coming from on high.

Will shivered. He wheeled his bike across the bridge and leant it against a tree on the opposite side. He would take a quick gulp of water before embarking on the second leg of his journey. He was a lot tireder than he thought he would be.

As he got closer to the creek bed, he noticed something strange. A light that was moving in a bizarre way parallel to the road. It was coming from the direction in which he had cycled, like a small meteor, only it was moving above the grassy culvert. He tried to reason with himself about the light source and what it might be.

He took a few steps back towards his bike. The light swerved off into the bush, dodging and going right through tree trunks.

'Who's there?' No response. He took a few steps towards the creek.

He was shouting now. 'Who in God's name is there?'

No one. Just the light moving in a bizarre way. A shiver of panic like a whiplash struck through his body. Geez, he didn't want to be a sissy knocked over by fear. Even a rabbit knew how to shake off a fright after being caught in a spotlight.

He started to tremble. He was chattering through his teeth. He might shake himself to death. The light was moving, slowly this time, towards the bridge. He took another step backwards.

He was no longer thirsty, he just wanted to know what the hell it was. It seemed to gather speed as he got nearer, then flashed off in another direction.

He wanted to get the hell out of there. Get away from the creek and out of there as quickly as he could. The bloody light seemed to be following him.

Just as he got to his bike, the light dived down into the water beneath the bridge, and disappeared, as if it had emerged from there.

Will didn't stop to investigate further. He jumped on his racing bike and sped, hell for bloody leather away at full speed.

He never looked back.

Every nerve in his body tingled and he felt that he'd escaped by the skin of his clattering teeth. Another second and he was a goner, from what? He had no idea.

Now it was terror that gave him the momentum. He sped along for three miles, faster than he'd ridden in his life before. He was almost pleased at the thought of the Page girls and his ordinary mother and father with their ordinary lives waiting for him back home.

It was something that he might carry with him forever, this incident, buried deep within, something that he couldn't share with a living soul, for fear of being thought mad. Or worse: a gutless, fear craven sheila. And he knew that, if he wanted to find an answer to such mysteries, he wouldn't find it in the Anglican church his father and mother attended, but beneath the cathedral like canopy of gum trees that he carried in his heart.

If only there were someone he could talk to about this experience. But there *was* someone—good old Reenie. He'd always been able to spill his guts to her. Even when he'd been sweet on her in school. Even when she'd gone off and married Len, closer in age, he could always count on her to listen.

He was panting and gasping for air like a stranded perch, as he saw his old friend's cottage, lit up like a beacon, come into view. He knew that his face was white as a bleeding ghost. He waited to get his breath back and regain colour before knocking on Reenie's door.

Chapter 6

It was several days after the movies before Bridie heard from Will about arrangements for the trip to Tumbarumbar. She guessed that he'd first needed time to broach the subject with his parents. Borrowing the car from his father was one thing, telling his mother about inviting the O'Toole girl to the family friends' cattle station would be the harder part.

She imagined the grim look on the mother's face when he mentioned the two horse-loving young women. *Why can't you choose a lady friend from among your own kith and kind,* her look would be saying. *You're too young for a girlfriend, anyway, you haven't got a penny to your name.*

Bridie's voice trembled when she answered his call. On the Sunday, he would pick her up in his father's ford and drive to Stella's place. He sounded nervous as he spoke, perhaps wondering if Bridie would like his old friends.

'I can't wait to meet your friends, Will,' she whispered. 'I'm sure you'll like Stella, a real horse lover.'

Her boyfriend was one of these sensitive souls, always anxious about things before he'd experienced them. He would be worrying about meeting Stella for the first time, no doubt.

They would pick Stella up as chaperone for the day. Will would relax at the sight of the friendly looking woman who was her best friend.

But would she, Bridie, take to his country friends?

As for the ominous meeting with his parents that she knew was coming, and that would be a make or break moment for their relationship, she dreaded it.

First up, though, she'd already arranged for him to come to Hilltop to pay a visit to the farm.

Bridie received Will in the loungeroom, and introduced him formally to her mother, even though she knew they'd met once before. It was her way of showing both of them that the relationship was acknowledged and accepted at Hilltop.

She'd go riding with him this day. It was the only chance they'd have to get away from Mumma and her far reaching gaze. And she needed to show him that she had a good seat on a horse.

'Want to come with us for a ride, Billy?' she asked her brother when he came up from the milking. 'We're going as far as the swamplands and back.'

'Sure thing, Bride.'

'I'll put on some proper riding pants first,' she said. 'Will is already saddling the horses.'

She now had a brand new riding set from McKittricks' that had cost her mother a packet, jodhpurs, riding boots, a tight fitting coat, and a brown suede skullcap that made her look like a million pounds.

Eliza found it hard to say no to her, that Bridie knew. She had begged her mother to buy the outfit for her. 'I'll go out riding more, I promise,' she'd said, while trying the clothes on in the store.

Bridie looked at herself in the mirror and felt good, even as guilt curled around her breast like a cat.

She'd ridden horses from the time she was three and could gallop and jump over logs. She'd learnt early how to jab her heels in the belly to make the animal trot, to shake the bridle to get up a canter, and how to sit up straight, thighs squeezed in against the saddle, in order to have a good seat on a horse.

But she didn't have the same passion for riding as did true equestrians, like her friend Stella. Riding was just the thing you did in the country.

Still, riding camps had been fun, and she remembered the thrill of rolling in the hay once with Bobby *something or other* from the public school. He'd been one of several sunburnt lads she'd allowed to kiss her. Innocent thrills, giving her the taste of something better to come.

Will whistled when he looked at her, all dressed up for a ride.

'Billy's going with you,' Eliza said, sniffing into her apron.

Billy rode ahead on Sancho, a fat-bellied piebald, who pigrooted from time to time. Bridie sat primly on Pal, a creamy coloured gelding, looking as if she should have been riding side-saddle. Will rode next to her on a bay mare called Lady.

'Now I believe that you can ride a horse,' he said, 'for a time there….'

'Did you think I was lying?' Bridie said, tightening the reins. 'Pal is a bit flighty, that's all.'

'Would you rather swap with me?' he asked. 'Lady is a dream.'

'No, I'm just a bit out of practice, need to find my rhythm with him.'

She stood up in the stirrups, stretched her jodhpur clad legs, and tried to relax her posture, sitting back properly.

'How is my seat in the saddle?' she asked.

'You look pretty good to me,' Will chuckled.

'Oh, stop that, Will Featherstone! Flattery will get you nowhere.'

She was secretly pleased and let Will know it with an open smile.

'What about a canter?' he said. Off they set across the grassy field towards the hills that stood out like sentinels, signalling one another in the blue springtime sky.

Billy had dropped right back. It looked like he would be a long time in joining them down at the swamplands.

She had gained the lead and Will saw that she was in trouble. She'd lost the reins and was no longer moving in rhythm with the cantering hooves, but wobbling around in the saddle as the horse moved into a gallop, clawing at the mane and forelock as she tried to retrieve the reins.

'Hang on, I'm coming!' Will shouted as he rode up behind her. With a quick movement of his arm and body, he grasped the rein and passed it to her, while pulling at the same time on the animal's bridle, in order to slow it down.

Bridie looked pale. 'Thanks, I thought I was a goner there,' she panted, 'let's get off soon and have a rest.'

At the swamps, Will dismounted and helped her down, holding her for a long moment in his arms.

It was a warm spring day but she felt frozen. She fell down onto the grass under the gum trees. Will stretched out beside her.

For a long while, they didn't speak.

'Thanks for saving my life,' she said, seeking his eyes, 'I could have broken my neck if I'd fallen heavily.'

She wondered if some part of her was feigning shock to get his attention.

'Well, then,' he said, perhaps only half joking, 'I can claim you as my own now.'

I wonder if he really means that, she asked herself.

'Come here and let me warm you up, my darling,' he murmured, pulling her towards him on the grassy verge, next to the floating hyacinths.

The delicate mauve of the flowers was in deep contrast to the dank waters of the swamplands on which they floated.

'You saved me from a bad fall,' she said, meeting his gaze. 'Oh, Will, how can I thank you enough, imagine….'

'Don't think about that,' he said, 'I'm just happy to be here with you, alone.' He reached for her hand and kissed it.

They lay back side by side on the grass and looked up at the sky. The two horses grazed.

'Yes, it is nice to be alone,' she said. 'You know, Will, things have gone downhill here since Dadda died.'

'What was it like before?'

'Sing songs around the piano, Ned and Johnny playing the mouthorgan, Mumma belting out tunes, me singing … even had corn harvesting parties with neighbours up until the war started.'

'Any … boyfriends before?' Will asked, trying to choose his words carefully.

'Not really, a couple of double dates, with Stella.'

'There was this girl at school. A bit older than me, I was sort of … fascinated.'

Bridie felt herself stiffen a little. Will pulled her close and kissed her full on the lips.

Should she pull away, she wondered, bracing herself again?

'I'm going to take you to Tumbarumbar, to the Finns'. Family friends on a cattle station, fifteen miles out west. They've got horses to ride, orchards of oranges, pecan and macadamia nut trees, and a creek to swim in, and further off through the scrub, a deep river with perch. The bush is thick and you can get lost in it.'

Bridie's eyes sparkled, even though she'd heard it from him before. She nodded and jumped to her feet, pulling on

Will's hands to do likewise. She had another date to look forward to now.

'Let's go and find Billy,' she said. They could see him at the side of the hill, sitting on a log and smoking a cigarette.

'Here, I'll give you a leg up,' Will said. 'Do you want me to lead your horse?'

'No, I'm alright now,' she laughed.

They met up with Billy and turned the horses' heads for home, Will careful to stay close to Bridie, urging her to hold tightly onto the reins in order to show the animal mastery. She knew Pal, if given free licence, would bolt for Hilltop. She tightened her thighs, pulled on the reins, and leaned forward in the saddle like a jockey. She forgot about her 'seat' for the moment and watched Will. His tawny locks blew in the breeze and she loved him even more at this moment.

Back at the farmhouse, Will dismounted and turned to help Bridie down. For a moment it looked as if he was going to kiss her. Billy pretended not to notice, with a grin on his face. He took control of the two horses and left them together there.

Will pecked Bridie on the cheek.

Eyes were watching from inside the house.

'Let's not keep your mother waiting,' he said.

Will was surprised to discover that he loved the rowdy, raucous way the family ate and talked, all at the same time. He couldn't get a word in edgeways. He watched as the boys shoved mouthfuls of home-cooked chicken into their mouths. He liked the way they ate, as if they relished every bit and mouthful. He gorged along with the rest of them, really savouring the taste of the well-cooked flesh and home grown vegetables.

In a quiet moment, he sat outside and smoked a Camel cigarette under the grape vine. With Billy there was no need for talking. Will preferred not to get him going with his stammer. But there was something he wanted to ask him.

'Does your sister go riding often?'

'Aw, gee, Will, sh-she's not one fer the outside, you know. She's a bit f-frightened ev frogs an' spiders an' things.'

Will was touched by Billy's explanation. It made him feel protective towards his lovely girl. He couldn't quite believe that she wouldn't like nature as much as he did. She would in time, he felt sure.

She was beautiful and funny and sexy all at the same time. Will knew he could change her, if she loved him, as he knew she did. She would surely come to like everything about him, all that he did, and all that he wanted. When she fluttered her long curled eyelashes at him and snuggled closer, he melted every time.

Will was one of those people who instilled confidence and a desire to unburden yourself.

'Will, it's great to have you in the family,' Billy said without a stutter. 'It's like you're part of it now.'

Will smiled. 'Billy, all I want in life is to have a property and animals, you're lucky to live on the land.'

'It's a tough life, Will,' said Billy as if he'd lost his stutter for good. 'Droughts and floods, and no money coming in. Working like dogs. I wouldn't wish it on anyone, mate.'

'I could make a go of it, if I had the chance. It just takes a bit of foresight.'

'I know you've got what it takes up top, Will. None of us had much schooling to talk of where I come from. An' when Dadda died, you know?'

'Yes, Bridie's told me about it. Must have been hard on all of you.'

'Yeah, it was a big shock, 'specially for Mumma. Never really got over it.'

'I suppose that's why she's so protective....'

'Yes, 'specially with Bridie. Dadda's last words before he died were *Look after the little one, Eliza,* even though she was becoming a young woman by then.'

'Talking of Bridie, let's get back, eh?'

When they got back inside, he saw that Bridie was looking out for them.

Out on the verandah after the meal, he and Bridie stood close together as Eliza prepared tea. Their bodies touched. She nestled her head into his chest. In the next-door paddock, the black stallion frisked with the mares and the fillies.

He put his arms around her from behind and kissed her on the nape of the neck. Then he was fondling her breasts through the silken blouse, lifting it. He felt the cherry-like nipples harden beneath his fingers.

She shivered at his touch. She turned towards him, brushing his chest with her breasts. She froze.

Eliza had appeared in the doorway and saw what Will was doing. 'Enough of that!' she snapped. 'Come in, Bridie, and help me in the kitchen.'

Bridie looked at Will's ashen face. She was embarrassed too, but more for him than for herself.

'I'm going home,' Will said. 'Pick you up tomorrow.'

'Can't you stay a bit longer?'

'No. Gotta get home.'

And with that he jumped on his racing bike and rode off along the bumpy track to the highway.

'Mumma, you've frightened Will off. He was going to stay for tea.'

'I've told you, girl, there'll be no goings-on under my roof! If you want to carry on like that you'll have to leave home, and get a job. You'll be with child before you know it, an' all on your own. He'll be off like a flash.

No Featherstone'll want to marry you, mark my words.'

Chapter 7

'Bridie's been telling me all about you,' he said as Stella, auburn hair gleaming like red gold, jumped into the back seat of the car.

'The pleasure's all mine, Will,' said Stella, holding out her hand and smiling.

'Maybe you'll like one of the Finn boys,' giggled Bridie, her eyes a-glitter with mischief.

'No match making, now, Bridie,' said Stella, laughing, as they set off, 'you know the trouble that's got you into before.'

'Tell me more,' laughed Will.

'Maybe for another time,' said Stella.

They drove westwards, the sun behind them, Will talking about some of the places that they passed on the way.

'Is it too early to call in on my old friend, Reenie?' he asked almost to himself. 'Told her I might be introducing you, Bridie.'

Bridie gulped inwardly, 'Yes, of course, if you think…'

'Come in, Will, girls,' Reenie said from the verandah, showing a broken tooth with a gaping smile. Where are ya orl headed?'

'Going to Tumbarumbar, Reen. Worried about springing a surprise visit on you.'

'Like last time, eh? You looked white as a sheet,' she said with a wink, not missed by Bridie.

Will introduced Bridie and Stella.

'Well, come in all, an' have a cuppa and a bit ev cake, before you go on.'

He reminded Reenie about the victory dance.

'Hello, hello. I thought you were still in love with me, Will.'

'I'll forever be that, Reen, we always were kindred spirits, weren't we?

'Ever since you first caught sight of me doing the vaulting at high school,' she laughed out loud.

'Before Len swept you off your feet,' chuckled Will, 'at least he was the same age as you.'

Reenie hugged Bridie in wiry arms, and said with a huge grin, planting a slobbery kiss on her cheek:

'Only joking, Bridie, he's been talking nonstop about you.'

'All good, I hope,' said Bridie, smiling back. She liked the natural, freckled look of this woman, who had Will's best interests at heart.

'That's for sure,' said Reenie. 'I've been hoping for him to come down off his high horse. Thinks he's too damned good for everybody round these parts.'

Reenie was chuckling as she said this, punching Will in the arm.

'He's been telling me about you and Len too.'

'Don't believe all he says,' said Reenie. 'He's a bushie, like me, and we only understand horses and cattle.' She laughed like a jackass at this and punched Will in the shoulder again.

'If it's not what you want, get out now, kid, while the going's good. And you won't say your friend Reenie didn't warn you, will ya?'

'Steady on there, Reen,' said Will. 'You'll frighten her off, if you're not careful.'

Bridie felt a shiver run up and down her spine at Reenie's words. Her face had drained of colour and she clutched at Will's hand. The obsessive thought....

Reenie came over close to Bridie's side and hugged her once again.

'Just kidding, Bridie,' she said. 'I'm a bit jealous of you two, you know?'

'I hear that your man's been away at war?' Bridie said.

'Yes, and I'm hoping he'll be found soon,' she sighed. 'It's the not knowing that tears at the ribs, you know, only married for six months before he got the call up.'

'I can't imagine ... how terrible that must be,' Bridie said.

Reenie took them down the back to see her horses. They sat on the creek bank and talked about first meetings.

'We chose one another as friends from the first day at St Joseph's,' said Stella. 'Neither of us liked the snobs in the school, especially the daughters of landed gentry folk, the Ogilvie girls and the Onslows.'

'Same for us, eh, Reen?' said Will, 'Never could stand the stuck up ones, who thought they were better than everyone else?'

'Yairs,' said Reenie, 'we even went to a school dance together, remember?'

Will bit his lip. 'Any other news out this way?'

'Heard some goons talking on the wireless about flying saucers in the district.'

'What d'you reckon about all that?' asked Will, taking Bridie's hand.

'Well my mob on Mum's side, the Bundjalung, talked a lot about *min min lights* that chased you. Scared us kids by telling us the lights would come an' get us if we were bad.'

Will gulped. 'Gee, Reenie, first I've heard about that.'

'Yeah, well I thought it was just dreaming, you know? But Dad, being white and a drover, talked about stories told around campfires as the herd grazed. Scared out of his wits he was by the crazy stories. Not everyone could see them, he said.'

'D'you think it could have been min min lights, the local men saw?' asked Will.

'They wez full as ticks, is what I reckon, after a stint at the local.'

'Guess you're right, Reenie. You always were the level headed one, weren't you?'

'Yeah, not that I could say the same fer you, always. What do you think, Bridie about these min min lights?'

'Well, I don't know, Reenie', she said, 'but there's lots of things hidden out of sight, that can't be explained, I know.'

Will said he'd ask the Finns whether they'd heard of any yarns about strange lights or sightings of UFOs in the district. 'But now we really must set off,' he said.

'Fingers crossed for that man of yours, Reenie,' he called out to the slim figure waving furiously from the gate. 'And let me know if you need any help. You know you can count always count on me.'

The three Finn boys jumped up and shook hands violently with Will. He introduced the two young women to them, and they all smiled and shook hands.

'Oh, so you are the little lady I've heard so much about from Margaret?' said Mabel, peering into Bridie's flushed face. How could that be? She hadn't even met Will's mother yet. Was she talking about another of Will's previous girlfriends?

'Pleased to meet you, Mrs Finn,' Bridie said, and she held out her hand to this woman with neat grey hair, home permed into a halo around a dimpled friendly face.

Will stepped forward and rescued Bridie. 'Mrs Finn, Mum hasn't met Bridie yet. I've told them all about her, that's all. Mum and Dad are both looking forward to meeting her, next week.'

'Oh, I see, so we have the honour of meeting her first. And her lovely friend, Stella.'

'Yes, I've been telling her all about Tumbarumbar, and all about you, my second family here.'

Bridie blushed at the thought that she had been the topic of conversation between the two matrons, twittering like birds up and down the wires, without the true facts being shared. *Oh what a tangled web we weave*, she thought. She imagined the telephone wire like a snake, buzzing with gossip about her and her family. It was not surprising that her boyfriend had been loath to admit the truth to his family about her. *Why couldn't people be honest with one another? You could choose your friends, but you were stuck with your families....*

Will put his arm around Bridie's shoulders and indicated a place next to his. He whispered in her ear, 'I was going to tell you when we were alone, Mum wants you to come to lunch next week.'

She'd had no idea Will had even mentioned her to his mother. What a strange world it was. But at least she felt at ease with the Finns, plain country folk that they were.

'In any case, she's as pretty as a picture, your Bridie, Will, and I shall be relaying the message back to Karrana. Yes, that I will ... pretty as a picture.'

Bridie's legs shook underneath her. Being discussed like this, it was a shock. She was already having kittens about meeting Will's mother and father.

'Come and join us at the table,' Stan shouted. 'Pull up chairs for the visitors, boys. There's plenty of tucker here for all.'

It was always like this, from what Will had told Bridie. He was part of the family, and everyone connected to him was welcome too.

'It's a paradise you've got here,' Stella said.

Stan and Mabel beamed with pride and nodded: 'You're welcome to come here any time, young lady ... Stella,' they both said, almost in chorus.

'How are your Mum and Dad, Will?' asked Stan.

'Just fine. They want to come out for a visit and a game of tennis soon.'

'We'd like that too. Soon as branding finishes, we'll give them a buzz about it,' said Stan.

Leon and Carl Finn suggested a walk to the river for a spot of fishing, well beyond the house. Perhaps to swim in fresh water.

Bridie was pleased to escape from the table, and the prying eyes of the lady of the house. Stella, too, jumped at the chance to see more of the property. Fishing tackle and togs were quickly packed in baskets for the walk through thick bush. They passed through citrus and macadamia nut orchards before they reached the rain forest.

Bridie and Stella saw how Will came to life in this garden paradise. He led them through the bush, pointing out the natural beauty of the flora on all sides. Soon there would be wattles blooming, he told them, adding to the concert of sight, smell and sound that always stirred up his senses in this secret nirvana.

You could hear the river tinkling over stones. Farther upstream there was a waterfall you could walk behind. Will recited the names of the fauna and insects they saw on the way: *Imperial Blue butterflies* and large *Monarchs* fluttered between sun and shade. Only the calls of native birds broke the silence, along with the gurgling water.

He pointed out the eucalyptus smell that floated in the air. Blue, ghost and spotted gum trees lorded overhead, forming a canopy. Casuarina and stringy bark grew adjacent to the riverbank that appeared suddenly before them.

Will shouted the praises of the crystal clear water, *clean, drinkable, really* .... before going off downriver in pursuit of his mates to catch some fish and have a swim.

Chapter 8

'I've never seen him so excited,' Bridie said, as she settled down next to Stella, who'd found a perfect shallow part of the river with a grassy knoll overlooking it.

'Let's have a bit of a paddle,' Stella said, 'before they come back.'

They'd taken off their shoes, and nothing else, and lifted up skirts to enter the shallows.

Sitting on the riverbank, they dipped their feet into the cool of the pristine river, sunning their legs and arms, and splashing the water over their skin.

'Talk about euphoria,' Stella sighed.

They lay on their backs and looked up at the sky, struggling to show itself through the cathedral like canopy overhead.

Sometimes, if you were quiet, Will had told them, you could catch sight of a male lyre bird doing its flirty dance.

They watched and listened.

The men were soon out of sight, but the women could hear them chuckling and chiacking, as they went further downriver to the bridge overlooking the deepest part. They were casting out their lines baited with cicadas caught along the way. By the sound of their cries, it seemed like they were having beginners' luck at fishing, as well as great fun.

The two friends imagined them hauling in dozens of shiny, slippery bodies of fat bellied river perch.

Soon the two women were walking towards the voices, to see if they'd in fact caught a barrel load of fish.

'That's enough for tea,' sang out Carl, showing the women a bucket with six fish, still jumping, inside.

'Poor things,' whispered Bridie, wondering if they could feel the place where the hook had entered.

Stella laughed at her.

'Let's have a swim before going back,' shouted Carl.

'Yeah, come on, mate,' called Leon with his nasal drone, 'see who's too scared to jump from the bridge.'

'No yeller bellies here, mate,' said Will.

They took turns to dive into the river from the bridge, aware of the two women watching them.

'Freshwater swimming,' cried Will. 'There's nothing like it.'

'Next time,' sang out Bridie. 'We're happy to relax and watch you from the bank.'

'Yes,' cried Stella, 'we liked paddling and listening to you lot skylarking.'

Stanley, the eldest of the Finn brothers was looking at his watch.

Bridie saw that the Finn brothers, shy in front of women, were loosening up a bit during the walk back to the homestead. They'd had a quiet yarn with Will, parts of which she'd overheard, while they were drying themselves with towels on the riverbank.

'So what do you think, boys?' he'd asked. 'How d'you like her?'

'She's a bonzer sort,' from Leon, 'and as for that Stella....'

'Well, come on and chat a bit. You need to get in some practice, if you fellows want to find a wife any time soon.'

Stella talked to them about her work, assisting the local vet in Karrana.

'Gee, I've never met a lady vet before,' Leon guffawed. 'You can come out here and help out with the calving whenever you like.'

'Not really a vet, more a receptionist, but I've gained the boss's confidence, coz I know a bit about horses and I love working with animals.'

Bridie had a private thought once again, that Stella, with her love of horses, would be a perfect mate for Will. Not to mention Reenie. She was sure they'd had some sort of a fling back in the past. But she pushed the thought out of mind.

He was hers now, and that was that.

Still, she'd like to ask him a little more about that time in his life.

Back at the homestead, the last rays of the sun had cast a pink halo around the red tin roof. Afternoon tea of homemade scones, jam and cream from the dairy awaited them.

They were so relaxed that Bridie had forgotten to remind Will about the time.

Stan Finn said: 'If you boys clean the fish, Mum will cook them, and we can all have a dinner of fish before you set out for home.'

'Afraid we'll have to leave before dinner, Stan,' Will said, 'Bridie's mother is expecting her back soon.'

While Mable was packing up goodies for the guests, Bridie heard how Mabel had schooled her three boys, and saw that it had served them well. They might've been a bit slow at socialising, but they were clever with their hands, and easy-going. Kind too, and Bridie saw what Will liked about them.

'It's been an amazing day, Mr and Mrs Finn,' Stella said.

Bridie agreed, her lit up face and eyes showing real enjoyment.

Stan and Mabel Finn glowed with pleasure. Mabel had filled bags with fresh eggs, home grown vegetables, macadamia nuts, oranges and stone fruits from the orchard for the visitors to take back with them.

'Next time, you'll have to stop for a proper meal,' she said.

'Oh dear, the light's already failing, Will,' said Bridie. 'I'll have to phone Mumma, so as not to worry her.'

Mabel took her inside to use the telephone in the hall.

The car bumped its way over the cattle grid. Stan, warning them to watch out for those *min min lights*, stood and waved, his arm around Mable's shoulders.

Will tooted the horn.

'They're such lovely people,' Stella said in the car on the way back.

'I love the house and the gardens,' said Bridie. 'I'll be happy to visit Tumbarumbar again any time.'

'Mum and Dad get on well with the family, too,' Will said, pleasure lighting up his words.

'But Mabel, she's so countrified, isn't she?' Bridie whispered to Stella, leaning over the back seat of the car and giggling, while Will was fiddling with the car headlights.

'You're too critical, Bridie,' Stella said. 'Don't forget those snooty girl boarders at school, not many of them, but those that were....'

'The Onslows, yes,' she said.

'It's really beautiful out this way,' Stella said. 'I could live here happily, if I had my horses.'

'But it's solitary, away from civilisation and all, isn't it?'

'You're too hard to please, Bridie,' Stella said with a sigh.

'I guess you're right, Stella, but I want to go up in the world a little, not become a bushie. And Leon looks a bit …

goofy, doesn't he?' It was the only word she could think of to describe her reaction to Will's best friend.

Still, she could see Leon settled down with a plain looking country girl wearing an apron in front of a kookaburra stove. Like Leon's father who'd married Mabel and made her happy. With his country gawkish looks, Leon would attract the likes of the Page girls Will had told her about, for the isolated life of a farmer's wife. She thought about how she might bring them together.

The Finns' life together, fossilised a bit like petrified wood, had been one of contentment. It's true that they seemed happy together, and after three decades.

She wanted more out of life, she realised. But just what, she didn't yet know.

She wondered for the umpteenth time if he was the right one to spend her life with.

She could not see past her raw feelings for him, and the pull like a magnet towards his well packed frame and earthy good looks. He smelt like the bush, the fragrant part of it that she loved and that would stay with her forever. Only problem was, she wanted more.

Will put the lights on high beam, as they were approaching Reenie's house, in total darkness now, but lit up by the glow from the moon.

'I really like Reenie,' Bridie said out loud. 'Such a warm person, and full of fun.'

'That's for sure,' Stella agreed.

'I'm glad you like her,' Will said. 'The best friend a man could have.'

'Let's put some of the goodies from Tumbarumbar on her front verandah for a surprise,' said Bridie.

'Well, so long as they're in a sealed box, so the possums won't get at them.'

He slowed down and did as he was asked. The dog barked, then quietened down. It seemed to know it was Will, by recognising his smell.

During the last few miles, Will repeated the invitation from his parents for lunch next weekend. He reassured her that they would love her, just as he did.

'I'm nervous about it, Will,' she said.

'You don't have to be, my dear,' he said. 'They're a bit old fashioned, that's all.'

Bridie looked at Will's profile and saw his chin and jaw stiffen a little, as he spoke.

Stella in the back was quiet.

'I'm still worried about it,' she said, her lips trembling now.

Around the next bend, a kangaroo jumped on to the road and was flung on to the dashboard of the car.

The two women screamed. Bridie covered her eyes with her hands.

Will put the brakes on and steered the vehicle into the culvert. The large furry body flopped onto the ground next to the Ford. It jumped up and hopped a little way into the scrub, then fell onto its side.

Will got out and followed the animal into the bush. Stella went after him.

Bridie watched from inside the car as they walked up next to the panting body of the wounded marsupial.

Stella touched the animal gently to see if it was breathing. Bridie imagined blood pouring onto the ground from its head.

Will was whispering to Stella.

He went to the boot of the Ford and returned with something hard and silver, some sort of a tool.

He followed the trail of blood back into the bush…to make sure the creature was dead and out of pain?

He knelt beside the kangaroo's soft body, still pulsating with life.

Stella was beside him when the blow fell on the animal's head.

Chapter 9

Bridie sneezed on the front steps of Honeysuckle Cottage. The sweet-smelling vines irritated her sinuses and she pulled back.

'You look gorgeous,' Will said to reassure her as he led her up the steps and knocked on the door.

She had on a checked gingham dress pulled in tight at the waist. This was her most chaste looking frock. Red suited her, she knew that. Her hair, swept back and up, was held in place with a tortoise shell clasp.

'Mum, Dad, this is Bridie. Bridie O'Toole.'

Margaret Featherstone wiped her hands neatly on a floral apron, before offering her hand.

From one look at the stern proud face and permed hair of Mrs Featherstone she, Bridie O'Toole, decided that she would never like this woman with her steely poise. Her manner seemed to be saying, *You have no place here, you'll never belong here.*

Margaret Featherstone emitted a nervous sort of laugh as she spoke.

'I've heard a great deal about you, Bridie. I hope you like Irish stew?'

'Oh, yes, Mrs Featherstone, it's one of my favourites.'

Will's two young sisters, were bringing into the dining room the antique plates laden with steaming stew and mashed potatoes, garden peas and carrots.

Henry Featherstone, with his peppery hued hair, and the Old English accent she'd heard in movies, charmed her. He said something like 'Broady' or 'Birrdy' when he said her name. It made her feel special, as if her name was out of the ordinary. She relaxed a little under his spell.

'I was beginning to think Will was making you up, Bridie,' he said, shaking her hand, 'so long it has taken him to let us meet you.'

'Did you like Tumbarumbar,' asked the lady of the house, 'and our friends, the Finns?'

'Oh yes, Mrs Featherstone. It's a magical place.'

The two Featherstone girls, plain and gangly, not at all like their handsome brother, stared at Bridie.

She took her seat between Will and Henry at the large shiny walnut dining table. Will touched her gently on the knee to reassure her. She concentrated on the silver cutlery. Would she be able to hold the knife and fork in her hands without wabbling or spilling peas on the floor? She felt her throat seize up.

'Not too much for us, Mum,' Will said, raising his hand in a stop sign, 'we're not starving, you know.'

Mrs Featherstone set a large helping of meaty sauce and vegetables down in front of him.

Bridie's usual healthy appetite had ditched her.

Thankfully, her helping was smaller than Will's. He patted her on the knee when it was time to start eating.

Bridie nibbled on her food and said nothing. Eyes were boring into her, sizing her up.

She felt like a rabbit caught in the spotlight. She must remember to close her mouth when eating. She would have to speak in between forced mouthfuls.

Her insides began to gurgle from the hot stew. Could they hear it?

'So, where did you go to school, Bridie?' asked Mrs Featherstone.

'St Joseph's Convent.' She blushed. 'On the south side.'

'I see.'

She felt all the better for the few words she'd managed to produce. They were watching her every move. She didn't want to look like a poorly educated person from the wrong side of the track.

'I had to leave school after my father died … to help my mother at home.'

A red flash came from somewhere within, energising her. She looked around her and said the only thing that came into her mind:

'I like your house, Mrs Featherstone. It's a lovely home.'

'Thank you, dear,' she said and smiled, a little too amiably.

'Tell me about your farm, Bridie,' said Henry with real interest.

'Well, it's just, jersey milkers that my brothers run, as well as cream making machinery… a trolley track up to the road … and crops.'

'It sounds,' he said, 'as if you are wholly self-supporting.'

'Yes, we grow our own vegetables, as well as keeping chickens and pigs.'

'That's marvellous,' and he sounded genuinely impressed.

'It's a great set-up,' said Will, 'corn fields, lucerne, mulberry trees, loquats and watermelons, as well as the dairy.'

'By the way, Will,' said his father, 'your mother and I have talked over the plans for your going to Sydney.'

Will looked up expectantly. His mother had been behind the idea from the start. That he knew only too well.

Henry cleared his throat. He didn't catch his son's eye.

'I have a proposal for you to consider, Will.'

Bridie knew instantly that it hinged on her. They'd thought up the plan before they'd even met her.

Henry still refused to meet his son's eye. He concentrated on the bright green and orange vegetables on his plate, as he sliced them neatly with his knife and fork.

'I shall pay for your course fees and lodgings in Sydney for the coming technical college term. It's an immediate start.'

Will's face showed no surprise nor pleasure.

'You mentioned mechanics. I've already made enquiries.'

'I had no idea that the term was about to start,' said Will, as if caught off guard.

'What about it, Son?'

'Of course I'd like to gain experience, Dad,' he mumbled, 'and mechanics is what I'm good at, but....'

'Your mother has found a boarding house near the college.'

In vain, Will sought out his father's gaze.

'I'll have to talk it over with Bridie.' He reached out and took Bridie's hand, which was shaking. 'This is a bit sudden.'

After dessert of blancmange and jam, plates were being taken away.

For the first time that day Henry met his son's eyes. He cleared his throat again.

'I propose that,' and he looked straight at both of them, 'if you two young people are still together in six months' time, or perhaps more reasonably, in one year's time, then we shall see about plans for your engagement.'

Will's sister's eyes shone at the prospect of being bridesmaids at their brother's wedding.

Henry proposed a toast for the adults, with a small glass of sweet sherry each.

'To your future course, Son,' he said. 'And may you both make the right decision about your future.'

'Thanks Dad.' Will took the glass of sherry, draining it quickly, and refilled it, slushing some into Bridie's now empty glass. He looked white as a spectre.

Bridie had swallowed something that felt hard and stuck in her throat. The second glass of sherry smoothed it out. The spirits inflamed her. *So sweet*, so *soothing*.

'Now, dear, why don't you show our young visitor around the garden?' said the mother. It was a signal of reprieve for both of them.

'We'll be off then, Mum, Dad,' he said. 'I'll drive Bridie home.'

Once outside, he put his arm around her shoulders. She was shaking.

'I'm sorry it had to be so awful for you,' he said. 'I'll try not to put you through that ritual again.'

'Come and I'll show you the tennis courts and the river.'

'It's just …,' she stumbled over her words, 'did he say in two weeks' time?'

'Yes, I wasn't expecting to have to leave so soon … a bit of a shock for me too.'

They drove further along the river, heading away from the cottage. The willow trees lining the bank at this spot filtered the strong sun's rays and spread a silvery sheen across the darkening water.

Bridie sniffled and sobbed, 'I d-don't want you to l-leave,' going through several hankies and asking Will to take her home. She hated him seeing her like this with smudged makeup and red eyes.

He held her to his chest. 'I just want to make you happy, Bridie.'

'They don't think I'm good enough for you, that's it, isn't it?'

'Darling,' he soothed, stroking her hair and breathing her in. 'It won't be easy for me, either. I can't bear the thought that I might lose you now, just as I've found you.'

This set off another outpouring from Bridie.

'It's for the best, darling. I'll be able to set myself up with a trade, not just depend on Dad for handouts.'

'Why can't you settle down here and forget about a career? We'll make do without money.'

'It's not that simple, darling. I want land. You'll see, I'll come back from Sydney better equipped for the future.'

What she could see was that Will was determined to stand on his own bloody feet. She was impressed, but sad and sorry…and angry.

If Henry had been a hands-on father…. It was all about money, not love.

'I don't care what they think. There'll never be anyone else but you, Bridie, and I think you know it.'

'They want to separate us, don't they?' Bridie said. 'I knew they'd hate me.'

'No, darling,' Will grabbed her, seeking out her eyes, 'they think, if he's going to pay me a higher wage, I need some qualifications.'

Tears were gushing out of her now. Was he out of her reach? Would he always be far above her like a giant towering over her?

Will sank into the grass on the riverbank and pulled her down beside him.

He pointed out where Hilltop would be, 'See, darling…,' although it was out of sight from here

'You don't even like working for your father, do you?'

'No, but Dad's right, anyway. I need to do a course. He's offered to pay for it, at least.'

'Oh, Will, I don't deserve you. You have such a good brain, and heart. I feel … worthless … beside you.'

'Don't worry, this trip to Sydney is for you, too. For our future together. I want you to have the best of everything.'

The easiest part of being in love was the making up after a quarrel. This time it was on the riverbank beneath the protective willow tree fronds that concealed them from view.

They took to kissing, as hunger overcame them.

Will was unable to stop himself, Bridie was drunk on love, and from the spirits she'd imbibed for the first time in her life.

She was giddy, too, from the spring sunshine on her head.

All she wanted at this moment was him. All of him.

She didn't care about his parents' gorgeous flower beds, the honeysuckle vines on trellises and the landscaped, mown lawns and the tennis court.

She forgot about all of that now.

There wasn't any blood afterwards.

Horse riding had seen to that breakage.

Part Two

Chapter 10

The day of his departure was looming. Bridie lay on the sofa in the lounge room, not having touched her lunch.

She'd wrestled during the night with thoughts of Will meeting up with girls in Sydney.

She'd started thinking about an engagement ring, could see herself opening the tiny box with a diamond sparkling inside. Will down on one knee, his hazel eyes sparkling.

She could barely put it into words ... what she wanted.

Would he still love her, now that he'd had his way with her?

Could he afford the ring that she desired?

Their relationship was stumbling against rigid blockades. Like in the fairy stories from childhood, wicked witches casting spells over princesses. Like in Camelot when love was forever unrequited or betrayed. It was no longer the Middle Ages, for God's sake.

They desired to have one another, body and soul. Mature enough to know love, yet no one gave them credence for the fact. Treated like children, they were, by both their families.

Eliza came and stood in the doorway.

'What is it, Bridie? I can see there's something bothering you.'

'Mum, how old were you and Dad,' she paused and sat up, 'when you met?'

'Just nineteen, love. Why?'

'Well then, I'm old enough to get married, aren't I?' Bridie's eyes flared with something akin to anger.

'Marriage is out of the question for you, dear,' her mother said and sat down across from her with a sigh. 'It's the Featherstone lad, isn't it?'

'Mum, I'm in love with Will. I want to marry him.'

'Yes, but you haven't got a footing…,' her mother stammered, trying to find the right words, 'to start a life together.'

'We're ready to make a go of things,' Bridie said with fervour, 'both feel the same way, about it.'

'Even if he asked you to marry him,' Eliza retorted, 'we haven't got any spare money for a wedding right now.'

'I love him, Mum, and that's all that counts for me,' Bridie cried out, her voice echoing around the dark walls of the room.

Mumma was talking fast now, not stopping to take breath, 'It's not just about falling in love, there are practical questions to think about … he's from a different … class to us, different … upbringing….'

Her mother was running out of arguments, Bridie knew. Eliza put a final cap on things, by telling her to ask Ned: 'He'll tell you the same thing, girl … there's no money for a wedding.

Bridie jumped up from the lounge and flung the words out into the room:

'In any case, he's about to go away to Sydney to do a course,' she said, her voice rising, 'for your information.'

'I told you not to depend on him, didn't I? I didn't want you to get hurt like this.'

'Mumma, he's coming back to me. It's just a term break … so he can get ahead.'

'A term cut-off, if you ask me,' she said, looking triumphant, 'I'd like to have a word in those Featherstones' ears, that I would. Thinking they're better than us simple dairy farmers. I have a mind to telephone that Mrs *High and Mighty* herself, and tell her what her son's been up to … in my house.'

'Mumma, you wouldn't have a darn clue,' she yelled, facing her mother, body stiff, screaming at the top of her voice: 'If you do, it's the last bloody thing you'll do, *ever*, before I leave this *God forsaken place* for good.'

There was a knock on the front door, and Stella's melodious voice rang out:

'Come on, Bridie. Will's here too. We're ready to go.'

Will had rung Stella and asked her to act as chaperone for a last urgent visit to Bridie.

'I hate bloody parents,' she shouted, as she raced out slamming the door behind her.

'Me too,' Will said, hugging her, as she fell into his arms.

Bridie led them around the side of the house and out to the back paddocks, without bothering to let them extend greetings to her mother, now standing at the door like a glum spectre.

The three friends saddled up the horses, and set off, Bridie's mood lightening as they cantered towards the river.

On the way Stella said, 'Look, you two, I can see you have things to talk about,' pulling on her reins and meeting her companions' gaze, 'I'm going to ride home, bring Pancho back tomorrow after work.'

'Are you sure, Stella?' Bridie asked, feeling great waves of love towards her friend. 'We'll catch up next week. Plenty of time then, that's for sure.'

'Yes, my friend, I'll be around.'

'Well, there goes our chaperone,' said Will, as Stella trotted off in the opposite direction, waving and yodelling. 'I wonder what your mother will think when we come back without Stella.'

'Well, I'm sick and tired of Mumma with her beady eyes. Let's go for a gallop to the old mill and back.'

They were both quiet while the horses cantered across the grasses to the far paddocks.

She knew that Will was just as worried about leaving Karrana as she, herself, about them spending ten weeks apart. His course, at Sydney Technical College in George Street, was supposed to be for their future together. She knew his parents saw it differently.

It'll be alright, she thought, trying to make herself feel better. Time apart makes the heart grow stronger. They'd be even clearer when he returned.

The horses had got up a good sweat.

At the river, Bridie unsaddled the palomino, got back onto her mount's golden back, and coaxed him into the water to cool off. The only risk was if the horses decided to roll over with riders astride and all. She'd be careful.

'Come on in, Will,' Bridie shouted. 'It's delicious.' Pal was gulping up mouthfuls of water and splashing the surface with his hoofs.

Will jumped down onto the grass at the side of the bank, pulled off the saddle and cloth before climbing back up onto Lady's glistening coat.

He had no trouble gently coaxing the bay in, the water soon lapping at his calves, and he was urging her out into the deep.

Bridie shivered at the sight of Will and his mount going deeper and deeper into the river.

When she next looked outwards, she couldn't see them.

'Will? Will! Where are you?'

Then she saw what looked like a horse's head, water darkened ears and mane poking above the surface, and Will swimming next to his mount.

Bugger, she's rolled. That's never happened to me, ever.

'Let's get out,' she shouted, 'before we both drown.'

The four waterlogged bodies of riders and horses scrambled up the bank. The couple sat amid the ruins of the stone mill buildings to dry off in the sun. The horses shook themselves all over, chewed on grass, and waited patiently.

'Don't be too hard on your mother, Bridie, she's only doing what she thinks is best for you.'

'I know, but she's so … ignorant, Will.'

'Same as mine, thinks she knows better than anyone else in the world.'

'She certainly thinks I'm not good enough for you.'

'And she's wrong there, too.'

'You know, Will, I think I could quite like your father, despite all.'

'Yes, he's always charmed the ladies. Has that *old world* thing about him, but don't be tricked by it. He's got a flinty side underneath.'

Will told her about his mother's maternal ancestor, Robert O'Hara Burke. How he'd died of thirst in the desert trying to fulfil an impossible dream. Ignorant lack of trust in the Aborigines he met, who knew and loved the land so well.

'That's what we're fighting against, Bridie, ignorance.'

'Your father and mother think that this will be the breach that separates us for good, don't they?'

'Well, if they do, they're going to be wrong, that's for sure.'

Tears rolled down Bridie's cheeks. Will hugged her wet body and she shivered at his touch.

'I wish I had a ring to give you, Bridie. That way, we'd be engaged at least, and you'd have to wait for me, wouldn't you?'

'I'd wait for you forever, Will.'

Kookaburras chortled in the gum trees overhead.

The sweet odour of sweat mixed in with river water, the muddy dampness of the earth itself, enjoined them in a rush. Was it rebelliousness, cheeky defiance…against her mother, her brothers and all of them? She'd show them, the lot of them.

The grass here was soft as a bed. He took her in his arms again and kissed her full on the lips.

'I really love you, Bridie,' he said.

'I love you, too,' she whispered into his nape.

They lay on the sunny bank of the river for as long as they could withstand it, the unstoppable urge, a gentle command to meld.

As it happened sometimes when she was sunbathing and the warm tingle between her legs surged upwards, she was feeling weightless and floating. She was slipping away from herself. She was melting into her boyfriend's aura. The surge of her own body pressing ever onwards into his…. Did she even want it to stop?

She was looking at the muted disk of the sun reflected in the river, trying to find herself in the depths of the dark coolness there. Surrounded by overhanging eucalypts and croaks of frogs, the pungent smell of gums and clay invasive as perfume….

All she could see was an optical illusion of herself, at once perfect yet grotesque, in the reflection distorted by the ripples made by the breeze across the surface of the water.

And here she was on the ground. Is this all there is? *Is this really what I wanted?* What about a ring and marriage, a house and children?

She heard the frogs calling, the lizards scuttling.

Wetness on the outside of her body became one with the moisture inside. She was opening up like a giant rose in the spring sunshine. A red beauty. All soft and velvety. How great and strong the physical pull towards the other. Like gravity itself.

Overcoming all obstacles of clothes, propriety and natural aversion, they sought out each other's body in a savage and determined push and pull.

She felt the juices from their wet encounter mingling with the smells of the river and the grass.

They were both naked now, and he fell onto his knees, pulled her over onto her back on the bank, and entered her, spilling his seed into her on the soft grass next to the water.

Flesh upon flesh, they became as one.

Chapter 11

The weather was warming up each day that passed. September turned into October, and spring fervour entered the farmhouse on breezes from the river. Bridie felt it through every pore in her skin.

She missed Will more each passing day.

She'd spoken to him on the phone several times.

She loved to get his letters full of stories about the 'big smoke'.

He told her about the throngs of people in the streets and on the trams; soldiers still everywhere; American accents mixed in with the Aussie ones.

Especially, he told about missing *her*.

He wrote to her every morning. Sometimes he wrote twice daily, remembering the next evening, after he'd sent the letter off, something he'd left out of the previous one. He'd been telling her of his course and his classmates, and about the tall buildings in George Street in the city where he went for his lessons.

Mostly, though, he described how lonely he was feeling, how he was missing her and how he loved her and would do so until the day he died.

After he'd been away for only a week and a half, she already had a pile of sixteen love letters from him, laying out his feelings for her in great detail, as he'd never been able to do in her presence.

She met the postman each morning as he rode up to the letterbox on his horse. A magical feeling wafted over her, soon as she spied the tell-tale blue envelope come out of the postman's bag. This empty feeling in her stomach, food only made it worse, sadness at being separated from Will.

I've really got it bad this time. *Little Bridie O'Toole, head over heels in love. Feels like I'm going crazy.*

By the time four weeks had gone by, slowly and agonizingly, Bridie had read and reread a pile of fifty letters from Will.

She thought of the time they'd 'done it' on the riverbank four weeks' ago, just before he left. She regretted a little the words of love that had tumbled out of her mouth, as they lay under the trees close to the riverbank. She would have to be stronger, resist his embraces.

She was the woman, *the fairer sex*, as they called womanhood. *What a laugh.* She knew that her feelings for Will were just as strong as his for her.

Her mother had said a man's love was like a carnivorous beast, able to sup on any flesh. Would he tire of her, as these words suggested, now that she'd given herself to him?

She tried eking out a tune on the old piano in the lounge room: Doris Day's *When I Fall in Love*. It only made her feel worse with longings for Will. His strong arms around her. His shoulders to lean on, warm voice in her ear.

She wished someone could have taught her about falling in love. What did it mean? Would she feel the same way forever? Her mother had been forced to marry in haste.

'No priest would marry us,' she'd told her daughter, 'unless I converted to the Catholic faith, an' we didn't have time in any case.'

The drudgery of farm work and successive birthings had consumed them, her father dying far too young at fifty-five.

Nat King Cole's voice *Will it be Forever?* kept ringing like a refrain in her mind.

Stella came over to go for a ride. They went towards the swamplands at the back of the farm, where the hills rose towards the western highlands.

'How are you standing up to the separation?' Stella asked. 'You look pale.'

'It's agonizing, Stella, waking up at night, just wondering what he's doing, if he's meeting someone else.'

'There wouldn't be much time for that,' said Stella quickly, 'all boys in the course, I imagine.'

'Yes, there's that, I suppose,' mumbled Bridie.

'Let's go for a canter,' said Stella, 'I feel like jumping logs again.'

Bridie followed after Stella, jumping over several logs, but she lacked energy, or was it spirit, today?

'Last time I rode with Will, we ended up in the river,' she laughed, 'and then we rolled in the grass together, all wet and....'

Stella had dismounted and was sitting on a log, smoking. Bridie followed suit but she didn't light up. She felt Stella staring at her. Bridie looked back at her friend.

'You didn't, did you?' Stella asked.

'Yes, we did.... Oh, Stella, I'm worried now.... What if I'm ... in the family way?'

'Surely not, after only one time?'

'Well, that's how it happened with Mumma, you know?'

'She might have been just unlucky.'

'What if it's the same for me? He's been gone thirty-five days, and there's still no sign of my ... period.'

'Look, Bridie,' said Stella, in her vet assistant's voice, 'there are only three days, right in the middle of the cycle, when it's dangerous, so to speak.'

'I hope you're right, Stella,' said Bridie, feeling much better now.

'You'd have to be ovulating just then, or the next day, and the fact that you got on horseback soon after, it's very unlikely that you're preggers after that one time.'

'So I'll probably expect my 'rags' to start any day soon?'

Bridie started running to the bathroom and to the lavatory to check for any sign of blood. She knew that Mumma would probably notice the to-ing and fro-ing, but hoped that the crimson river would flow before too long. She'd think it was fretting for Will Featherstone, since he'd taken off so suddenly, that was causing discomfort and upsetting her tummy.

Day after day, with the nausea increasing and the lack of any sign of red, she had to admit that something was wrong. There was a strange 'downwards pulling' force beneath her navel. It was a new sensation.

'No thanks, Mumma, I feel sick,' as she pushed the plate of bacon and eggs her mother had placed before her on the polished table.

She was running to the lavatory every few minutes.

'What did I tell you?' Eliza hissed. 'That young fellow has got you in the family way and run off to Sydney an' left you to deal with it.'

'No, Mumma, Will writes to me every day. And he's been ringing me, as you well know. He won't leave me in the lurch. He's already hinted at getting married when he comes back.'

'A lot of poppycock! His family won't hear of it!'

'It's not up to them, Mumma. Will loves me and that's all that counts. Even if we have to live here with you.'

'There's no room for that, and you know it, my girl.'

'Well, I'll go and join him in Sydney. We'll stay with Aunt Annie till we get married and on our feet.'

Eliza O'Toole coughed and turned away at the mention of marriage and her older sister's name. 'I warned you about this, a bastard without a father for support.'

Bridie gasped inwardly. She longed for her boyfriend's deep voice. His soothing words. Four hundred miles separated her from him in his Glebe boarding house. Four hundred lonely miles, echoing now the distance she felt from her mother. It was words that she needed. Comforting words. She wondered if he would ring that night. Nausea was easier to bear than the harshness of Eliza's words. Would she be able to find the right words to tell him the news, without giving in to tears that she felt welling up inside her?

Bridie decided that she would write a letter to Will about their situation. She sat down with pen and paper and began the task. Easier to do on paper, rather than over the telephone. She hoped that the act of writing would help her get her thoughts in order. Yes, she could express herself well in writing. It was one of her greatest strengths.

My dearest Will, she began. She continued the task by explaining their situation, telling him as simply and as honestly as she could, that he was to be the father of their child, already forming inside her body. She had no idea how they were going to get on, but she knew he would support her in her decision, either to keep the child and to live with her, in Sydney or in Karrana, as an honest woman, or….

In other words, she was indirectly accepting his proposal, which he had already let her know he was on the point of doing, on his return.

Bridie could see that her mother was itching to set the fox among the fowls in the chook yard, and call Will's parents.

'I'm going to ring those Featherstones, and let them know about this, Bridie,' she said.

Bridie screamed at the top of her voice: 'You'll do no such thing, you madwoman! I'll look after this myself.'

She remembered Eliza telling her that Aunt Annie had helped her with her plans to have Baby Ned in Sydney. It was time to stand up for herself, time to make some hard decisions.

Bridie filled her chest and invoked all the saints the nuns had taught them about. Especially Archangel Michael, who'd always come in handy at exam times and other periods of high nervousness. He'd give her courage to stand up to her mother, to Ned, and to all of them.

She gulped in deep draughts of air, before speaking in a cool crisp voice:

'I'm catching the overnight train to Sydney to stay with Aunt Annie,' she said. 'She'll help me decide what to do. As she helped you, before.'

It was like history repeating itself for sure, she thought.

Eliza looked like a balloon deflating.

Bridie rang Will to tell him the news before he'd received her letter. He was ready to cancel his studies and return to Karrana. She burst into tears. They were tears of rage. Against destiny. Why was this all happening over again, as it had for her mother and father?

'Stay there, I'm getting on the mail train tonight,' she said, 'meet me at Central Railway Station tomorrow morning. We'll talk and decide what to do.'

'Right, of course I'll meet you. I'd move heaven and earth to be with you now.'

'I can stay at my Aunt's place. In Dover Heights.'

Eliza tried to talk her out of it: 'You don't have to do this. He should be the one to come to you.'

'Not after the meddling and lack of support from everyone.'

'We were only trying to stop this from happening.'

'Well, you can help some more by phoning your sister. You wanted to phone around, so you can blooming well set it up with Annie for me now. Just tell her I'm coming to stay for a while. I'll tell her why when I get there.'

'I've always done what I thought best for you.'

'Have you forgotten how you and Dad started off in life?'

'I was trying to protect you from that very thing.'

Bridie just wanted to get away from her mother and Ned and the lot of them. Her elder brother would have to drive her to the station, though. But if he said one word about … *things*, she would … scream at him … and jump out of the car.

Guilt and shame, more than the sickness, was making her powerful.

It came over her in waves now, terrible remorse and her misery at the whole unhappy saga. Her dreams of a ring and a man on bended knee were far out of her reach. They would have to make the best of a bad situation.

She'd begun to think of this tiny creature growing inside her like one of those vines that curled themselves around the tree trunks at Hilltop.

It was native mistletoe, stifling the trees, their produce and growth.

Chapter 12

The trip in the smoky dragon that was the Mail train was uncomfortable for Bridie. She felt nauseous and could not sleep as it rattled and swayed along the steel tracks.

The other women in the compartment ate sandwiches and fruit that made her feel even sicker. The smoke trundling back past the windows of the compartment added to her queasiness.

Young men roamed the corridors smoking and staring in at her.

She thought of her mother's journey on the high seas, long ago, carrying a similar guilty secret

She tried to imagine her sufferings, and felt a little sorry for the cold fury she'd unleashed on her before she left.

She was thankful, at least, that Mumma hadn't blabbed down the line to Will's mother.

Will was standing on the platform waiting for her when the train pulled into Central Station. He threw his arms around her and kissed her on the lips. He could never keep his hands off her for long. She felt the same stirrings of hunger for him in spite of her swollen belly.

His skin on hers sent tingles throughout her whole being; she could melt into; become one with him.

'I've missed you, missed you so much, Bridie darling,' Will sighed into her ear.

He stroked her stomach, 'How do you feel?'

'Don't touch me there,' she said as she brushed his hand away. 'I'm sick as a dog. Make me a cup of tea, then we'll go to Aunty Annie's place. She's expecting me. Oh, Will, what are we going to do?'

'Let's talk about it later. For now, I just want to look at you, breathe you in.'

He picked up her brown suit case and, still watching her with smiling eyes, led her towards the exit. 'God, how good it is to see you again.'

At the Glebe boarding house where he was staying, he dropped off his course books and things. Bridie looked over his lodgings, the single room, the dark wood wardrobe, reminding her of her brothers' dressing room back home.

The landlady said, 'Your mother's spoken to me mother about your lady friend's visit.'

She made it clear by the stern look on her face that there would be no carryings-on allowed on her premises.

In the taxi on the way to Dover Heights, Bridie sank into his body and laid her head on his shoulder.

Everything seemed busier and bigger than she could remember from her one visit before.

'So your folk back home know, too?' she said.

'Yes, I told them the news by phone yesterday.' He spoke the words as if there was no guilt, no shame, a simple matter of fact.

The taxi passed by the famous Bondi Beach and wound in and out of streets that seemed to branch off in all directions like a labyrinth. The cars and the noise of the city made her feel sick. She would have liked to revel in the sights they passed on the way, swoon over the tall buildings, the fashionable shops, and the masses of well-dressed figures on the streets.

'My family all know, she said, 'apart from Aunt Annie.'

'Let's talk about it later on, don't worry, I'll take care of you,' he whispered into her ear.

She breathed a sigh of relief at his words.

Over a cup of tea in Aunt Annie's house on the cliffs of Dover Heights, Bridie told him how pleased she was to hear his voice at last.

'I look forward to meeting your aunt before long,' he said.'

She pushed him further about his parents' reaction to their news.

'What did they say about what we should do?' she asked.

'You can guess, can't you?'

'No, what?'

'Oh, Bridie, I don't want to say the word … they thought we should consider, you know, seeing someone. Dad knows of a doctor.'

She had heard from a friend about how some girls got rid of their unwanted babies using knitting needles, or even wire coat hangers…. Will was talking about a medical procedure. She hesitated from saying the word 'abortion'. Surely it was illegal, wasn't it?

Yes, Will admitted, it was. And expensive. His father was sending money to pay for it. He'd given him the name of a doctor who performed these operations, and had even made an appointment for them to see this man soon.

Will was adamant. If she decided that she didn't want to have the baby, wanted to get rid of it, then he would pay for the procedure himself.

Bridie had started to see the glimmer of a way out of her predicament. The dark clouds that had shrouded the light of her happiness in recent days parted a little.

She couldn't think of this tiny pin prick of a thing growing inside her womb as a real child.

She wasn't ready to swell up like a watermelon and display her unwedded state in a humiliating fashion before the world. Especially not for Mrs Margaret Featherstone to gloat over in a *told you so* fashion.

The last thing she had wanted was to follow in her mother's footsteps—the shotgun wedding and all that it implied. Nor did she want to spend nine months fostering a child in her womb, only to give it away at the end.

She wasn't ready to be a mother. She simply couldn't bear it. There was a part of her that lacked ... toughness. This parasitic thing growing inside her could strangle her future, choke the plans she'd made for herself to go up in the world.

She had to grasp the nettle, no matter how much it hurt, and rid herself of this unwanted cargo before it was too late.

Her impetuous decision was tempered by an urge deep within that warned against rashness. She would go to no backyard butcher, nor would she risk doing the procedure herself. No, she would let Will pay for the expensive doctor and have it done safely and quickly. They could tell their folks back home that she'd had a miscarriage.

Her aunt, who led a busy life, need know nothing. She had come for a holiday and to buy some clothes. She would indulge in a little shopping, after the event, to make herself feel better. The morning sickness had already begun to subside.

'You're tough, my girl,' Will said and he hugged her as if he would never let her go.

'When is the appointment you mentioned?' Bridie asked.

'Day after tomorrow in the evening,' he said. 'I'll pick you up in a taxi.'

Aunt Annie was a matron at Sydney Hospital. She lived alone now, after the premature death of her husband, a tailor.

She had to go to bed early every day, to be ready for morning shifts at the crack of dawn.

'He's a nice-looking young man,' she said as she sat with her niece at the kitchen table.

A spray of white hair falling across her forehead made Annie's sad eyes even more wistful looking.

'Just make sure he doesn't get you in the family way, like what happened to Eliza.'

Bridie's insides did a somersault; she felt as if Annie was staring through her and might know. Perhaps her mother had told her?

'You don't have to worry about that. We're going to wait until we're married,' she said, which was partly true, since that was her intention from now on.

'That's the way, good girl.'

It was as if the oldies had forgotten how difficult it was, the pull of the body's will, its hormones and juices surging, as powerful and as unstoppable as the great machines of industry, yet silent and out of sight.

'We're spending time together after his course each evening, so I won't be back until late.'

'Alright, dear. I'll see you in the morning. I don't have a shift then.'

On the way there in the taxi, Bridie held onto Will's hand as if it was her life line. She knew that what she was about to do was akin to murder in the eyes of the church, no matter which one you belonged to. It was awful, but she could see no other way out. Why bring an unwanted child into the world? Would God want this?

And adoption would ruin her whole life, as it had for that other aunt, who'd given her baby away forever, never to fall pregnant again.

She clung to him like a vine, until her knuckles were white and she felt that she might never be able to free herself ever again.

'It's going to be all right, sweetheart,' he said in her ear. 'We'll start afresh after this. No one will know anything about it.'

The house in Glebe was a white building not far from his boarding house with a tower, as if wanting to proclaim ascendancy. Ironic given the circumstances. Pitch blackness surrounded them. There was no one home. It looked abandoned, the family all gone away for a holiday. She and Will crept around the side of the large white structure to the back, as they had been told to do. A light flashed on, illuminating concrete steps leading up to a verandah.

They knocked on a green door. A stooped man in his fifties with down-cast eyes showed them into an annexe. Will handed him the envelope with the money inside and sat down on one of the plush armchairs in the room.

'Come in to the surgery,' he said to Bridie, 'and close the door behind you.'

The room was decorated in a homely fashion, and looked a bit like a granny flat. There was a sink, a toilet and a bathroom, but little else. The lights were dimmed. The doctor had access to a brighter light that he used once Bridie was lying in place on the bed. He was brusque yet pleasant, focused on what he was doing. He had a job to do and he intended to do it with the least fuss and time consumption as possible.

'You're already eight weeks,' he murmured, 'perhaps even more.'

Bridie sat up. She'd started holding onto her stomach and imagined she felt a twitch from deep inside. A seahorse flickering its tail against the sides of her womb.

She announced, as if to the whole room: 'I've changed my mind.'

She met the man's gaze, steady as a sentinel, and pushed his charitable hand away.

Yes, she felt a little dizzy as she climbed down from the bed, but not weak. The overwhelming sensation was one of relief. She wouldn't need the pads that she'd brought for the homeward journey.

She smiled and said 'Thank you for seeing us. I'm sorry, I don't want to go through with this.'

The doctor didn't seem at all surprised. He looked around the room, as if searching for someone hiding in the corner. He handed back the envelope. He led her out to the ante-room with a nod towards Will.

'I changed my mind,' she said, and gave him the envelope. He hugged her, his huge frame and dark eyes showing relief, as he bounded to his feet and half carried her out to the waiting taxi.

On the way back in the taxi, she felt elated and downcast all at the same time. Will reached for her hand and squeezed it. She snuggled close to him, but it was her turn now to soothe him. He looked to her as if he were on the point of crying.

A terrible sadness had come over him in the waiting room; he'd wilted like a plant in the midday sun. She saw that he'd taken on himself the full responsibility of the decision to terminate their child.

He could have stopped it if he'd wanted to, he told her. Could have at least tried to. She heard his guilty words, indicating that he had complied and participated in the destruction of this seed of possibility.

A tiny acorn that would have grown into a man like himself.

He felt sure that it was a son. And he had gone along with it like a gardener destroying weeds; a woodcutter toppling old growth trees in a forest.

He felt terribly culpable, sad and tired.

And he had a sense, from deep within, that he might end up having to pay for this decision in some way. He knew it from his closeness to the bush that you didn't get away with wilful destruction of nature. He didn't know exactly what he meant, but he sensed a mysterious force at work in Nature, knew that She always had the upper hand.

'We'll start over,' he kept mumbling. 'We'll get married now. We'll start over.' And she was patting him on the back of the head as he leaned in to her, and comforting him with soft gurgling sounds from deep within her throat: 'Umm, mmm ... ahh ... ahh ... shh....'

Chapter 13

Will got down on his knees and asked Bridie if she would marry him.

'Oh, yes, Will,' she chimed.

She fell into his arms and they collapsed together into the swing chair on the balcony.

She looked out at the wild sea. Everything looked new to her.

She was high on her emotions.

'Let's get married tomorrow,' she said. 'You've got enough money for a ring now, at least.'

'Well, yes, there's that to it, but I wanted to give you a proper engagement, and a country wedding back home in Karrana.'

'Let's not worry about that and just tie the knot,' she said, 'before I start showing too much. I think I'm over the morning sickness now.'

'You've lost weight, darling, instead of gaining,' he said, 'no one would know you're ten or more weeks.'

'Yes, I'll stay here until your course finishes, talk to Aunt Annie about it,' she said, 'it's only a few more weeks.'

'We'll surprise them all back home with a *fait accompli*, save on the expense of a wedding for them,' Will said. 'By the time we get back, we'll be Mr and Mrs Featherstone, and summery days and Christmas celebrations will be upon us.'

'Yes, and no one will have had time to think about anything but harvesting back home at Hilltop,' she said. 'Oh, Will, I'm so happy.'

The dark waters down below, the stars in the sky, the new moon and her gentle giant of a boyfriend's face, all looked gilded with expectation of good things to come. She knew that she'd made the right decision.

Will with his soft edges complemented her in her ability to make quick and right judgments about things.

She sometimes felt that she was in touch with a greater reality that lay just behind this one, an ability to see beyond the contours.

'Will, do you think we're ready to start a life together?'

'We've got our love, and that's all we need to begin with,' he said.

'I want to live in a big house with conveniences like this one.'

'One day, you will, my darling.'

'I love the view out onto the wild sea,' she sighed.

Will approved, but secretly he preferred the quiet peace of the countryside back home.

'I love you,' he said. 'I'm speaking from here,' and he placed one hand on his chest, and with the other drew her close to him. 'Can you hear it beating for you?'

She remembered how he'd pulled her close to his chest at the dance that night. It's what had drawn her to him in the first place, the size of his chest and shoulders, enveloping her. She imagined a giant's heart beating inside that chest of his.

'Well, what's it like, your dream home?' she said, disengaging herself from him. 'You tell me first, and I'll tell you mine.'

'It's high upon a hill,' Will said as he closed his eyes. 'There's views of water way off in the distance, a river.'

'Go on, tell me more. I love to hear you speak, Will. Love your way with words.'

'There are Norfolk Island Pines lining the route all the way up to the homestead. And a gravel road, because it's far from the town.'

'Sounds a bit lonely, that....'

'There's a dam down the back on the flats. The homestead stands on a hilltop, see.' He narrowed his eyes and stretched his hand out towards the horizon, as if he could really see the vision up there in the clouds.

'Are there any neighbours round about?'

'Yes, but far enough away for it to be private. No rubber necks here,' he said. 'Bushland all around where you can get lost. A large herd of Herefords. And closer to the house, a citrus orchard, macadamia nut trees, stockyards, a barn, a creek and horses and....'

'What's the house like, Will? Is it big and smart with all the mod cons?'

'Yes, it will be brand new, built especially for you and our children. It will have everything you'd ever desire, and there'll be ponies for the kids and wild animals, possums and koalas in the trees, kangaroos.'

'Not too wild, I hope? Snakes is what I'm scared of, and dingoes and spiders an' things....'

'I will take care of you always, my darling red red rose.'

'That reminds me of a song *Always* by Bing Crosby. Can you sing along with me now, Will?'

Will put his arms around Bridie and whispered in her ear: 'I love you, Bridie O'Toole, I'll give you the world, but I can't sing very well.'

She took a deep breath of sea flavoured air and sang the words of the song that had filtered through into her thoughts, *I'll be loving you, always....*

The country twang that Aunt Annie had parodied when she kissed her on the day of her arrival, disappeared when she sang, drawing out the vowels and imitating the American accents.

Her face shone in the moonlight, and the sweet notes of her soprano's voice floated out over the sea in the wake of the cool breeze.

She knew that he was the one, the one to drag her out of the mud and swamplands of her background.

'Bridie, I have to tell you,' he said, 'that things will be pretty tough for a while. Until I get on my feet.'

'I know, Will. Don't worry about it. I'd live with you in a tent,' she cried, never dreaming that those soaring feelings could be felled in an instant, like the trees her boyfriend would chop down in bush paddocks to clear the land for the beasts he would raise.

'And the ring,' he said, 'I'll buy you a proper one when I have the money.'

'I love you, Will Featherstone with your funny name.'

'I want you, Bridie O'Toole, every little bit of you, to be my life's companion, and marry me.'

'Oh, Will, I'd follow you to the ends of the earth.'

'That won't be necessary', he said with a chuckle. 'I'll rent us a house on the south bank, close enough to Hilltop, so you can run home a bit. We'll be happy as pigs in mud.'

Over an early breakfast of Billy's tea and toast, Bridie avoiding the marmalade, she told Aunt Annie about her engagement.

'I'm glad you've someone who'll care for you,' she said. 'Such a nice young man. Well brought up, too! I do hope you two stay together.'

'Mumma thinks I'm too young to marry. Says he won't want to settle for a girl from a dairy farm.'

'Well, it's for Will to decide, isn't it? Not your mother, nor his people, either. She tells me they're well off, eh?'

'Yes, but Will wants to strike out on his own. He wants to save up for a block of land to run cattle on.'

'I understand that. But how do you feel about living in the country, far away from the town?'

'Oh, Aunt Annie, I'm scared. I don't know. What if I make a mistake? How do you know when he's the right one?

'You just know, my girl. You just know!'

'Tell me about your marriage to Len. Was it happy always?'

'Yes, happy but short-lived. Because of the accident. I always wanted to do nursing, which was why I'd come to Sydney. Len, the brother of my best friend I'd met at the hospital was from a well to do north shore family. He could have done anything with his life. Had just finished his degree when we got engaged. Head over heels we were!'

'Were your parents happy about it?'

'My father, no. He wanted me back in the country. Couldn't understand how I'd prefer the city to country life. I think it was just meeting Len that decided me. And then…the accident. It was such a shock.'

'How did you find out about it?'

'I was on duty when he was brought in. They stopped me from attending to him. I was hysterical. He'd been so full of life. We had friends and plans for the future. And then one day, he fell under a tram. The doctors tried to save him, but he'd lost too much blood. The only blessing was that I was able to tell him I loved him. Before he went.'

'Oh, Aunt Annie. So sad!'

'I threw myself into my job from then on. Became the best nurse in the hospital. Knew I'd never find another Len.'

'Did you think of returning to your family?'

'No, I wanted to be near Len. It sounds silly, but I felt his energy around me all the time. His family became mine. I was bridesmaid for his sister. Bridesmaid but never a bride.'

Bridie felt a mixture of sadness and awe as she looked at the proud strong features of her grey haired aunt, who was now lost in thought. She prayed silently that she, too, might be granted wisdom without, however, having to be tested in the awful crucible that had been her city aunt's destiny.

She had a sense that her own person was made of flimsier stuff than the strong substance at the core of her beloved aunt's breast.

An image of her boyfriend's robust features came to her then, and she had an irresistible urge to fold him in her arms and keep him safe forever.

'We're getting married before we go back to Karrana, that is, if you will let me stay here, Aunt?'

'Of course, dear, but why the rush?'

'Oh, Aunty,' she murmured, looking down and touching her tummy....

'Darling, no...? You're with child? Of course you can live here with me. I'll talk to your mother about it.'

'Thanks Aunt Annie, I'd love to stay here, but Mumma knows already, about the baby.... And Will's not one for city life. Wants to get back to the country as soon as possible.'

'And what about you? Did you want to have a family ... so soon?'

'Oh no, in time, but I'd have liked to experience life first.'

'It's good to have a job in case something happens to the breadwinner.'

'I don't know what I'd do, apart from secretary. The nuns at the convent taught me typing and shorthand. I haven't worked yet, as Mumma's needed me at home.'

'What would you like to do?'

'I love clothes. Know what looks good on me. If I had the choice, I'd like to work in fashion. I've got a good sense for it, colours and patterns whirling around in my head. If only I could do a course, I know I'd be good at it.'

''Well, it's never too late, dear, as they say….'

Chapter 14

Those months leading up to the end of spring were a time of harvest for the family back at Karrana. Hours and hours of back breaking work, hardening them against fate and the weather. Since Charlie O'Toole senior's death, things had gone downhill for a bit. This time, they'd hired a seasonal worker and accepted help from neighbours. Trying to keep the farm from going under.

Lucerne and corn harvesting had been accomplished, but without the sing songs around the piano afterwards. The threat of war had added to the gloom and Johnny had stopped playing the mouth organ.

Mumma no longer belted out tunes on the old piano to entertain the workers.

'How will we celebrate harvesting this time?' Johnny, always ready for a party, had asked.

'With a dinner like always,' Ned said, nodding towards his mother who'd have to prepare it.

Silent now, the four members of the family and the three helpers devoted themselves to savouring the home-grown pork and vegetables, to breaking the bread hot from the wood fired oven, the clink clink of the cutlery, the only sound to disturb the peace that settled over the old dining room. Eliza O'Toole slaved away at the hot stove, resigned to the heat and to her role as matriarch. She was her family's keeper, after all, no matter what the season.

'When's the married couple coming back?' asked Billy, who, with his child's heart, missed his sister the most out of the brothers.

'My daughter has accepted the hand of Mr William Featherstone,' crowed Eliza, coming out from the kitchen with steaming plates of plum pudding for dessert.

'She is to be married in St Patricks' Church in Belleville Point, on the last day of spring,' she exclaimed, as if reading the news from the gossip pages.

'We regret that we cannot be present at the ceremony, due to harvesting needs, but the bride will be given away by a family friend, Doctor Gabriel Kelly.'

This friend was another 'gift' from her sister Annie, who seemed to pull things out of the air when required, like a magician manifesting a white rabbit out of a black hat.

The priest, Father Patrick O'Shaughnessy, sought out by Annie, had been willing to overlook the groom's Protestantism. 'I'll marry you in my church,' he said when Will and Bridie had met up with him, 'if you can bother to help me with a little donation.'

He'd stuttered and slurred his words, obviously inebriated, but only too pleased to oblige.

'That can certainly be arranged, Father,' said Will, shaking his hand.

'Oh, Will, thank you,' Bridie whispered once out in the street. 'It means such a lot to me, as if Dadda will be present, watching over the ceremony.'

'Well, let's get you back so you can tell your aunt the good news.'

She'd begged Aunt Annie to keep some of the details secret from her family back home

What Eliza did hear about was that her sister had run up a gown for the bride from parachute silk, gifted by a wounded paratrooper. Decorated with sequins and lace, it would be something special and Bridie had enthused: 'Thank you, Aunt, my fairy godmother! Please make it simple, a sweetheart neckline and softly padded shoulders.'

Luckily, she probably wouldn't be showing for a while, this being her first. Annie was pleased that some good news was reaching her sister and family back home. And she'd heard some positive news in the reverse direction.

Ned had been keeping an ear and an eye out around the district for rental properties. He'd found one that might suit the couple on a bit of land close by.

'That's a relief,' she said when her aunt told her, 'they seem to have accepted things now.'

'Yes, Eliza has been on the line whenever she gets a chance. Perhaps you'll feel like ringing her soon.'

Bridie was not quite ready for that. She thought of the teasing from Ned, how he'd guffawed about Will chasing sheilas at *The Troc* in Sydney. She'd fought back, told him he was jealous of Will's good looks and brains.

'A shotgun wedding!' Ned had cried out, relishing the twist that the story had taken, not minding so much that his sister was pregnant out of wedlock, but liking the fact that they now had something to hold over their future brother-in-law.

'Bull,' Ned called him, 'couldn't wait. Forced himself on our sister.'

The brothers were secretly pleased, because Will was from the better side of the tracks, and would bring respect and status to them: A Featherstone in the family, pure English blood.

Will's parents, too, had acted like irritating grasshoppers blighting the crops. They'd hoped that the separation might fix the problem once and for all. How terribly mistaken they were. It had only served to intensify the irresistible attraction that pressed them together.

Will had known that his feelings would be boosted by the forced waiting. Nothing to do with the city pleased him very much. He hated the rattling trams competing with cars and bodies. It was too noisy. There were too many people rushing about like stupid mice in a cornfield, not knowing where they were going. Why were they in such a hurry? What's it all about, this life, he wondered? It was dangerous, too, with tram accidents happening every day. And the sight of poor people, often dark-skinned, struggling to live well amid the city grime, disgusted him. He longed for the peace and quiet he found in the country.

And for his beloved Bridie. How am I going to survive this place for the next few months? he'd asked himself daily.

The main distraction for him had been his studies. As he travelled back and forth from his boarding house, words and definitions rattled around in his brain, competing for reinforcement: *Sump pumps, regulators, alternators; Alloys are mixtures of a metal with other metals or non-metals, e.g. brass is an alloy of copper and zinc.* He knew he would pass his exams with ease, and would return home with a certificate of entry into an apprenticeship. Perhaps with his father or one of Henry's friends. He'd work at two jobs, if necessary, so as to get ahead fast and fulfil his dream of land. Still, it was going to be a tough road ahead for the next few months without Bridie. Often at night, as he lay alone in his dark room, he was beset by jealous thoughts of what she was doing, where she was and who she was with. Was he going to be able to cope for the next three months without seeing her?

And he knew that his mother still refused to believe that her only son was going to wed the O'Toole girl from a dairy farm. One of his sisters suffered from thyroid problems. It gave her a bulging eyed, look. She knew everything, was a constant companion for her mother, and told them what she knew.

'He's going to marry her, Mum,' she said. 'Hope I can be one of the bridesmaids.'

'He hasn't spoken to us of such a thing,' snapped her mother. 'Surely he would inform us first.'

All this talk of marriage irritated his father. He maintained his mask of propriety for the sake of peace. Devoid of emotions either positive or negative, this allowed him to live in a state of near meditative calm.

The O'Tooles, descended from a rich assortment of Catholic and Protestant Irish, including convicts, and poor immigrants, a bushranger or two by association, drew Will to them by dint of contrast.

As it turned out, they'd been separated by a mere five weeks in all, by the time of their forced reunion.

'How many weeks are you?' Aunt Annie had asked as they continued a conversation that had begun on a sunny morning in early November.

'Eight weeks or maybe more, we're not sure. Back home, they think we've come to get rid of it, you know?'

'Oh, that's awful,' Aunt Annie said, and hurried inside, returning with a small box. 'Look, I've got just the thing for you. I want you to have this, it's my engagement ring.'

Bridie opened the box and gasped in delight at the shining diamond on the silver ring.

'Oh, Aunty, it's gorgeous. We were worried about how to afford a wedding ring,' she said and hugged her aunt and kissed her on both cheeks. 'Now we can have both.'

Bridie watched Aunt Annie draw a grid of the streets of the city centre, showing where the great department stores were: 'Here's George Street, Pitt, Castlereagh and Elizabeth Streets, all parallel. And Market, King and Martin Place cut across them like this. Trams are the best way to get about in the city.'

'Well, I've got to rush off now,' Aunt Annie said, looking at her watch. 'I'll see you tonight. We'll make plans for you two to have a proper ceremony, with or without parents.'

Bridie caught the tram from North Bondi terminus for the city centre. What an adventure it was going to be. She felt like a grown-up for the first time in her life.

Soldiers in uniform, many with American accents, were lolling around the streets and in the shops, eyeing her appreciatively.

When she found Elizabeth Street and walked into the David Jones store, she was dazzled by the lights and chandeliers. She felt like a princess escaped from her castle for an outing.

Bridie knew that she was different from Will in this regard. She loved the brightness and artifice of the city. She went straight to the women's fashions and over the space of two hours, searched through dozens of dresses, blouses, hats, shoes and lingerie, knowing that she couldn't afford them, just enjoying trying them on. There was a sleeveless little dress in ivory with burgundy lining that had first caught her attention. *Oh, divine,* she thought as she slipped into it. *I'll have that.* Glancing quickly at the price tag, she did the sums in her head.

Next was a chic and classic frock for evening wear, in black, set off by a lacy white neckline decorated with costume pearls.

Bridie primped in front of the mirror in the fitting room, imagining herself on Will's arm on the way to a fine dining experience.

I love it ... love it. She mouthed the words to her reflection in the mirror. All thought of morning sickness was gone. So ladylike. There's nothing like this back home.

Sadly, as well as the black dress, she had to choose between a lingerie set in ivory and a lacy camisole and tap pants in peach. Afterwards, having chosen the 'wedding night' lingerie set, the spending money Mumma had pressed into her hand as she was leaving, was depleted.

She'd meet Will at the appointed time for lunch in the café here, then set off by tram back to Dover Heights to try on her fashion items.

She was as bubbly as a schoolgirl when she paraded in her new dress for Aunt Annie that night.

'Well, you do look the part in that!' her aunt cried, 'a real mannequin, that's for sure.'

But that wouldn't do for a wedding.

Chapter 15

The Friday of the wedding had dawned with end of spring sunshine blessing the day with its balminess, helped by a light breeze.

Bridie sighed with relief. Perfect spring weather. A good omen.

Will, chafing at the bit for the ceremony to begin, arrived early, and had to wait in the vestry. Annie, the Fairy Godmother, sensed that the groom would be early and waiting at the church for his bride. Stella had come on the overnight train to act as bridesmaid, and a friend of Will's from his course would be a witness.

No bad fairies turned up. Bridie wore the gorgeous long gown Annie had made from white parachute silk, plus a single layer net veil, attached to a headband of white roses. A white pearl necklace was her only jewellery. Her lustrous hair dropped down in cascades around her shoulders. She carried a very large bouquet of red roses interspersed with greenery. The groom's corsages matched this. The handsome groomsman led the bride up the carpeted aisle to the font where the smiling groom, dressed in a dark rented suit and sporting a colourful tie chosen by his bride-to-be, waited patiently. Stella was in a similar style dress to the bride, but with short sleeves instead of long, and in a rose pink shade. She wore a garland of white flowers in her hair, and carried a grand bouquet like that of the bride.

Two tiny flowergirls 'on loan' from Annie's nursing friends, and dressed in floor length puffy pink skirts, primped along behind the bridal retinue, carrying baskets of white rosebuds. A gorgeous page boy dressed in a tuxedo style suit, brought up the rear.

It didn't matter that there were no close relatives in the congregation. Once again Annie had come to the party, inviting her friends from the hospital, doctors and nurses, who enjoyed the ceremony hugely. And curious people dribbled in from the street.

The bride entered the church on the groomsman's arm, to the sound of *Nearer My God to Thee*. Bridie exuded light. Joy lit up her face. She smiled broadly at the sight of the packed congregation.

How on earth did Annie manage it? Perhaps my father, watching over me?

Annie and Stella had chosen the music to be played in the church well in advance: Bach's *Jesu Joy of Man's Desire,* fell on their ears as they entered. Later it would be *Ave Maria* by Schubert, and Beethoven's *Ode to Joy*. The two women had not only helped Bridie with choices, but had wanted to present the readings themselves, having chosen the most popular ones, Psalm 33 for its positive message: 'The earth is full of the goodness of the Lord'.

Even Will enjoyed the ceremony, inserting the word 'love' in his mind instead of that of 'God' or 'Father'. The women read with passion, and *became*, during those minutes, wedding pastors for the Catholic Church. The wedding ceremony was full of signs and symbols for Bridie. The rings, the psalms and the music—all of these spoke of the beauty of marriage and its permanence. Even the pastor appeared to be sober, and mentioned the need for patience in marriage. He talked about how the liturgy that celebrates the marriage of two Christians speaks of a *God of love* who draws human beings into this passion in a profound way. He reminded the couple that the vows they say at their wedding day are all in the future tense 'until death do us part', and that above all, the wedding is only the beginning. He used the example of Pope Pius XII and his great patience during the war, the Holy See choosing to remain 'neutral,' and wait out the end of hostilities. *Even Popes cannot all be saints*, he seemed to be saying. Bridie wondered if he was excusing his own frailties, along with those of the Pope, who'd kept silent throughout the years of atrocities committed by Hitler.

It's all due to fear, she thought, and sayings about *throwing the first stone*, or *walking in someone else's shoes* were competing for proper expression in her mind.

How could anyone have true courage in the face of such brutality?

And then came the best part, the rings to be exchanged, the veil lifted and 'You may kiss the bride' and that first delicious meeting of their lips as a married man and woman.

After the ceremony it was time for photographs on the steps of the church, as the congregation thinned out, and only friends remained, surrounding the bride and groom.

'How shall we celebrate now?' asked someone.

'You're coming home to my place,' Annie said. 'Will's father has generously financed light refreshments for the occasion.'

Bridie, and Will himself, were surprised to hear of this. So his *old man* had come good in the end and let the moths out. Telegrams would no doubt be awaiting them back at the house, too. And here was Annie whispering in her niece's ear about a honeymoon.

Saturday was the first day of summer, and their first day as a married couple. Aunt Annie and the Hilltop family had all contributed money for a honeymoon for the young couple at the Hydro Majestic in the Blue Mountains. One week would have to do. In any case, Will's course had to be wrapped up and there was to be a graduation ceremony. They would be staying together with Aunt Annie, now that they were a respectable married couple. For Bridie, it was like one prolonged holiday, the worry about her pregnancy being over, she felt more in love than ever, and she was one of these lucky women for whom morning sickness was not a problem.

From the date of conception in the early days of spring to the wedding on the last day of that season, before the hot and humid weather struck, the couple had few days to spend together, before the tiny shadow of multiplying cells was shadowing them. Not that either felt in any way inhibited by this unseen presence, as they luxuriated between the crisp sheets of the Hydro Majestic. Bridie had youth on her side, she was supple and felt every cell in her body alive and bursting. Nothing had prepared her for this heady rush towards arousal. At the point of climax, she felt a flow of clear fluid gushing from *down there, between her legs,* mingling with the semen and soaking the sheets.

How could this be? Is this what happens to a woman, too?

Will lay back and looked at her. And saw surprise, mixed with gentle concern, on his face.

'It's alright,' she said. 'Maybe my bladder … gave way.'

'Thought it might be the baby,' he murmured.

He was nearly as innocent and chaste as her. Neither had tasted real love before.

She wanted him more than ever at that moment and moved her body closer and clung to him, sucking in his aroma of salt and earth.

She'd never been happier than these days spent with Will in *The Mountains*.

It was what she imagined Europe to be like. The freshness of the air, even in early summer, the greenness of the vegetation and the beauty of the native waratahs and the imported tulips all blooming together as a positive omen. She imagined, too, that this was to be her lot from this time onwards. Only joy and happiness. That's what life promised, now that she'd found her soul mate.

Bridie was looking forward to returning to Karrana and celebrating Christmas as a couple — with a sumptuous lunch at Hilltop on the twenty-fifth of December. Her mother was phoning Annie, telling about plans for a Christmas celebration at Hilltop, with all family members present, including the Featherstone seniors if they so desired.

She'd heard about the cottage Ned had found for them near Hilltop. It was in bushland, not much clearing had taken place for farming, but it was a start. Will could run a few poddy calves and wieners there. Bridie only hoped the cottage would be better equipped than Hilltop Farmhouse, that was all.

Will told her that he could persuade the owner to drop the rent, give him a bedrock bottom price as a good start to married life. *Old Man Farley* was in no position to barter with him, and he knew that he had the upper hand in terms of brain and will power when it boiled down to it. He felt in his bones that he came from better stock than all of these old codgers trying to eke out an existence on the farms around the place. It wasn't snobbery so much as a sense of entitlement based on self-knowledge; he knew that he had strengths that he had not begun to utilise. He had only been in need of motivation. Finding his true love had given him the piston, to propel him towards his goals.

She was going to have to lose her man for a couple of weeks so that he could look over the place and see how much the owner wanted for rent. He'd stay with his parents, and ask his father about increasing his wage, now that he was a certified motor mechanic. Not to mention his skill in regard to sales.

Feeling the little bump in her abdomen now, she looked down at her figure and thought of her mother's lowboy frame. How seductive she, herself, was by comparison. That was why she had never asked her mother about birth and sexual fulfilment.

She'd never forget the thrill of the honeymoon weeks in the mountains, and that first coming together on the riverbank. They'd been lost in one another, swept away on a ribbon of pleasure almost as intense as pain.

Only pity was it'd ended in a pregnancy.

The little cottage had beckoned him, before he'd seen it, like a beacon on the high seas. Big enough to run a few stock and several horses. He'd realise his dream of land and a life partner who set his heart aflame. He wanted nothing more nor less than to protect her and their baby and to live a true but passionate life. A little creek at the back of the property sounded like a dream. Described it all to Bridie from his imagination. Shy bush creatures, lizards and platypuses, scuttled and hid in the soft clay banks.

She was enthralled and hugged him fiercely, before they found one another's bodies again, for the umpteenth time.

Chapter 16

Bridie's return to Karrana was celebrated by a Christmas lunch at Hilltop. She offered to help her mother dishing out the hot dishes for the table of five. Eliza shooed her away, as she always had, happy to sweat away on her own in her chosen domain. Pleased, at least, to have her daughter back under her roof for a time.

Only Will's family couldn't be present, having gone to Tumbarumbar for Christmas, in response to a long-standing invitation.

Now that he was a member of the family, Will enjoyed the rowdy Irishness of the get-together and was butting in just as the others did.

Billy had caught and killed the rooster that Mumma had baked, along with home-grown potatoes, pumpkin, peas, and chokos, all spattered with buttery sauces and with generous servings of rich brown gravy and seasoning. The aroma coming from the kitchen, fuelled by a wood stove, was amazing, even on such a hot day. Eighty degrees in the shade.

The first course consumed, Christmas pudding and custard was served. Afterwards everyone swaggered outside and lay around on the grass underneath the grapevine trellis at the back of the house. A welcoming breeze off the river began to ruffle the leaves on the vine.

Ned shouted to Will, beckoning him to follow. 'See the mark on the ground over here, Will, it's a trapdoor, see,' he shouted. 'That's where we would'er gone had the Japs come over in their bombers. Underground. Built by a civic group, working in the dead of night.'

'Had no idea,' said Will. Nor had Bridie, who was stunned by Ned's claims.

He went on to boast of an enemy plane being shot down, in the western highlands, not too far from there.

Bridie was shocked at these revelations, at how close the War had come without her knowing it. It was always hard to know how far Ned was prepared to sacrifice the truth for a good story. But she felt that they were at last treating her as an adult now that she was married.

Everyone talked quietly about their hopes for news of Charlie and Shaun, still among the missing.

Once the food had settled, the farmers placed a large watermelon, rich pink inside, on the grass. They cut it up with a cane knife and shared slices around. Stories became more and more far-fetched as the men reacted to the beer they'd imbibed.

One tale was about an old Irish hermit known as *The Prospector* who lived in a hut not far from Hilltop. He looked after the hut, set dingo traps and fossicked for flakes of gold in the creek bed. He made regular trips into Karrana on horseback to pick up supplies, including a small wooden cask of rum and flagons of whiskey. He told pub goers of sitting alongside the hut at dusk, when a naked woman, dripping with water came towards him. She was headless, but she was carrying her head in her hands. Two weeks later, his corpse was found by the creek, next to the empty bottles of liquor.

Bridie was four months pregnant when she saw it for the first time. The rented weatherboard cottage was situated two miles from the O'Toole farm.

In midsummer, the humidity coiled around the cottage ruthlessly. It had a ramshackle verandah at the front, along which a native creeper had taken a stranglehold on a honeysuckle vine, then grasped its way across and up into a lilli pilli tree. Peach and orange trees in need of attention dotted the backyard. To the north, a ghost gum stood with its white trunk and olive green leaves overtaken by a predatory mistletoe vine.

'I know there's a bit of work to be done to make it liveable.' Will's eyes shone with excitement as they pulled up in front of the quaint cottage with the vines almost choking the façade. 'But we can move in straight away if we want. Be together, for good, at last.'

'Yes, there's that,' said Bridie, trying to hide her disappointment.

'And it's near to your mother's place,' Will said, pointing in the direction of Hilltop. 'To help out with the baby and all.'

Will picked her up and carried her inside. He placed her gently on the old sofa in the lounge room.

Hilltop Farm for Christmas lunch had been fine, but once they were man and wife, they'd needed privacy. They'd just spent a couple of pleasurable weeks at the plain but comfy Pioneer Hotel in Karrana. In town, they'd found one another's bodies eagerly, the sheets left soaking wet from the mingling of fluids once again.

Bridie wondered if they could stay there for another week or two, before settling into the new cottage. She knew she was trying to put off the inevitable.

She screwed up her face at the sofa she was sitting on. A squat brown lounge suite with markings like an ugly toad's back did not belong to her. To some other woman with a tight head and steel wool hair.

Bridie smiled up at Will's sparkling eyes in the open, suntanned face above her.

She looked around her.

Her spirits sank.

Her dream home was modern, not running down around your ears. And it was in town, preferably on the riverbank north side.

This was no better than what she had come from. Worse, in fact.

'Will, dear, it'll just have to do, until we find something better.'

'Oh,' he murmured, 'will I ever be able to satisfy my Bridie?'

She felt his sting of regret. For now, she would just have to ignore her pregnancy and start doing the old place up as soon as possible. Making the best of things.

One day I'll be free to decorate my house the way I like it.

The outside with its honeysuckle vine had a certain charm, she secretly admitted.

For the first couple of weeks, it had been bearable. She'd revelled in being wed to this handsome, hardworking man. Now that she'd been married for two and a half months, the honeymoon was well and truly over.

He'd handed his wages over to her each week. The first pay package had lasted a fortnight. Up until then, she hadn't had to spend much money on groceries at all. They'd lived on sausages, eggs, milk, bacon and vegetables provided by the two families—the one along the road, and Will's parents on the north side of the river, a good ten mile drive across the bridge.

The door into the master bedroom squeaked as she opened it, and peeped in at her sleeping husband. She felt a stab of remorse, as she thought of the initial rush of pleasure when her nipples stiffened to Will's touch, and his erect penis thrust into her moist vagina. But she hadn't felt the same euphoria from their love making for some time now.

Backing out of the bedroom onto the yellow linoleum floor of the hallway, she entered the second poky bedroom. She pulled on the chord that switched on the globe. She tried to imagine a cot and baby things in there.

The lavatory was down the back. A tippy tin and newspaper cut into squares for wipes. A cesspit, even worse than the one along the road at her mother's place.

She slipped into a silky nightgown and went out onto the front verandah. It was little more than a few boards, worn and splintered in places. She lit up and blew a series of circles up into the air and shivered. She tried to make out the lights of the town far away in the distance on the north side. That was where she'd hoped he would take her, instead of to this hovel on the south side of the river.

It was a typical summer's evening, the sky at five o'clock pearly and bright. He was the happiest man alive. Willow trees fringed the dark waters of the riverbank. The vista of flying foxes going over in throngs of thousands delighted him. Everything lightened his heart, like the cool clear waters as he dived in, to wash off the grease and dirt. Before he went home to his wife.

He'd longed for his Bridie all day at work. Saw her perfect face and features everywhere, even as he sprawled beneath the cars on the greasy cement floor. Her brown curved legs in the short shorts that she liked to wear. The full lips and eyes like ponds. He couldn't wait to get back home to her.

Every man and boy between the ages of twelve and ninety noticed her. Blokes'd called her *The Million Dollar Baby* when they saw her driving the Pontiac around the town. But they were wrong…. Will knew who she really was beneath the outer layer.

She was his soul mate, and she was all his.

After the swim, he walked back through the tall grass to his bicycle. He wondered what Bridie had prepared for their tea. He was hungry, hungry for food and for his young wife's body. He thought how he loved every little bit of her. If only he could tell her somehow. It was words that failed him at times, the right words to say at the right time.

He walked in with a smile as broad as the river. Bridie ran to him and threw her arms around his neck, little girl style.

'I'm glad you've washed, at least,' she giggled. 'I can still smell the garage, though. Poo! I'm a bit nauseous, and it's all your fault.'

'Come on, give a man a break,' Will laughed. 'You didn't seem to mind when I was courting you. What's for tucker?'

'It's sausages and mash again, I'm sorry.'

'What? You didn't manage to do any shopping?'

'Yes, I drove the jeep to McKittrick's store. Take a look at this,' she said, holding up the pretty blue ashtray she'd spied with her artist's eye in the shop. 'I couldn't resist it, and it only cost sixteen shillings.'

'Sixteen shillings?' Will's face went from white to red and back again to a yellowy pallor. 'But, but, that's three quarters of the housekeeping money.'

'I said I'm sorry. I wanted something pretty to brighten up the house with. I spent it before I knew what I was doing.'

'Next time, for Christ's sake, take a list and tick items off, stocking up on the necessities of life. Flour, sugar, white bread and meat.'

'But the war's over! Surely no need for rations anymore?'

Will put his head in his hands and groaned. She was like one of the frisky fillies he'd learnt how to break in out at Reenie's place. He would have to teach her about budgeting, and it wasn't going to be easy.

He was in for a long hard haul if he wanted to realise his dream of land. All a man needed, after all, was a good feed in your belly, and shelter. Saving was easy if your needs were simple.

Later on, after a meal and a wash, all his worries evaporated. She was lying there on top of the sheets, naked and in wait for him.

Outside, the leaves of *the elephant ear tree* tapped on the iron roof. The cow mooed softly, and something scuttled in the grass. There was just him and her in the whole world. He looked at the full moon afloat in the sky outside the bedroom window, switched off the lights, and knelt over her. She wrapped her beautiful legs around him, and he entered her, forgetting about money, and coming almost as instantly as he felt the soft plush flesh meet his.

They both felt the water overflowing.

Will was soon asleep, dreaming of Bridie and him, in a *trundle bed boat* in the sky, an image spun from his sleeping soul like the golden thread of a silk worm, busy at forming a cocoon in which to protect them.

Chapter 17

Will stood at the back door of Mistletoe Cottage and watched the first rays of sun pierce through the gaps between blue-green foliage. Scuttling sounds from the undergrowth reached him. Almost certainly wallabies or goannas. Frilly shapes of banana trees and native palms dotted the yards closest to the cottage, welcoming golden shards of sunlight in their outstretched arms.

Pride swelled upwards from his abdomen, filling out his chest, as he surveyed the property. He was master of his own domain at last, even if it was a rented weatherboard cottage set back from an unsealed road. The 'tithe' he paid *Old Man Farley*, who called fortnightly to collect it in his ute, was a temporary nuisance.

He walked around to the front verandah and peeped in at Bridie still asleep. She looked angelic. He'd always remember her like this, innocent and sweet. He thought back over their lovemaking with pleasure; how she'd enjoyed it, making little bleating, animal like sounds. And how he was getting better at pleasuring her, extending the foreplay and climaxing together. It was all about timing and rhythm, like the movements in nature. Nature was fecund all around them; in the rich olive green of the gum leaves; the bulging tree frogs croaking their mating calls; kangaroos and possums feeding babies in pouches; birds calling and carolling.

It was summer and Will fell into it through all of his senses; the humidity trapped in the air and the moisture sucked out of the ground by towering eucalypts energised him. All spoke of new growth and rebirth, the opposite of where he'd come from in town. He was going to visit Hilltop to talk about his plans. He walked along the dusty road rather than drive the ute. Being here, surrounded by nature, took him back to his first taste of the bush; his parents sending him off aged four to Tumbarumbara, to convalesce from a bout of pneumonia. He'd remained faithful to that first love affair with the bush to this very day.

Obscured from view by ghost gum trees that stood like proud sentinels on both sides of the road, Hilltop Farm, with its rolling, tree cleared hills, came into view after half an hour. There was a good chance that his two brothers-in-law might consider taking him on as a partner in the dairy farm. He had business nous that he'd inherited from his father. He could make improvements to Hilltop if they'd let him. He'd help put order into the farm and increase profits tenfold. One thing they all said about him was that he had a good business head on his shoulders. A well-shaped head, it was, too; he was proud of his lion's head of hair. That was his only fear, that he would go bald like his father.

He breathed in great gulps of the health-giving air, spiced as it was with pungent, aromatic scents from diverse species of eucalypts, and heard the whole bush thrumming, as if in unison with his plans.

He'd rear calves at Hilltop. Have separate paddocks for weaners, barns full of hay to help fatten them up. He'd put his shoulder to the grind. He'd be good at it.

For the moment, he'd just have to keep working at the garage to make enough money to pay the rent.

Will thought how much brighter he was than the lot of them, these O'Tooles. They needed him, and they would realise it in an instant, if they saw what he could do. After the marriage ceremony, his place among them had been legalised, and he felt like another son, ready to take his place in the family. Accepted as one of them.

He'd slipped into their easy-going rhythms that he now belonged to, forever more. No gloomy old father in charge, stomping on spirits, only a reckless duo, Bridie's brothers, and her soft willed mother.

Higgledy-piggledy lantana vines on sheds met his sight as he approached the farm from this angle. The black bull stamped and snorted behind barbed wire. Would he really toss an invader like a cracker night dummy, high in the air, if he got the chance? Yellow jersey cows roamed the paddocks and hay was drying in the sun, ready to be stacked away in the immense barn.

Far away towards the western slopes, he visualised the swamplands, the delicate mauve of the *bog hyacinth* blooms afloat on the surface, depicting the duplicitous side of nature.

When he got to the farmhouse, Billy came up from the dairy and showed him the litter of newborn terrier puppies, eyes closed and squirming, latching onto their mother's teats. There was always something of interest, something going on like this at the farm—yellow ducklings and chickens, a red and white newborn calf on tottering legs, the old sow and her hungry piglets. The farm would, in time, become *a magic castle* for his kids, too.

He followed Billy back to the dairy yards.

'Hey Will! How you going?' Ned, his head pressed against the flank of a jersey milker, jumped up from the stool, and pumped Will's hand. He sat down again and tightened, with jerky movements, the leg rope on the cow's leg, pushed his head against the flank and pulled frothy milk from the teats into a silver bucket: *plink, plonk, plop, shhhh....*

Will waited until Ned had finished with the cow. He leaned against the fence, chewing lazily on a grass stalk.

'I'll give you a hand to make this place pay if you'll take me on as a partner,' he said to Ned. 'I could run a weaner or two here myself for fattening.'

'I know you're clever, Will, a good brain on your shoulders, good business sense, too. But this place is too small,' he said shaking his head, 'It's already three of us, with Mumma, Billy and me.'

Will looked at the dairy shed and yards, and saw, through a shrewd eye, how it could be improved: 'You need more tanks and wells to collect water, a dam, mechanised dairy and a mixed stock of breeders and weaners; grazing herd as well.'

He paused, looked at Ned's bowed head, and then went on, 'You could eventually spread out further west. I could arrange it with my friend, Saul, and we could, together, do the bidding and selling at the saleyards.'

'Arrgh, dunno, Will. It's a risky business getting involved with friends and relatives. Better you go your own way, an' we ours.'

'Talk it over with Billy and your mother, anyway. See what they think. We could really make a go of this place if we put our heads together. Even erect a trolley on rails up to the road for milk and cream drums to be collected.'

On the way back home, he thought how he'd ask Bridie to back him up in talking to Eliza O'Toole about his plans for Hilltop. He had no idea, for the moment, of the scene that would soon take place back at the farm.

'He wants to take us over!' Ned bellowed at his mother. 'Thinks he's too good for us, with his stuck-up air. Tight-arsed, too!'

Eliza said nothing before the onrush of words. It was she who advised her sons on their personal affairs: 'Make sure an' come home before dark,' she'd say to the boys, even when they were well into adulthood and, much later on when she thought Ned needed a wife to look after him: 'She's a nice woman, that one behind the counter there, the sort you could think to marry.' But in affairs of land and property, she left it all to Ned.

Billy, too, was easily influenced by his older brother. The idea that Will was a scheming go-getter who was hard on his wife quickly took hold.

'Yes, he's egotistical, just like all men,' Bridie replied, 'but he'd be an asset to you and the farm. He's brainy and good with figures. Why don't you give him a chance?'

'Nah, he's got a job with the garage. He can save up for land of his own,' said Ned.

'He hates it there with his father. Just give him a chance, why don't you, Ned? He's a whizz with machinery and mechanics, got a certificate to prove it.'

'No, too big a risk, it is, Bridie,' said her mother, backing up her son.

Bridie found it hard not to be persuaded by her family. She knew she was whining a little now.

'I'm not in the race when he makes up his mind. So I have to go without, and he wants to pour money into buying land.'

'You made your bed, now lie in it, Bridie,' her mother said.

'I'd like to work just like all those women did during the war. A bar job, anything, but Will won't hear of it.'

'Especially now that you're pregnant, girl,' her mother said. 'You need to settle down and prepare for the baby.'

She shuddered at the sight of him now, coming home with black grease from scrabbling underneath cars. She told him the disappointing news of her failed efforts at changing her brother's mind. She kept to herself the parts where she'd been taking their side against her husband.

He'd told her how he'd have to siphon away income each week to put down as a deposit on a block of land. This dream of land he saw as being for the future good of his family. She'd heard it all before.

A small property, a herd of cattle, a homestead on a hill at the end of a tree lined road.

Bridie had other ideas.

She told him about her desires as he washed for dinner. She longed for a modern, Spanish style home within a stylish suburb near the riverbank. She'd seen photos in the *Home Beautiful* magazines. Her talk seemed to wash over him like the water running through his fingers just now.

She continued to whinge at the table. She'd had enough of dirt and mud in her childhood years, and deserved a house that was easy to keep clean. She knew not to add *and a clean shaven man to show off to my friends.*

Over dinner, he reminded her how happy she'd been when he was courting her. *Remember the time he'd done a backflip from the bridge walkway into the river to impress her?* How all she'd wanted was to be spending time alone with him?

They laughed together at the memories.

She'd fallen for him, too right. But she'd also taken a shine to the idea of a classy lifestyle. Moving across the bridge to Riverdale, on the north bank there had been one of her dreams.

He'd fallen hard, and that was a fact, same as her. Things had changed … the taste of it was like bile in her mouth.

The truth was, she'd come down in the world since marrying Will, not up, as she'd hoped.

She'd have to make him see what her needs were. In a few months' time, there'd be a baby, for God's sake. They hadn't planned on the pregnancy bit. She knew he'd had no choice, but to bring her to live in this hovel. This didn't help how she felt about it.

Will was getting ready for bed in order to rise early the next day and go off to work.

Surely the old boy, Pa Featherstone, would come to the aid of his only son, if he asked for a helping hand?

'Not bloody likely,' Will had said when she brought it up. 'I won't be beholden to him in any way. Ever.'

What a darn foolhardy way to live, Bridie thought. If you've got a bit of spare cash, why not spend it?

She'd never imagined that the fiery passion could be wiped out so fast, that some intervening event, such as a surprise pregnancy, a rundown shack, could dampen the ardour of first love.

Chapter 18

Bridie was pleased that the last stages of her pregnancy were happening in autumn, not summer. The days were getting shorter and that nippy feeling in the air foretold the onset of winter. A relief, really, as the previous months had been extra humid and hot. Still, she had an uneasy feeling about the winter birth that was fast approaching.

It'd been a good omen to have tied the knot in spring.

Will's American friend, Chuck, talked about 'fall' with his funny accent. She had *fallen* pregnant by accident in spring, and next she'd be birthing a baby in midwinter. She knew her musings were silly, and wondered if she'd been spending too much time alone of late. Her days had been taken up with sweeping, dusting and teaching herself to cook, trying to get the house ready for the new arrival.

Nesting, she mused, *like a honeyeater she'd seen building a cup-shaped nest from matted grasses lined with roots and mammal hairs. Making the most of its flimsy dwelling.*

She couldn't help thinking about how she'd wanted to get rid of the baby at one stage, to save herself from embarrassment. Now, sitting at the kitchen table next to the wood stove, she put her arms protectively around her watermelon tummy.

Will was absent more and more these days, spending his weekends scouring the district for land to purchase. If he kept working at his second job selling used volkswagons, he'd soon have enough money saved up to buy something.

He was grinning widely when he came in and announced the news to his wife, and swung her around, before remembering to mind her swollen tummy.

With the help of Chuck and his country friends, he'd examined a property suitable for beef cattle raising at Mounttain Ridge, not too far away from Karrana.

'Good for you, old codger,' she laughed, pushing him away, 'but when are you going to share some of your time with me? Soon there'll be another little being competing for our attention.'

'I'm taking you there right away, if you're up for it,' he said, beaming. 'There's still plenty of light if we set off now.'

'Anything to spend more time with you,' she said, not relishing bumpy roads that she knew would be ahead.

'Hop in the jeep and we'll be off, then.'

They drove westwards, Will conserving petrol by cutting the engine, and allowing the landrover to find a rhythm, gliding up and down hilly slopes and rises in the road of its own accord. Bridie placed her hands over her belly and pushed back with her feet and head. She remembered suffering from vertigo on a scary ride at a country fun park once.

They turned off the bitumen five miles out of town and went through scrubby terrain for what seemed like forever. Climbing up a near vertical rise in the land, the vehicle was skidding sideways. Bridie's stomach was churning. Will said that they were nearly there.

The bumpy track opened out onto cleared pasture lands where beasts were grazing.

Bridie got out gingerly and looked at the view. From the tabletop ledge they were on, you could see right down to Karrana River behind them.

Not a bad site right to erect a modern house right here, for someone who liked living away from civilisation.

She hugged Will and told him how clever he was to have found his *Shangri-La*.

'Yes, and look at this perfect spot,' he said, pointing to the site Bridie had noted, 'for a house to stand in time, eh?'

'I don't like that steep ascent for getting here, though,' she said. 'Is there another way out we could take on the way back?'

'Yes, there is, but it'll take much longer going home.'

'I can't stand the thought of that vertical drop,' she said, 'let's go the long way round, or I may deliver the baby right there on the track out of sheer terror.'

'I don't remember you suffering from vertigo before, darling. Must be the nipper inside you causing it.'

The dark was falling when they left. Her teeth started to chatter on the punt crossing the river. Will wrapped a blanket around her shoulders and hugged her in his arms to warm her and the baby up.

A little boy shot out of Bridie's womb in the middle of winter at Camelot Hospital. It was eight months to the day after their springtime wedding.

On the cusp of watery Cancer and the fiery Leo sign, a straggling infant, not at all sure of its destiny, lay in his bassinet next to Bridie.

'The baby's come early,' she told her mother when Eliza called the hospital for news. 'It's a big boy.'

There was quiet at the other end of the phone.

'It was awful, simply horrible, the pain,' she said into the mouthpiece, trying not to whimper, 'and the doctor insisted I go through it without pain relief.'

A sudden warmth for her mother enveloped her, thinking of her births.

'Mine all slipped out onto a double bed,' said Eliza. 'Only a midwife present, usually my sister or aunt with some nursing skills.'

'I can't believe you went through this six times, Mumma', she said, 'don't know if I can do it again.'

'Hummph,' said Eliza. 'You youngsters, you've lost yer backbone, that's fer sure.'

In spite of the long and painful birth, Bridie fell in love with the boy at first sight. Staring up at her from a bruised head and face was the most beautiful pair of unwavering, Buddha like eyes she'd ever seen. She was enraptured. Soon Bridie saw that he had olive skin and dark eyes. *His hair is jet black, and he's like me.* He looked like he should be called Heathcote, or Tristan, so perfect were his features and his crown of thick, dark hair. Part of her was shocked at the voracious way he sucked on her. Still, she liked the feel of the pull and throw.

He was hers, more beautiful than any of the other babies. She hugged him greedily.

In love with her husband, if not in the first throes of passion, Bridie wanted to call the baby after him, *Little Will.* She was annoyed when her mother-in-law disagreed, as it was not his baptised name. Margaret had read somewhere that Albert meant 'noble', 'bright' and 'famous'. She felt that the child had such a mature look, those dark eyes that shone with intelligence, suggesting he *took after the Featherstone side of the family, bright as a button.* She mentioned the English kings and queens, and pointed to the faithful 'Bertie', Queen Victoria's consort, as a positive role model.

Bridie disliked the name instantly.

Margaret brought up *Richard the Lion Heart,* who had shown no fear in conquests across the known world at the time of his reign. Pa Featherstone was not so sure, pointing out that this brave warrior king spoke French, not English.

Bridie arrived at a compromise with her mother-in-law. They'd baptise the infant *Richard Tristan,* incorporating the second favourite names of each.

She said to herself: I can always call him by his second name of Tristan, if I want. Let him be Richard on paper for the in-laws' sake.

Bridie didn't like to think about the war, now that it was over. She'd prayed constantly, in secret, for the safe deliverance of her family, the farm and her country. She'd felt safe and secure here on this island continent, far from the action. *In a quiet bushland setting.* She'd known deep within herself, at some secret place, it would all turn out for the best in the end. The Japs had come close, though, bombing Darwin and entering Sydney Harbour in submarines.

Four of her unmarried brothers, including Johnny, had had to undertake three months' compulsory military training, introduced by the Prime Minister, Robert Menzies.

Charles and Shaun had volunteered with the Australian Infantry Force for overseas duty. 'We'll stop the buggers before they get a chance to come here,' Charles'd said before leaving.

There were compensations, she'd realised, of living in the bush, away from the action.

Now it was harsh, though. She'd have to wash nappies in an outdoor wash house. First she'd have to light the copper to boil water in. Then she'd have to wring the clothes out through revolving rubber rollers, after she'd stirred the wet items around in the boiling water with a stick.

To make matter worse, Will had been keeping a calf in the laundry shed at night. It'd been a gift from Billy O'Toole: 'Here, Will, your first calf to rear,' he'd said. 'See what you can do with it. Fatten 'im up and add him to your future herd.'

Bridie was shocked when she opened the door to the wash house, and found soft pads of calf manure all over the floor.

Having to get poo out of soiled nappies was one thing, but slipping around in calf muck at the same time…. How had her life come to this? She'd have a word in her husband's ear that night.

There was to be no extended family celebration of young Richard's birth. Will had heard the bad news first from Eliza O'Toole, shortly after his son's birth. He knew he couldn't keep it from his nursing wife forever.

He'd often thought back to that day when reports of German soldiers marching through the *Arc de Triomphe* in Paris in the northern spring were relayed. It was the day the French, much to their surprise, lost the war. Will had learned that Germany, like a wounded lion, had struck back with fangs and claws lashing, hell-bent on a quick revenge.

France had lacked the will to re-arm, after the horrors of the 'War to End All Wars'. Shocked Parisians wept in disbelief; winners became losers, and the Germans struck across the Meuse.

French had been one of Will's best subjects at school.

He had read posters calling for volunteers to join the AIF. *The last bloody thing I'd want to do is fight in a war overseas,* he'd thought. *Too much to do here. I'll join the part-time militia if things get worse.*

Two days following Richard's birth, a boy rode up to Hilltop on a bicycle. Eliza was in the wash house humming 'We'll meet again, don't know where, don't know when,' in a sad lilt, her grey wisps of hair sodden and clinging to her pale face as she lifted the wet clothes from the boiling copper. She heard the knock on the door and saw the 'angel of death' standing at her back steps, yellow envelope in hand.

His open book face told her the bad news. 'Ned!' she screeched. 'It's news of the boys!' Ned caught his mother as she fainted and he lay her in the shade beneath the grape trellis.

'I'm sorry, Sir, it's from the War Office,' said the boy, as he handed Ned the telegram:

This is to inform you that your son, Shaun Francis O'Toole's remains have been recovered, along with documents and personal effects. We can now confirm that he was killed in action at Gona in New Guinea. A letter to follow.

'Sorry, Sir,' the youth repeated, 'really sorry.' He wheeled off on his bike, Ned's sobs echoing through the back yard and waking his mother up as she lay sprawled on the grass.

They'd suspected that Shaun had been killed in action. Now that the news had arrived, and a body had been found, the watershed of grief they'd been holding back, was able to be released.

Will comforted Bridie with words and caresses that night.

'You're right, Shaun died protecting us, and he's a hero forever.'

'He was so keen to go and fight them over there,' she cried, 'to stop them from coming here. So brave.'

'It'll all be over now, darling, and our boy may never have to go off and fight. Once the world wakes up to the destruction caused by wars, it might start to go in the right direction towards peace.'

Bridie cried long into the night after Will and the baby were asleep.

Poor Mumma. What's the point of giving birth to gorgeous sons, just to see them killed in a useless war? I hate war so much.

Within two weeks of the first telegram, Eliza had received news that her second son, Charles Patrick, who'd been fighting in Kokoda, had been found in a hospital in Port

Moresby, wounded but alive. A Japanese mine had thrown him and his mates into the air. But he was one of the lucky ones. At least her Charles would be coming home.

What they didn't know at the time, was that he'd be coming home with only one leg. Fated to hip-hop around for the rest of his life on crutches and a wooden leg.

Chapter 19

Will burst in later than usual, eyes twinkling and red-cheeked from a beer at the pub, and picked Bridie up in his strong sun-browned arms: 'What has my little darling been up to today?'

'Put me down, you smell of beer.' But she was pleased with the attention.

'What have I done? I'll tell you what I've done today! Cleaned the house, swept the leaves up, done the washing in the dirty old copper, cooked your dinner and minded the baby. No one to talk to except myself, and you wonder why I'm going stark raving mad.'

'I'm taking you to the pictures tomorrow night at the Palace, Bridie.

'It's about time, 'ol man!'

'Get your mother to mind the baby....'

'He's Richard, Will. We've got to stop calling him 'baby', especially him being so bright and all.'

'You're right, Bridie. Young Richard it is from now on.'

'Yeah I've been up to my neck, too, as you well know. That cow bloating from too much clover was the last straw.'

'That wretched old cow down the back in the sling! Skin 'er I say!'

Will had slung up the bloating cow in a makeshift sling, trying to save it from bursting with the clover it had over-indulged in. And they laughed together at using the names of their closest neighbours, the Skinners and the Turners.

'That's right, darling: Turner and Skinner. That's what I should do with that bloody beast.'

They shouted out the refrain again: 'Turner an' Skinner.' And just for a moment, they were as happy as they'd ever been before the arrival of the baby into their lives.

In the beginning, Bridie played with him constantly, sang to him, nursed him and blew raspberries on his tummy and kissed and teased his worm-like appendage with the tip of her nose to make him giggle. She revelled in his squeals of delight, sang and cooed with him, until he fell into a deep sleep on her shoulder. He was her playmate, her little *Dicky Bird*, on those long days when Will was away at work or in the bush.

Will came in dirty and tired from working in the new paddock that he'd bought. He was a little grumpy to see the baby suckling at her breast. *Too big for that*, he muttered to himself. Will realised that he was being childish, but he couldn't help it. This slurping parasite of an infant had taken Bridie away from him, always too sore and bruised 'down there' to make love.

'Why don't you get him off your breast and onto a bottle, darling? You're always so tired.'

'Think I will before too long,' she said with a sigh. 'Maybe in a few weeks' time. Cows' milk is just as natural, after all.'

She was also thinking that her figure would get back into shape, if she weaned the child.

Over tea, Bridie told him about the black snake that had been sunning itself in the garden while she was waiting for Richard to wake up from his nap. She'd had on one of her silky numbers that day, a floral dress she'd bought in Sydney last year, thinking to drive into Karrana with Richard to do some shopping. She was about to hang out washing on the line, which was a rope slung between two forked tree trunks.

Something caught her attention in the grass near one of the makeshift posts. She'd glimpsed the sight of a shiny form glinting in the sun. Without taking her eyes off the snake, she picked up a shovel. Raising the heavy tool above her head, with one quick movement she brought it down hard upon the shiny black body as the reptile tried to slither away. The red belly flashed into view and the creature writhed in the throes of death, the severed parts still wriggling even afterwards, like a spirit trying to escape.

Again and again the metal pounded down upon the pieces of the snake, which divided endlessly into smaller and smaller parts until they were a mockery of the original animal.

'I hate snakes,' she shouted to the bush around her. 'Slippery, horrible creatures, no business coming near the house and my child.'

Will had tried to tell her about the highly developed sound detectors of the reptilian creatures that were emerging from winter hibernation; that they scuttled away at the first soft tread of an interloper.

Bridie refused to hear, and lived with the notion that a snake might jump out and devour her baby whole.

She still longed for more creature comforts. Places and spaces where she could escape from the outside world if she wished. Where she'd feel safe for herself and her loved ones.

'I'll build you your dream home one of these days, my Bridie,' he said. 'You'll see, I promise you that.'

That's what she'd started to pray for these days. He was a kind and loving God, the one she prayed to, not a cruel and punishing man. How could she believe in hell, now that she'd given birth to such a cherubim. She saw God in the image of her son, as well as in that of her father before he'd died. Always giving and compassionate.

Love could never die, she saw that now.

She had prayed for a healthy child, too. She'd prayed to the Catholic God and to the Virgin Mary that she hardly believed in. Secretly she'd wanted a boy, and it seemed as if her prayers were answered when he arrived. After the birth, though, Richard remained attached to her like a baby quokka. She was exhausted much of the time. The baby would only sleep if she brought him into bed with her. This was not at all what she'd envisioned married bliss to be.

She might have prayed too hard and too loudly to this unseen God to deliver a special child. Richard's career as a genius began when he was a babe in arms. It was aided and abetted by Ma and Pa Featherstone, who held education in high esteem.

This day, Bridie had left the baby with her mother-in-law, and had gone to do some shopping in town. Ma sang nursery rhymes to get the baby back to sleep:

> *Ding, dong, dell,*
> *Pussy's in the well.*
> *Who put her in?*
> *Little Johnny Thin.*

Margaret cried out when Bridie returned: 'He's clever, Bridie! He sang the words *in a well ... in a well ...* after me. Have you ever heard him?'

'Yes, oh yes, I'm sure you're right, Ma,' she said. 'He's bright alright.'

There was at last something that they agreed on at last.

'Just look at him', Bridie enthused to her friend, Stella when she visited. 'We've got a smart one on our hands here.' She couldn't take her eyes off him, this brightly shining light.

'He's a gorgeous looking boy, and clever too, I'm sure,' said Stella, 'but I just want to hold him close like this.' And she hugged him to her chest, rocking and singing.

'I sometimes think he looks like a Buddha, with that big head and serious expression,' said Bridie, taking him back from Stella, and holding him close to her heart. The baby gurgled, revelling in the attention, especially from his mother.

Stella had already tired of baby talk, and went outside to saddle up and ride off on her favourite mare.

'Everyone says he's bright for his age,' she said when Will walked in from outside. 'We've got to send him to school early on. Takes after your side of the family, brainy like Pa.'

'Dad never went much further than you or me at school,' Will said. 'He came out here as an orphan, when he was sixteen.'

'Maybe he takes after me, then,' she said jokingly. 'Have I ever told you that I gained the highest aggregate score at the end of year exams at Saint Joseph's in sixth grade?'

'Yes, over and over, but your mother pulled you out to help at home, before you finished high school.'

'Yeah, no need to rub it in, old man, that's right. And I wasn't any good at arithmetic, anyway. That kind priest dressed in a skirt, pointed out my mistakes with a fat finger on the right answer, I'll never forget that.'

'So how did you do so well?'

'I was good at stories, that's how I came top, and from that bit of help from Father Malone.'

'I didn't like school,' he said, 'always wanted to fix things with my hands. Mechanics, and *Ag* studies were my strong points.'

'But you've got a good brain in that head of yours, everyone says so. It's what attracted me to you.'

'Your figure, Bridie, is what I long for. How about it, tonight, when the kids are asleep?'

'I'm tired, Will,' she sighed. 'Exhausting, looking after a baby who wakes for bottles throughout the night.'

'A man will go mad if he doesn't get love-making, Bridie.' And he wondered if he could make her change her mind, come round to his way of thinking with a night out at the cinema.

For Bridie, the next night seemed like she was stepping out to a gala event, a fairy-tale ball. It was so long since she'd been anywhere without Richard hanging from her breast or clinging, possum like, to her shoulder.

She'd dressed up in her green frock and was hoping to be seen.

They entered the building through a Roman arch surrounded by columns.

Bridie remembered learning about such things from the nuns at school.

Chandeliers lit up the entrance foyer to the movie theatre. Colourful posters of Hollywood stars splashed colour around the walls.

Bridie's eyes widened as she drank it all in. She felt other eyes following her as she walked on Will's arm up the narrow stairwell to the top floor. Faux marble columns decorated the upstairs area, and she took it all in—the plush red seats, the velvet curtains, the candy bar....

An attractive woman dressed in a black and white uniform showed them into the enormous decorated auditorium. Bridie noted the lit up stage framed by red curtains as they followed the usherette's torch down carpeted steps to their seats.

Will went out to the sweets bar to buy Peters ice-creams that he knew Bridie would like to eat with the dainty wooden spoon provided, and jaffas to take home to Eliza, as well as the chewy fantales in wrappers with stories about Hollywood stars on them.

She imagined she was a star herself, an Egyptian queen seated high above the rest of the world. She felt her heart rekindle towards her husband that night, as she nestled into his comfortable shoulder.

As the child grew into a toddler and beyond, Bridie told everyone how clever he was. Richard would sit cross-legged on the floor in front of the wireless in the lounge room, listening to the *Chickabidees of the Air* on Radio 2KF: '*Sing a song of sixpence, a pocketful of rye, Four and twenty blackbirds baked in a pie.*'

'He recites the rhymes, claps his hands and answers when he hears Miss Finch's voice.'

She thought how her darling, handsome boy was going to get the best that was on offer. She would see to it. Will had found an army type jeep for his wife's special use. She would enrol her firstborn son in kindergarten at the Catholic school, even though it would mean a longer trip, driving him there and picking him up every day. But for now, it was teaching him at home, and watching his starring role on Kindergarten of the Air.

Bridie told Grandma O'Toole: 'Richard's ahead for his age, needs to go to school as soon as he turns four.'

'Not good to be too brainy,' Grandma said. 'There's a fine line between genius and madness, you know.'

'I want to get him into singing and piano lessons early on. He's a star in the making.'

And there was another sign to this clever boy that she would become aware of in time.

Part Three

Chapter 20

Bridie calculated that she'd conceived exactly five months after Richard's birth. She'd just given up breast-feeding, because she was forever tired. Will's seeds quickly found their target and one of them stuck.

Fall pregnant she thought, it's a bit of a misnomer if a girl *wants* to be pregnant again. I'm not sure if I do or I don't, but it'd be nice to have a playmate for Richard.

Will, too, was unsure of his feelings about a second baby coming on the scene; he'd be competing for his wife's attentions even more.

'Perhaps it'll be a girl,' he said, 'completing our little family.'

'I think it'd be good to have another boy, for Richard's sake,' Bridie said. 'Make him less spoilt as an only son. He needs a playmate.'

'Well, yes, there's that to it. I'd like to have sons to help me on the land, too. But a daughter is what I hanker after,' Will said. 'Proves a man's a man, they say.'

Bridie could think of nothing but her firstborn. How would Richard react to another child in the family? She felt a slight sense of pulling away from her husband.

'Where do babies come from, Mummy?' Richard asked early on when she was carrying the second child.

'From my tummy. Here, feel the baby moving in there.' He put his brown hand on his mother's 'watermelon' as he called it.

'No I didn't.'

'Where did you come from, then?'

'I come down in a rocket ship. From way up in a castle. In the sky.'

'What sort of castle?'

'Silver one. And glass.'

'Who was up there? In the castle.'

'An old man called Bert. He had red cows and a black spotty dog.'

'And what else was there?'

'A lady called Mary.'

'Did they say anything?'

'They give me a letter for you, is all.'

'Where is it? The letter?'

'I dunno. Left it there.'

'What did it say?'

'Love to mummy and daddy, from Mary and Bert.'

Strange, Bridie thought. My great-grandmother was a Mary, and her deceased father had been baptised Bertram. He'd run a herd of cattle on one of the hills to the north of Karrana. But they were jersey milkers, a yellowish colour.'

She told her mother about the conversation.

'Bert was my father's name. It's just his imagination. You need to keep that in check. Don't want him going funny or anything, do we? A thin line, you know, between genius and madness.'

Will looked startled at first. 'Spooky,' he murmured. He explained it all by saying that Richard must have overheard his grandmothers talking about ancestors, as they often did. Some of them kept herefords, which were a red and white sort of colour.

This made no sense to Bridie, but she thought no more about the mystery.

'That boy needs to come out with me and learn how to ride and rough it a bit. Out in the bush. Mustering cattle.'

'He's too young for that, Will. We can get him a Shetland pony to learn on. Soon as he's three.'

Charles Edward Featherstone, ginger headed with green eyes, was born on a spring morning in October, 1947. Will took one look at his second born son and fell heavily for this child's exotic looking, large green eyes staring up at him.

'He's special, Bridie. A little gem.' He noted the thick mop of hair, the colour of ripened pumpkin, and wondered if it was a throwback to the Scottish genes on his father's side.

The new baby was strong and lithe, and he'd slipped out of the birth canal easily, causing her little pain. She forgave him for taking after some throwback Viking or Scottish individual in the family tree that she didn't know about. He'd be able to use his hands to make his way in the world, despite his colouring.

'Mum said my hair changed from auburn to dark later on,' said Will, 'but his spirit is all yours, my darling. There's rebel Celtic blood flowing in his veins. Just look at him.'

'Most of my Irish ancestors were peace loving folk,' she said. 'But alright, there were a few black sheep, and a convict or two … maybe a bushranger, to boot.'

Will laughed and picked up the squirming baby in his arms. He tried to make eye contact with him. The child's head fell gently on to his father's shoulder and nuzzled there, as if recognising him from his scent.

Bridie watched as Will rocked the bundle, wrapped now in a bunny rug, back and forth, as she'd never seen him do with Richard at the same stage.

'He'll be helping me with the mustering and branding before too long, that's for sure,' he said. 'What a bonny young fellow you are! Look, Billy,' and he showed him off proudly to his brother-in-law who'd just come in to see the new baby.

'B-but there's no r-red hair in our f-family,' Billy said as he stared at young Charlie in his father's arms. 'G-green eyes too.'

'He takes after the Featherstone's, Billy,' Bridie called out from the kitchen, where she was preparing a pot of tea. 'Don't worry, I didn't flirt with any woodcutters while Will was away in the bush paddock.'

Charlie bellowed then, and Bridie came running back in from the kitchen, asking Will to finish preparing afternoon tea. 'Time for another feed,' she said, sitting down on the couch and placing the infant to her breast. 'Ouch!' she cried, and the baby pulled away from her.

'It's alright. Let's try again,' she whispered in the baby's ear, and gingerly placed his eager mouth around her sore nipple, trying to ignore the pain. I'm going to have to put this one on the bottle, she said to herself.

The next day, only three weeks after the birth, she was back in hospital with a raging mastitis.

Ma Featherstone had offered to take care of Richard for a few days. Will dropped the boy off on the way to the hospital, then helped Bridie settle in with the new baby, to be treated until the infection and the pain subsided.

The scorching pain in her pus filled red and swollen breast was so severe that she had to give up feeding the new baby and seek help from staff to prepare bottles.

The pain in her heart was worse. Why did she have to fall pregnant again with a second baby, while the first was still so young? She felt guilt as well as sorrow.

When Ma Featherstone brought the young boy in to see his mother, he was afraid and clung to his grandmother's skirt, peeping around at the nurses in their starched uniforms.

'I want my Richard,' Bridie sobbed. 'He doesn't know me anymore.'

'Wanta stay wif you, Ma,' Richard cried, clinging to Ma's skirt.

'He's forgotten me,' Bridie wailed even louder in grief. The doctors and nurses came and gently suggested that Mrs Featherstone should leave with the child.

By the time Bridie was to be released from hospital, Richard and Charlie were home and in the care of their father, who'd taken time off work to feed the baby.

'It's the best thing to do,' the staff at the hospital had said, 'to keep the baby away from the smell of the mother.'

Bridie's mother had offered to prepare bottles for Charlie, but Will had insisted on caring for the baby himself, and invited Eliza over to look after Richard.

'I'll cook a meal for you to have tonight now that Bridie's coming home. And you can all come over to Hilltop for a baked roast on Sunday.'

Will realised that Eliza had thawed a little towards him, perhaps pleased that he'd brought her daughter to Mistletoe Cottage to be nearby.

'Thanks Eliza, we'd like that. When the baby's asleep, I'll drive to the hospital with Richard to pick Bridie up. If you'd stay here until we get back.'

Bridie was overjoyed to see Will enter the foyer of the hospital with Richard. She ran towards the boy and clasped him to her breast. 'I've missed you, darling boy!'

Richard now responded, smiling like a cheshire cat, as if he'd only just left his mother's care.

'It's the hospital atmosphere that upset him … you in bed, and the nurses dressed in white uniforms that put him off,' Will said.

'Where's the baby?' Bridie asked, looking around.

'Home wif gramma,' Richard said.

'I can't believe you weaned him yourself,' Bridie said.

'Baby's weaned now,' Richard chirped in.

'Yes, darling, and you're a big boy now, too.' She was slightly miffed that her husband had been able to undertake the wifely duties without a hiccup. But she was pleased not to have any more excruciating pain, and to be back with her firstborn, who hadn't forgotten her after all.

'What do you want to do with Mummy when we get home, Richard?'

'Play with my train set, and meccano,' he chirruped.

'And I'll read some story books after your bath.'

Bridie could see that her firstborn son would be reading the books himself before too long. She sat in the back seat, cuddling her boy and ruffling his hair.

'Mumma says it's not good to be so clever, you know, Will. What a funny old thing she is. How can you not want your child to excel at school and in every way?'

'Well, she's had six of you, so she's not lacking in experience,' Will said, as they drove towards Mistletoe Cottage. 'Gee, it's good to have you back, my Bridie.'

'And it's heaven to be home with my family,' said Bridie, smothering her boy's olive cheeks with kisses, until he was pulling away from her, screwing up his face and scowling.

'I's a big boy, too much kisses,' and pushing her off him.

Bridie frowned at the sound of his speech, that had slipped since she'd been away.

When they got out of the car, they heard Charlie's wails ringing out over the treetops.

'I'll go to him,' Bridie said.

Will was already out of the car and running towards the door. As soon as he took the baby from Eliza's arms, the child quietened down.

'Mumma, thanks for your help,' cried Bridie.

'Don't thank me, girlie, it's your Will that's done it. Something I never had was help from the ole man, that's for sure. Dinner's heating up on the stove.'

Will was already feeding the baby with the bottle Eliza had prepared. There was hot water in the bathtub that she'd filled from the outside copper, ready for baths. Bridie would bathe her son before reading to him in his Christmas pyjamas, all made so much harder by the coming of Charlie into the family.

Will made enquiries and arrived home one weekend with a tiny black Shetland pony with a star on its forehead that Bridie named, immediately, 'Gem'.

'He's gorgeous,' she said, 'but we'll have to lead him with Richard on him for a while.'

Bridie led the quiet animal around with Richard laughing gleefully in the saddle, sausage-like legs with boots kicking heels into jet-black flanks, toes in stirrups already like a pro. 'Steady on, old boy,' she warned. 'Take it easy. You have to learn to walk before you can fly.'

'That's my boy,' Will enthused as he watched his wife leading the little black pony around with their firstborn on his back. Such a good, docile little pony. The two would learn together, boy and boy horse, to love one another.

When Eliza visited, Richard took her outside to find Gem. 'He's a confident mite, Will,' she said of her grandson afterwards. 'He puts out his hand and the pony trots up to him. He pets him on the forelock and wants to jump up onto him.'

'Yes, we're still leading the pony around, but our boy'll be catching and saddling him before too long.'

The dark had begun falling over the tin roof of the cottage as Eliza left on foot for Hilltop. She hoped there'd be no more babies for a while. It was tiring for her daughter, not to mention for herself. The haunting sound of a mopoke fell on her ears from the canopy of trees as she hurried homeward along the dirt track.

Chapter 21

Bridie drove Richard off to kindergarten that year. She was pregnant with her third child and summer was a scorcher this time. She stayed with him as long as possible, often with Charlie in her arms. She felt her firstborn needed the stimulation from other sources, not to mention social skills, but she was unhappy leaving him in the clutches of Miss Hanna, whom Richard called 'Honey'. No matter how sweet was this tall, educated woman with the gentle manners, Bridie was loath to hand over her boy.

The teacher had to almost push her out of the classroom. 'It is time for you to leave now, Mrs Featherstone. It's best if you leave smartly, for your child's sake,' Miss Hanna said the first time Bridie had overstayed her welcome. Even then, she stayed outside the building, peering in through the curtains to see if Richard was crying for her. He never was.

She was always there on the dot of two o'clock to pick him up. He seemed happy and relaxed. She checked with Richard to see if he'd liked his day at school better than with her.

'How did you like school?' Bridie asked him when she picked him up. 'It's good, but … too many … little bits … an' sitting down on the floor.'

He was unused to the discipline, she knew, but he lapped up lessons like a hungry cat.

'He's bright,' Miss Hanna said. 'Will do well at school. Buy him books and things to interest him.'

Bridie did that, and she bought him musical instruments and toys that would stir his imagination. Many of the educational books and props came as gifts and surprises from the older Featherstones.

Richard was far ahead of the other children. He could read books and do sums in his head. He'd easily be able to keep up with the first class pupils. Bridie decided she would broach the subject with the teacher about moving him up. The boy floated above his peers, above his father, above all of them. She imagined him soaring high over the earth on a magic carpet from Aladdin's epoch. Born aloft by the gift of a great intellect, bestowed on him by fate.

Bridie swelled with pride.

Bridie had come into the room just after the incident and had heard the slap. Baby Charlie, was lying on a rug on the floor, screaming. Richard had slapped his brother hard on the back. Bridie ran to pick him up in her arms, scowling at Richard. 'Don't dare ever hit the baby again.'

'Mummy, naughty, naughty baby.'

She was at a loss as to what to do.

'Take him back to the hospital, Mummy,' he cried, 'don't like stupid baby.'

Bridie was ignorant before the onslaught of the green-eyed monster 'Jealousy'. She felt sure Richard would get over it once he learnt how to read books.

She was careful to keep her eye on the new baby girl when she arrived the following year, and not to leave her alone on the floor.

She encouraged Will to take Richard, at three, out riding as much as possible.

'He's certainly not born under the star sign of horses,' Will told Bridie at night, 'whatever that is.'

'I think it's Sagittarius,' she said, 'and no, he's not. His signs are Cancer and Leo, watery and fire signs, both, which is where he gets his brains and looks from, no doubt.'

Richard was learning quickly how to master the art of trotting, then cantering. But as soon as Will allowed him to ride ahead, without the rope connecting them, the boy wanted to gallop.

He lacked something essential in Will's eyes, that subtle union between man and beast. Will worried that he might be knocked off by an over-hanging branch, or fall off, if Gem stopped too quickly.

'Steady on, Son. You have to learn to walk, before you can run.'

By the end of the year, Richard could read all of the picture books at the library. He'd outgrown *Winnie the Pooh* and *The Tales of Peter Rabbit.*

She started borrowing older books from Karrana Library and reading them to him at night. *Gulliver's Travels* enraptured him, as did *The Sword in the Stone* and *Journey to the Centre of the Earth.*

'I want a story, Mummy. Wanta find out the ending.'

She imagined myriad pathways in his brain, linking up like the roads on a map of the district, like the Karrana River system, starting high up in the Queensland ranges and rushing southward, breaking into tributaries, curling westwards and eastwards, flowing towards the Pacific Ocean on the seaboard.

He often refused to sleep until his thirst for mental stimulation was sated. He bawled if she stopped at a crucial moment in the story, 'Keep going, Mummy, don't stop....' He wouldn't go to sleep, before he'd had his fill of the story.

This night she watched him as he looked at the pictures of Robinson Crusoe in rags stranded on the island. She was realising, gradually, that her son was reading the words, not just remembering the stories from the picture books.

Richard's head was growing faster than the rest of his body, she saw. He was like an old man already at four. 'I'm tired, Richard,' she murmured. 'Let's get some sleep.'

'No, Mummy!' he shouted. 'Want this book. This one!' He shoved *Robinson Crusoe* into her face.

'Alright, Richard. Why don't you try to read it for yourself? Mummy's tired.'

Richard looked at her, then at the book. He started mouthing out the sounds, deciphering the words underneath the pictures.

He's away, she thought. Mary Mother of God, thank you!

She made the sign of the cross on her tired brow and chest.

From then on, Bridie was released from the task of reading to him aloud for long stretches at a time. She felt released from a sort of prison.

Richard was soon gorging well into the evening on *Robinson Crusoe*, *Treasure Island*, *The Magic Pudding* and *Wind in the Willows*; and all the Rudyard Kipling stories.

Even *David Copperfield* was soon within his grasp.

One Saturday, Will took both boys with him to the high property. He rode on a sturdy piebald pony, a full bellied old nag that he trusted to behave. Richard followed on Gem, and Will carried Infant Charlie in a homemade structure on his back, which Bridie had used when she was doing housework with each baby. She'd sewed the pieces of cloth together from a pattern Will had drawn up; he'd then attached the fabric around a light cane frame and strapped it on her back. It was inspired by American Indian and Aboriginal artefacts he'd read about in a *Reader's Digest* magazine.

This day the infant crowed from his place on Will's back. He loved being out with his father and brother.

Charlie was drawn to animals of all sorts from the beginning. Richard trotted past them, always happy to be the first in line.

Will'd named his property at Mounttain Ridge 'Deep Creek', after the gurgling stream that ran through it. He'd purchased some low priced weaners, and Billy had given him poddy calves that he'd reared by hand to add to the herd. With the aid of the Finn boys, Will had built stockyards and a bush hut down on the flats. There he kept bridles and saddles, as well as tools and basic food stores.

Bridie went with them some Sundays, and liked to watch, as they swam in the creek. Richard was already dog paddling.

Today Bridie was having a break from the boys and focusing on catching up with housework. She also wanted to visit Hilltop to see how Eliza was coping, now that Charlie was back home, limping around on crutches.

'Dad, I wanta gallop,' Richard shouted. He liked to push the pony, digging in his heels and urging him forward with a flick of the reins.

'Alright, but just for a little while. It gets a bit rough up ahead.' Will was impressed by Richard's confidence. He didn't want to quash it, but kept a watchful eye at the ready to caution him. The boy was a risk taker.

They reached the creek, hot and sweating from the ride in midsummer's heat. Richard threw off his clothes. 'Last one in's a scaredy cat,' he screeched as he ran to the edge and jumped in.

Climbing onto a branch overhanging the bank, he jumped in, over and over again.

'Stay in the shallows, Richard,' his father warned.

Will sat on the edge and let Charlie splash his toes in the cool water. The ponies, unsaddled, shook themselves and munched on grass. Cockatoos screeched in the gum trees overhead. A kookaburra laughed at something and Richard imitated it.

It's damned near perfect, Will thought. The sun's rays filtered through the foliage overhanging the banks, as his two little boys splashed happily in the pure waters of the creek.

A niggling worry kept popping up, like a lizard's head on the creek bank. It was something to do with Bridie. He wondered if he could ever really possess her. Their love making wasn't bad, but he felt that she was trying too hard to please him. Was she feigning a climax, rather than reaching a peak of pleasure, brought on by his moves?

His ease with tackling and taming the rough bush and the beasts was one thing. He was already an expert at horse breaking, droving, branding and breeding cattle. But he was lost when it came to the female of his own species.

All he'd ever wanted was to have a mate. He thought he'd found one in Bridie. Now, sometimes, he doubted if he could ever make her happy.

What am I thinking? he chided himself. At least we're alive, the war hasn't affected us too badly, and we've got all the eggs, meat, milk and vegetables we can eat. We've got two sturdy boys and another child on the way.

If only Dad would step in with a loan, I could buy this place outright, build her a better house to live in. A house of our own. On top of the hill with a view over the river. Bedrooms for the kids, better appliances.

As it was, she was always tired, and so was he.

He'd have to have a yarn to Reenie about it all when he got a chance. She'd been his confidant for years now, and he always felt better after a cup of tea and a talk with her. She understood him like no one else.

Still, that empty feeling in the pit of his stomach returned, like a snake curling up within his gut, strangling his attempt at reasoning away the doubts.

He doubted that his old friend could help this time.

Chapter 22

By the end of the next year, three children had joined the Featherstone parents at Mistletoe Cottage, each born little more than twelve months apart. Will'd been mustering cattle at Deep Creek for two years now, while working towards earning his own livelihood on the land.

She'd missed him almost as much as she had during their courtship days. She'd wanted him as a lover so badly that she forgot his sometimes clumsy lovemaking. She'd yearned for the touch of his wiry body and salty lips, his penis like a battering ram seeking its target.

Hungry for his wife's body after Charlie's birth, he'd wanted her all the more, soon afterwards. When he returned from the high paddock after the birth, she noticed a difference in her own feelings. She'd become angrier, too tired, bored with the housework, to make passionate love.

She was surprised, nevertheless, at how easy it had been to fall pregnant once again. It must have been because Charlie had been bottle fed from early on, that she fell pregnant for a third time so quickly, in spite of a dearth of coital events.

Will drove Bridie to Camelot Maternity Hospital with the first signs of labour pangs early on a Friday in late 1948. Once she was inside the sad, two storey building that looked out shamefacedly from closed lids like a house of ill repute, the contractions stopped. Will had to return to Mistletoe Cottage with the boys.

Bridie lay back in the narrow bed, thankful for the respite from pain and from housework drudgery. Meals and magazines were brought to her as she lay back and rested. She saw that the cover on the out-of-date *Women's Weekly* magazine was of a war plane cockpit. It was filled with stories about rations and 'Cheery Letters from Prisoners in Germany and Japan, Home to their Parents.'

Please, God, make it a daughter this time, not another boy, who might have to go off and fight overseas one day.

A subtropical summer storm was raging outside as Bridie's contractions returned that afternoon. Two hundred and thirty-three points of rain had fallen in the previous week and the river was starting to overflow its banks. Bridie had always hated storms. Towards evening the contractions got stronger, but now the storm in her body was worse than the one outside. The doctor would not let her get up and give birth like the cows on the farm, opening up and flowing in rhythm with the tide, naturally. She had to lie flat on her back. Prostrate, obedient, the nurses falling in line behind their master commandant. She felt that she couldn't even scream. It was forbidden. No painkillers allowed, either.

The pain of birth was a woman's lot, they all thought. The baby's head was bigger than the two boys' had been at that stage. Her birth was slow and tortuous as a result. Bridie was aware through the pain, as the baby—*It's a girl!*—was yanked, mewling from her womb, held upside down, puking and bruised, black and blue. Forced from warm spring waters where she'd swum and floated, mermaid like, oblivious; flung out into a harsh element under cold cruel lights. Miserable, mute, the rush of air heavy and sharp upon raw skin. Slapped on bare buttocks by the family doctor, screaming, then. He, pleased now, as he cut the warm pulsating cord that held her to her mother, tied it quickly in a knot with cool fingers.

A grim faced band in white starched uniforms, staring down at them. Hard eyes sizing them up. Exhausted, everyone.

Bridie was too tired to hold her daughter as she came into the world. She went instead from the disciplined hands of the family GP, Dr Turnbrow, who commandeered the operation, refusing all drugs for the mother, and into the arms of a stiff nurse at *Camelot Hospital for Women* at the end of summer in 1950.

She caught the first glimpse of her daughter and gasped, cried out to the nurses: 'That's not my daughter, there must be some mistake. She's so,'... she stopped herself just in time from saying *ugly* ...'fair.'

The girl baby had thick red hair down to her shoulders, and hazel green eyes. Her skin was pale. It was clear to Bridie which side of the family tree the baby belonged—the Scottish Featherstone one.

She looked away and felt like sobbing.

Will broke the news of the birth to Richard and Charlie, as they woke up early on the morning of the twentieth. 'You've got a little sister with lots of red hair.'

Eliza came from Hilltop to help mind the two boys, so Will could visit Bridie and the baby girl in hospital.

He was besotted at the sight of his daughter.

'She's like Charlie with that hair. Adorable.' He couldn't keep his eyes off her fiery red crown.

'The hair's a lot redder than Charlie's. Charlie's hair is strawberry blonde, not red,' Bridie said.

'If she's half as sweet natured as Charlie, she'll be perfect,' Will said. 'That boy entered the world with a grin, and it hasn't left his face since.'

With her own dark haired good looks and wide eyes men could drown in, Bridie felt that this changeling of a child was a bad reflection on herself, having been told since childhood that she was unusually beautiful and sensual. *Of model material, really.*

'She looks like the *Virgin Queen Elizabeth* with her white skin and red hair,' Bridie said, 'I don't feel like she's mine.'

'Don't be silly, darling. She's a little beauty.' He held his baby daughter proudly up in his arms and kissed her.

'Mum and Dad will be pleased. They always liked red hair. It's on Dad's side.'

'She's like a baby cuckoo in the wrong nest,' Bridie said when she held the baby to her breast. 'With hair like that, she'll have a temper, I'd say.'

'Let's call her Olivia,' said Will, remembering the name of one of his favourite actresses, Olivia de Havilland in *Gone with the Wind*. 'If she turns out anything like her namesake, the actress, she'll be doing great.'

Bridie liked the name 'Olivia' and agreed with Will's suggestion to give her a second name, 'Elizabeth', after the famous queen.

'A daughter at last,' said Billy when he heard the news from Will over the telephone. 'They say it proves a father's manhood, Will.'

'Yes, Billy,' said Will, 'and she's a little beauty, with lots of gorgeous red hair.'

On the way home from the hospital, Will drove them to pay a visit to his parents' cream and green bungalow on the riverbank not far from the hospital.

Once inside, Bridie placed the baby in a bundle on the comfy floral sofa in the living room. Charlie called out in terror as he caught sight of the felt toys on the lounge: 'Don't leaf the baby there, or the mices will get her.'

Ma Featherstone laughed, as she picked up the toy mice she'd made as gifts for the new baby.

'It's alright, Charlie, I shall put them up here on the mantelpiece. Which names do you fancy for your little sister? We must name her now, boys.'

'I think, maybe *Rubicon* or *Jellybean*,' said Richard in his old man's voice.

They all laughed, and Ma said it wouldn't do for a girl. She preferred something a little more exotic and romantic, and wanted to call her 'Philomena' or 'Elizabeth'.

'Will suggests Olivia,' said Bridie. 'It's theatrical.'

'Olivia's not a bad name,' agreed Ma.

'And maybe 'Elizabeth' for a second name,' said Will. 'We knew you'd like it, too. There, we've decided, Bridie and me.'

'Look at the long nose and fine hands. We have a future piano player here,' said Pa, in his dignified voice. 'And that hair reminds me of someone in the family photographs. On my side.'

'It's your mother, dear, with that thick red hair,' said Ma Featherstone to her husband. 'She's like young Charlie here. Just lovely, isn't she?'

Ma, with a nervous sort of laugh as she spoke, her own hair turning coal black, asked her husband if he agreed with her.

Pa, who held a pipe in his mouth, nodded in agreement and said: 'Hmmm! Well, may I nurse the baby?'

'Not if you're smoking,' said his wife. 'Here, give her to me.'

The baby was passed from person to person, then back to Bridie once again.

Later on, they sipped tea from fine cups and nibbled on Anzac biscuits and tea cake from old English china.

'Is she sleeping through the night?' asked Ma.

'Not yet,' said Bridie, 'I'm breastfeeding her every three to four hours.'

'Well, dear, the latest Tresillian approach is to allow the baby to cry itself to sleep. They learn self-control that way. Our niece is an expert in the field of mothercraft.'

'I don't like to hear a baby scream,' said Bridie. 'I run to her every time.'

'Well, I come from a large family, twelve children in all, although some did not survive. It was a question of necessity, a case of survival for Mother. All well cared for, too, as well as educated.'

'What did those ones die from?' Bridie asked, interested.

'Diphtheria was the killer of the day,' whispered Ma, remembering.

'Mumma had a family of six, and none died,' Bridie said.

The next day at Mistletoe Cottage, the extended family stood around the cradle, peering in at the baby. Eyes and faces staring down, sizing her up, counting her fingers and toes, noting her features, whom she looked like. Richard and Charlie were playing with the meccano set, unaware of the words flying backwards and forwards across the space above their heads.

'Where does the red hair come from?' asked Bridie's brother, Johnny. 'Nothing like that in our family. All dark an' Irish on our side. Strange, that....'

'From Queen Elizabeth the First,' snapped Bridie. 'And she did all right for herself, eh?'

'Yeah,' said Will, 'it's from my side of the family tree, a real little beauty, isn't she?'

'Can I nurse her, Bridie?' asked Johnny.

'If you sit down on the lounge chair, here,' said Bridie. She was anxious, fearing that her brother might drop the baby on her head, leaving her brain damaged or crippled, as well as red-haired and plain.

Everyone gathered around Johnny and the baby on the chair.

Johnny's words cut through the air, 'It's her red hair that spoils her, Bridie—such a shame....'

'Don't be a drip, Johnny,' said Will. 'She'll be a true beauty one day, you'll see.' And he took his daughter in his arms, held her up against his shoulder, and danced gently with her around the room.

Bridie, watching this display, thought of their first waltz together, when Will had held her in those strong arms of his, and she'd fallen for this confident yet gentle giant of a man. Was it happening all over again?

It was now Bridie's turn to experience, as she stared at them, and the baby seemed to surrender and fall asleep on Will's shoulder, a feeling akin to some leftover relic. A strange childhood anguish had invaded her being for an instant. Was it envy, abandonment or simply that green eyed monster jealousy?

Coming in to see her locked in a synchronous embrace with Charlie, lying asleep on one side, and the new baby at her breast, he'd balked like a startled horse, a shade falling down over his face. A third marsupial like creature was attached to her cherry red nipples. He stood there and watched for a moment. A pale creature, lips closed around the purple fruit, greedy cheeks puffing in and out. Suckling at—*his* breasts.

Bridie looked up and noticed. 'You all want me so badly, that you're fighting over me,' she said with a laugh, and motioned for him to come and sit down next to them on the bed. The baby pulled away from the nipple, stretching it out like an elastic band, and Bridie yelled in pain.

Olivia looked up at Will. He picked her up and sought those gorgeous green eyes as if he was drowning in them. How could he be jealous of his infant child? His own flesh and blood? He held her to his heart and thanked the universe for giving them three healthy babes, and this one a daughter, to boot. Two of them with hair the colour of pumpkin and fire.

He felt his heart swelling in that moment of realisation. There was nothing to be jealous about. It was all a case of expansion and growth.

Chapter 23

Bridie felt all eyes on her from the other mothers in their shapeless floral dresses, and especially from their husbands, who ogled her as she strutted across the asphalt to find Richard with Gem. Two little red-headed toddlers ran at her feet, decked out in matching sailor's outfits, Livvy's hair curled into long sausages with a roll on top of her head. At three, Charlie's hair was long and wavy, his father not wanting him to lose his baby hair just yet. They looked like twins, Livvy being tall for her age.

It was the Annual Pet Show at Karrana Catholic School. Bridie had decided to send her firstborn son here because of the emphasis on music and the arts, as well as its solid pedagogic record.

Richard, in third grade, had been fast tracked up the scholastic ladder. He was especially good at arithmetic and reading. Comments on his first school report were always 'excellent pupil', 'highly motivated' and 'confident'. He was a good all-rounder, successful at sport, as well as public speaking and music. The school valued his skills, as did his mother and paternal grandparents.

Bridie felt her breast fit to burst at the thought of her son's successes.

A large crowd of boys and girls had gathered around Richard on his pony. They stroked Gem's shiny black belly and patted his forelock, hoping, no doubt, that they would get to have a ride on the pony. Bridie doubted that Richard would let anyone mount his special pet. Charlie and Livvy ran around the playground, devising imaginary games. They stuck together like Siamese twins. Bridie thought of Hansel and Gretel, those tiny children lost in the woods, as her two carrot headed tots tripped around together, mischief in their eyes.

She saw that the two had started to play a game of jumping over a row of miniature rose bushes, when her gaze was pulled like a magnet towards Richard.

She'd dressed him up as a cowboy

'Will had to go to the saleyards,' Bridie told Billy who'd ridden all the way to the school, leading Gem with a rope.

'You'll have to take the pony back home, too.'

'That's alright, Bridie,' he said, 'I've got time. Something your Will hasn't got at the moment, with all his jobs and duties.'

'Yes, he's trying to buy more machinery and property. When will we have some cash to spend on necessities of life?'

'He's got a good business head on his shoulders, Bridie, and you should be grateful for that.'

'What, grateful for living in a dump with no *mod cons*? I'm sick and tired of it, Billy.'

'Stick with him and it'll be your turn in time, Bridie. I'll give you a hand to plant a flower garden at the front of the cottage. It's not so bad, you know.'

'That's what my friend Stella says. Calls it romantic, would you believe, with its parasitic vines clinging to the trees?'

Children had brought bantam fowls, rabbits, guinea pigs, persian cats; and spotted dogs that snarled and barked at the cats, showing their teeth.

Dressed in a black waistcoat and chaps over jodhpurs, and seated on a tan saddle with a red and yellow striped rug, Richard was the star of the show. He sported a felt hat with a silver sheriff's badge on it, with boots and spurs adding to the cowboy look.

Gem, frightened by a brindle mutt, pigrooted, tossing Richard off onto soft grass.

Bridie, eyes never far from her handsome son, ran out onto the field in her silky dress and high heels.

Livvy, had scratched her knee on a rosebush thorn and was crying in her mother's arms at the time.

'It's okay, Bridie,' shouted Billy, who'd already picked Richard up and hoisted him onto Gem again. 'He's embarrassed, that's all.'

They watched as Richard pulled on Gem's reins and galloped off across the expanse of grass to show off his bravado and riding skills.

Kids watched, open mouthed in admiration.

He's a real hero, that child, Bridie thought. He'll go far in life. One of those kids that'll make a difference, maybe prime minister or save the world, who knows?

Ma Featherstone turned up at that moment. 'I've come to see our young master in his schoolyard realm,' she laughed. Bridie had started to warm a little towards her mother-in-law, seeing how much they shared admiration for Richard's scholarly successes.

'Glad you could make it, Ma,' Bridie said. 'He's just gone for a gallop on Gem. Go and talk to his teacher about his marks. She raves about him.'

The prize winners were announced at the end of the afternoon. Only then did Richard dismount from his pony and give a Cheshire cat smile, as he went up to collect his prize for bringing along the largest animal.

He refused to allow any children to ride on Gem, saying 'He might throw you off,' as an excuse.

'It's his special pet,' Bridie said in a firm voice. 'Maybe you can come to our house and have a ride.' Richard was shaking his head.

'Show me your prize,' Charlie said, pulling at the parcel in Richard's hands.

'It's a book,' Richard said. 'Too hard for you to read. No pictures in it.'

All the way home in the car, the two younger children grizzled that Richard wouldn't show them his book.

'You'll tear it,' he whined, 'you kids make me sick.'

'You're all tired, Bridie cried out. 'Why do you have to fight all the time?'

'It's not me, it's them two,' shouted Richard. 'They won't leave me alone for a minute, always wanting my things.'

Bridie sighed. She wasn't in the race when it came to sorting out conflict among her brood. She'd never learnt how to get on with others in a civil manner, having had to fight back and compete with five older brothers.

'If you don't keep quiet, I'll tell your father you've been naughty,' she said.

'No don't,' cried Charlie, who hankered after his father's approval, and didn't want to disappoint him. 'Don't tell Daddy, please.'

'I don't care,' said Richard.

Livvy had fallen asleep, her hair spread out like a halo around Charlie's lap.

Richard stuck his nose in his book. There was peace and quiet until they reached the cottage.

The next Sunday the whole family went along the road for a birthday dinner for Bridie's brother, the one who'd lost a leg in the war. This day, as well as Grandma, Billy, Ned and Charles, there were other uncles who'd come to stay at the farm for the celebration. Wally, the short fat uncle with the gruff voice was there from Taree, and Cyclone Johnny had come up from Sydney on the train.

Charles O'Toole was now able to walk on his prosthetic limb, partly with the aid of crutches. His wavy hair and smiley face drew the children to him. They stared, boggle eyed, as he pulled up his trouser leg and showed them the pinkish artificial leg underneath.

'D'you want a go with it?' he joked as he pretended to take it off, and offer it to Richard.

'No, no, thanks,' said Richard. 'I want to be a soldier like you when I grow up.'

Bridie shivered and said: 'No, you don't. You'll be a doctor or something if I have my way.'

There was a lot of shouting and roaring as Bridie and her brothers laughed and joked in their *deaf* Irish way. Will tried to get a word in edgeways, but didn't stand a chance.

'How is the milk run going, Billy?'

'N-not bad, Will. Prices are down, but.'

'Have you given any further thoughts about diversifying, Ned?' he asked *The Godfather,* (Ned's brothers took great delight in teasing the firstborn with this nickname), 'running a few weaners for beef, as well as the cows?'

'Nah. Not enough time as it is, Will,' he said. 'To do the milking and crops, and all.'

'I'd be willing to step in and help set it up, if you want.'

But Will knew it would fall on deaf ears, as it had in the past.

Everyone, especially the kids, wanted to know about *The War* from Uncle Charles, but he was tight lipped when it came to that. He'd told Grandma O'Toole about the nightmares he was having, and a little about *the cruelty of the Japs*. He spent long periods lost in thought, mute to the world. A possible career as a primary school teacher awaited him. He'd be the first in the family to ever gain an education.

The kids raced outside to see what Uncle Billy was about to do. He'd grabbed the biggest rooster, the bird squawking like a banshee, from the chook yard. He laid its neck out on the wood heap block, and, with one swift movement, chopped its head off.

Livvy came out, just in time to see the headless rooster running around the yard.

'It's still alive, with its head off,' Richard gasped.

Livvy screeched, as it fell, still pulsating a little, into a crumpled, feathery heap on the grass.

'No, it's dead, now,' Billy said. 'Don't worry, kids.'

He plucked the feathers from it then and there, while the kids stared, open mouthed. He called out to his mother to take it inside to cook. He beckoned to the kids to follow him.

'Now, c-come an' s-see the baby ducklings.'

Next it was the red and white newborn calf on tottering legs that he was feeding by hand from a tin bucket.

'Let me do it, Billy,' Charlie shouted.

'You're too little on your own, Charlie. Here, I'll help you.' The serrated tongue of the calf sucked on their hands with fierce vigour, and bumped its head into the milk bucket, almost spilling the contents.

As a special treat, he took them to the slip rail gate that led into the far paddock to look at the dark brown bull.

'Will he chase us, Billy, if we go there?' asked Richard.

'Aw, gee, yeah. Don't never go near the bull.'

'A cranky look on 'is face,' Charlie said, and he mimicked the fierce expression.

'Just s-stay away from 'im, you'll be alright.'

Charlie chuckled: 'I'll duck under the wire if he chases me.'

Livvy cried out: 'Me too.'

'I'll climb up the mulberry tree,' said Richard, 'and stay there till he gets tired of waiting for me to come down.'

'Yeah, well jus' don' go near'im!' said Billy.

After a rowdy lunch, they went outside and had watermelon underneath the grape vine trellis. They gorged on the brilliant pink flesh until they were sick, lying bloated on the grass. They snuggled up close to their uncles, who'd begun to tell tall stories to make everyone laugh.

In the lounge room later on, Bridie played the piano and the mouth organ, while they all sang along with her *When Irish Eyes Are Smiling*. All of a sudden Johnny pulled a white handkerchief out of his pocket and started to bellow out loudly the words of the song *Cry* in a near perfect rendition and impersonation of Johnny Ray.

Actual tears came into his eyes, and he sobbed louder and louder, until droplets were gushing out, and he was howling and blowing his nose, and the kids were sure that they were real tears pouring forth.

Chapter 24

A year had passed quickly, with the three children growing into sturdy little beasts like the animals surrounding them. Bridie and Will stood in the middle of the ochre coloured road and watched their two youngest children setting out for Hilltop.

'Just look at those babes in the wood,' Will said as they watched the children tripping along, Maggie the dog following closely on their heels like a chaperone.

Livvy, in Ma Featherstone's gift of a little red coat, protecting her from the dying kicks of wintry cold, was carrying a basket full of flowers to give to her other grandma.

Bridie waved to her, blowing kisses, as the little girl followed closely on Charlie's heels. As they'd grown, Livvy had stuck to Charlie like a vine to a trunk. He was her hero and they became inseparable.

Black and white birds flew around the treetops, magpies and currawongs, competing with raucous crows. The mixed chorus of sounds descending from above was both melodious and jarring to adult ears.

'Remember to look out for snakes, Charlie!' Bridie called to their receding backs.

'Yeah Mah!' he yelled, guessing what his mother was saying. He had no fear of snakes.

'Yes, this place is safe for our children,' Will said, 'so few cars, and the only danger is deep water, far enough away from here, at least.'

'Of course, darling,' said Bridie, snuggling up to his shoulder, 'you don't have to worry, Billy and I have drilled it into them for a long time now. *Don't go near the river without an adult. Ever.*'

Will shot around as a bushland chorus rang out above them. 'Just listen to those blackbirds cackling. As if they know something we don't. Birds are messengers, you know.'

'Where's Richard, I wonder?' asked Bridie, a sharp spasm in her stomach, reminding her, perhaps, that it was time to prepare lunch. 'Hope he's alright.'

'Probably jumping over logs on Gem. The will of the devil, that one, when he's out to win, even competing against himself now.'

Bridie told her husband about having taken Richard to the appointment with the family doctor, the previous day. Doctor Turnbrow had been impressed with Richard's intelligence and reading ability.

'He's well above his age group of six,' he said. 'Intelligent children are often difficult when it comes to obedience.'

He'd met other children like Richard, highly excitable with nervous dispositions.

Bridie thought how it sounded a little bit like her own temperament.

The doctor'd said that there was no cure for this syndrome, which was in great part hereditary. Catholic education would certainly teach the child discipline, that he couldn't get away with everything he wanted to. The keenness of school exams, group sports and other activities would also assist in mental focus and alertness.

She'd walked out of the surgery and taken him straight to the newsagent to choose a book as a reward for behaving well during the doctor's appointment. He'd chosen *Mrs Piggle-Wiggle's Magic* about a woman who cured children of bad habits.

She hoped that he had not somehow gleaned that they thought of him as 'bad'. It was only his excitable behaviour that worried her.

She tried to imagine her husband's true thoughts about Richard's conduct, as they sat down to lunch on the back verandah. She didn't know how to ask the questions that were percolating in her mind.

Bridie had sparkled with renewed hope and vigour after the talk with Doctor Turnbrow. She'd always had great respect for doctors, and had a secret wish to belong to their social group. She knew she'd never fit in. Not while Will had no such desire.

It was Sunday. Bridie had talked Will into staying home today. She was wanting to talk some more about Richard. Sitting together on the back verandah, she knew he was champing at the bit to get back to work at Deep Creek.

'You know, Will,' she said, 'I reckon we ought to talk to Richard about the dangers of galloping and jumping.'

'Bridie, you know the saying, *boys will be boy,*' he said, 'It's good that he's fallen in love with the pony, at least.'

Will might have chosen the wrong word, 'love', when applied to their elder son. At some level she blamed herself for Will not having bonded with Richard properly at birth. On a deeper level, she knew that Richard might have been born this way. She was loath to admit that her husband disliked something about his eldest child.

Will hadn't warmed to his firstborn, who seemed to take after Pa Featherstone's flinty side, not at all like the other two.

The expression 'set in stone', like some rocks hardened by the sun she'd seen on the property, came to mind. So different from Charlie's twinkle eyed grin.

Her thoughts took her back to courting days, when they'd conceived the baby, who was now this sturdy six-year-old schoolboy, an iron will stronger than his father's. Could it be punishment for having thought of getting rid of him?

She knew she was being illogical, that it was superstition, but she felt on a deep level that the law of cause and effects had been disturbed…. She knew Will would scoff at her foolish thoughts. *Surely, a loving God would understand their predicament and forgive them?*

Still, the thought persisted, and still she bit her tongue when she thought of telling him.

'I'm worried about Richard, too,' said Will.

'But he's a star, you must admit that,' chortled Bridie, 'reading far ahead for his age. Your mother borrows books from the library for him, says he's a genius.'

'All war books at the moment,' said Will. 'Are the teachers aware of this?'

'Yes,' said Bridie, laughing, 'Douglas Bader with his tinny legs and funny walk, *Jack Simpson and his donkey*, *Lawrence of Arabia* … I'm learning from him, too, you know. The teachers don't care, so long as he gets high marks in the exams.'

She remembered her son asking why *Will* hadn't gone to fight in the war. As if he'd lost respect for his father for being a coward.

'I'll have a word with him, but I think he's more likely to listen to his teachers,' Will said, trying to reassure his wife.

On the Deep Creek property, they'd watched one day their son galloping the pony downhill, jumping over potholes, while reciting *The Man From Snowy River* as he rode.

The boy's courage and enthusiasm for life, both impressed and worried them.

Apart from riding, Richard's other love was playing with his giant electric train set, fiddling with all the little signals, lights and toy stations. So many different ways that he could connect the tracks for the train to run along. So many games that he could play on his own. So many treasured pieces that he wouldn't allow anyone to touch.

Bridie thought of the connections taking place inside their clever son's head.

It was a Saturday toward the end of winter. They happened to be inside when Richard raced in shouting: 'Mummy, Daddy, come and watch me on Gem.'

They went out to the backyard.

Richard had set up a series of jumps from logs and planks he'd erected in a circle, covering thirty square metres, Will having cleared much of the space, so that snakes and other wildlife would stay away from the house.

'Watch Mum, Dad. I'm getting good at show jumping.'

Bridie watched, her heart in her mouth, as her son cantered around the clearing, urging the pony over ever bigger and bigger obstacles. She clutched at Will's hand.

'I'm afraid,' she whispered, her voice going hoarse.

That night, Bridie had had a luminous dream. She'd seen the five of them, standing transfixed, side by side, next to the river. A fiery ball above the horizon grew larger as it hurtled towards them. She watched, the end coming nearer, with a fatalism she hardly knew she had, protected by her family and their great love.

She reminded herself to tell Will about her dream, which was troubling, yet radiant.

'Perhaps you and Gem need to have a rest now, son,' called Will. 'Come and have something to eat and drink.' It was as if the child didn't hear his father's voice, and he continued pushing the pony in and out and over the obstacles.

Just as the boy and his pony were about to jump over the last, highest log, a wallaby shot out from behind a bush. The pony baulked, Richard flew over Gem's head and landed on his back on the ground. He didn't move.

Bridie screamed and went pale. Richard was lying on his back, looking up into the sky, except that his eyes were closed and blood oozed from his head near his left ear. Was it a large stone she saw next to his head? She placed her hands over her eyes, to blot out the sight of her injured son. *If he dies, I'll die too.* She wished she could drift into a slumber next to the body of her son.

A stoic calm had descended on Will, countering the near hysteria that was enwrapping itself around Bridie, who was sobbing now. Will placed his coat over the young boy:

'Ring for the ambulance, Bridie. A doctor … to come straight away.'

Bridie, white-faced and on the point of collapsing, summoned her last bit of energy phoning for medical help. Then she rang her mother:

'Quick, Mumma!' she gasped. 'Come quickly. Richard … a fall.' And with that her legs wobbled, before giving way under her, and she sank into a heap on the kitchen floor.

'Daddy, Richard is bleeding!' Charlie cried out. 'Look,' as he pointed to the red fluid mixing with Richard's dark hair, and pooling on the grass beneath his head.

'Yes, son. He's got a bump on the head. The ambulance will take him to hospital to fix him up.'

'Probbly just a cut,' Livvy said, reassuring her brother with big eyes.

'Now, you two go inside with Mummy and wait for Grandma.'

'Mummy's lying on the floor,' yelled back Charlie from the kitchen.

Bridie sat up, and started praying when Eliza arrived: 'Please God, if you save Richard, I will do anything … anything you ask of me. Quick, get down on your knees and pray, Mumma, Livvy....'

She asked her mother for a sip of brandy and stumbled to the sofa in the lounge room.

'Is Richard dead?' Livvy asked Eliza. 'He's blooding on the grass.'

'No, silly, he's just sleeping,' said Charlie, 'Daddy said he's going to get fixed.'

'Like Humpty Dumpty?' squealed Livvy, putting her hands over her mouth.

Bridie closed her eyes again and was drifting off once more. It's the shock, Eliza whispered to herself.

'Is Mummy dead?' Livvy whimpered. 'Is she going to the hospital too?'

'Mummy will be alright once the doctors arrive to fix Richard,' Eliza said, hoping against hope she was right, though she didn't like the pallor on her grandson's face, as she glanced through the window.

Will told her that Richard was still breathing, and he didn't want to move him in case of spinal injuries.

'I'll stay here with Bridie and the little ones,' Eliza called out.

'Thanks Grandma. I'll follow the ambulance to the hospital and stay near Richard.'

Eliza would feed the children leftovers from last night's meal, and let each child choose a favourite book, reading aloud to them and singing lullabies. That way, they'd drift off into slumber, the sweet, sad refrains of their Grandma's voice soothing and reassuring.

'Come in!' she cried out from the bedroom, as she heard the doctor's quiet knock on the front door.

Bridie woke up just as the sun was setting. As she opened her eyes, she was staring into an olive skinned face fringed with brown curls. She thought at first it was a dark angel. He was leaning over her, as he placed smelling salts beneath her nose.

'Where's Will and Richard? Is he all right?' she asked the beautiful apparition that knelt before her.

'He's gone in the ambulance to the hospital,' Doctor Goldblum said calmly, 'with your husband. Your little boy is going to be well cared for. And you must get some rest so you can be strong for him. I'm going to give you something that will make you sleep.'

His hand was cool on her skin, as he touched her forehead. He administered the injection that would allay Bridie's unbearable anguish until the morning.

She shivered slightly, before responding to his touch and drifting off.

Chapter 25

Will pushed through the front door of Karrana hospital. The smell of ether was so strong it knocked him off balance for a moment. So different from the eucalypt and natural scents of the bush. Here, everything was spick-and-span, scrubbed and polished. He'd been told that the family doctor, Dr Turnbrow, had been called in expressly to look after Richard. He wondered if his son was in the operating theatre now, about to go under the knife. Would Doctor Turnbrow agree to see him before he operated? Please Lord let him be able to see his son beforehand.

The receptionist at the desk directed him to the ward where Richard would be brought after the operation. He followed the long cream corridors connecting sections of the hospital. Nursing staff in starched uniforms, medicos in white, and anxious visitors moved silently through swing doors. The matron on duty in the children's section spoke kindly to him. 'Doctor Turnbrow is examining your son at the moment. I'll see what I can find out.' Will poked his head through the door into the ward. He could see rows of small beds and cots lining both sides of the long room in the children's ward. It made him think of wartime hospital wards that he'd seen in photos. Most of the children were asleep.

'We're going to have to operate,' said Dr Turnbrow. He offered a clean white hand for Will to shake. 'There might be a bit of pressure from the skull, given that there's a fracture. We'll only know if there's any intracranial damage once we have a look inside. Sometimes it's the jolt that the brain receives on both sides, rather than at the point of impact, that's the concern.'

'How long will he be in the coma?' asked Will. 'What are the chances of brain damage?'

'He's a strong little fellow,' said the doctor, 'and his skull is rock hard. All signs are no long-term damage. But you must expect some short-term changes. Mood changes, irritability. Laughing one minute then crying the next. The coma at this stage is the brain's way of regenerating itself. The longer he stays comatose, the worse the damage is.'

'When can I see him?' asked Will.

'You can visit him in the ward, straight after the operation, if he's doing well.'

A cloud of gloom had descended on Will after having talked to the doctor. He felt that Turnbrow was trying to reassure him, holding back a little. He wanted to shout at him: *Fix my boy! If not for me, for my wife's sake. She'll die if he's brain damaged.*

The doctor was already walking towards the operating room where Richard now lay, preparing, Will imagined, to cut the knife through his son's skull towards the densely coiled grey matter, location of the boy's super intelligence.

What if there was damage on both sides of the brain, as the doctor had intimated? What if the jolt had thrown the squishy matter against the hard skull on two sides of his head?

Will sat down at a table in one of the hospital café lounges with his head in his hands. Someone brought him a cup of tea and a scone. He tried to read the newspaper. He remembered stories of his mother's cousin, Mick, a large, pasty man with no future, who'd suffered brain damage from a bicycle accident, and who'd become loopy afterwards. 'Go to your room, Mick,' the father would say when visitors were there. It was embarrassment for the family, a damaged son.

What if there were learning problems? It might take weeks and months of therapy, maybe years, to get him back to a shade of what he'd been.

Bridie would be devastated. He remembered the doctor's warning: *The brain can bounce around, slosh inside the skull, which can be a problem.*

He dozed off.

In the critically ill medical section, Richard lay with eyes still closed and with a white bandage round his head, his face as white as the cloth. Tubes protruded from his throat and from other places beneath the sheets. It was not a pretty sight for a father to see. Tears rolled down Will's cheeks. How could this be the confident, active boy who'd jumped over logs with his pony a few hours ago?

'The operation was a success,' the doctor had said. 'We've relieved the pressure on his brain and we've done all that we can do. It's now up to him.'

'Thank you,' was all that Will could mumble.

'You'll be more use to him if you go home now and have a good rest, so that you can visit tomorrow.'

Will could see the logic in that. But what was he going to tell Bridie when she woke up? That her son might have brain damage from the fall? That they'd just have to wait and see what happened next? Would it be good for her to see her son in the state he was in?

Before leaving, he took one last look at his sleeping son, and thought, I'd swear he's aware of what's going on, the young tinker, if I didn't know any better. His eyes seemed to be moving underneath the lids. He looks as if he's fighting to stay, to not give in and surrender. Don't be silly, he chided himself. He's in a deep coma. Sometimes people don't wake up from these states for months or even years. The thought horrified him. As he stared at the pale face, he had a sudden intuition that the boy might pull through, and quicker than anyone expected. He's a fighter, he thought. His competitive nature might be just what gets him through.

As he drove home through the darkened bush, creatures, perhaps marsupials, scuttled in the undergrowth, owls hooted and the moon shone wanly. A voice in his head chided him: *It's the brain, the brain, the brain ... it's the brain....* Until he felt that his own mind was being pulled out of shape. 'I've got to get to bed and rest my brain,' he said out loud to the surrounding bush, 'He's a fighter, he's a fighter, you know, and he'll pull through, you'll see.'

The next day, Bridie steeled herself for the visit. Folding the striped pyjamas and placing them in neat piles with slippers and toys in a small brown port to take to the hospital, she fought to hide the tears. Charlie and Livvy had never seen their mother cry. They watched, open mouthed, as large silver droplets welled up in her eyes, clung to long lashes, and fell down her face. 'Is Richard dead, Mummy?' Charlie asked. He looked at her eyes, red and swollen. Livvy started to cry: 'Want my big brother back.' Grandma took the children outside, tears held back within her stout frame. 'He's in hospital having a long sleep. The doctors and nurses are making him better, that's all,' she told them.

Will was ashen faced, Uncle Ned hiding tears behind snorting noises. 'You know it's a bad sign, Bridie, if he hasn't woke up yet?'

Billy was wandering around down by the creek where he could cry without shame.

'You all think he's going to die,' Bridie shouted. 'Well I know differently. Just get down on your hands and knees and pray. Everyone. Now!'

And at that the two farmers, Grandma O'Toole and Bridie got down on their knees in the loungeroom and prayed quietly to a God that none of them believed properly in.

Please, God, bring him back to us, Bridie mouthed to herself.

Will waited for her in the car to drive towards the hospital.

Doctor Godblum came up to Bridie in the hospital foyer. Will was checking to see if they were able to visit Richard.

'How are you, Mrs Featherstone?' He put out his hand and said, 'Myer Goldblum. I saw you after your son's accident.' He smiled, showing perfect white teeth. Bridie felt as if she knew him from somewhere. An image rose to the surface of her mind, like an iridescent spirit emerging from a lake— *here was the visitation she'd seen after she fainted.*

'I think your son's going to be all right,' he said, contacting her with those earnest dark eyes. 'He's got the best care he could have here. And I'll keep an eye on him. Here's my number. You can phone me with any questions you might have. Turnbrow and I are working together.'

Bridie felt a little better after having spoken to this doctor. He had such kind and gentle eyes. She felt he could be trusted.

But when she saw Richard, lying there as if tethered to the bed, with all the tubes showing above the tight sheets, instruments recording his every pulse, she clutched at Will and sobbed quietly into his shirt. 'Oh, Will, he looks awful. That's not my Richard. So white and still. *Please, please God, let him come back to me.*'

Bridie stifled her sobs. Her face drained of all its blood. I've got to be strong for him, she thought. She rushed from the room onto an adjoining balcony and let the deep, heaving sobs escape from her chest like a levee bank breaking. Mustn't let him hear, she thought.

Will thought it best to leave her sitting out there until she was ready to come back in. If ever, he thought. Poor darling, I knew it would be hard for her to see.

Again Will had the sense that Richard was listening to them, recognising their voices.

'At least he's still with us,' Bridie whispered, coming in from outside, 'and that nice doctor says he's going to get better.'

'Go and talk to him, Bridie. Touch him, tell him you're here waiting for him to come back.'

She knelt by the bed and placed her cheek near to where she knew the little beating heart would be: 'I love you, Baby. It's Mummy here. We all miss you so much. Please come back to us. Your whole family, we're all praying for you.'

On the way out, she took one last look at the sleeping form and imagined that he was waving to her. *It's awright, Mum, I'll be back home and on Gem again, soon as you can blink an eyelid.'*

On the way back home, Will said, 'Bridie you'll need to expect some brain damage. Doctor Turnbrow mentioned that he might be erratic, spacey for a while, but that they'll get him the best treatment and give him the best care they can. Even if it means going to Sydney to find the best specialists in brain damage, we'll find a way to bring him back.'

'He doesn't look any different from the outside, does he?' she said.

The next day was cloudy and muggy, with showers expected later in the afternoon. The Hilltop relatives and the younger family were shrouded in gloom. Bridie had telephoned the hospital, and spoken to the matron. 'He's still in a coma, I'm afraid, Mrs Featherstone. The doctors and nurses are doing all they can. We'll ring you as soon as there's any change.'

The whole extended family was at Mistletoe Cottage, sitting outside under the trellis Will had erected for protection. The small children were playing hide-and-seek around the outside of the house.

'The passionfruit vine has grown so fast, Will,' Billy said. 'It'll be great in midsummer to keep the sun off.'

'Yes,' said Will. 'I'm pleased with it.'

'I feel like shooting that horse,' Ned snarled, as he watched Gem feeding tranquilly in the further reaches of the property.

'Don't be silly, it's not Gem's fault,' said Will. 'It was an accident.'

'You know there's no joy if he lives, either. Could be an idiot.'

Will shushed Ned as Bridie was coming in. She'd prayed for Richard this day, instead of visiting him in the hospital. She felt closer to him that way. She asked them all, once again, to please do the same.

'I feel God is on our side,' she said. 'I had a dream that these golden rays came down and touched Richard on the head. He's going to wake up, I know he is.'

Ned and Eliza threw a glance at one another, then looked down. 'Be careful what you wish for,' Ned muttered underneath his breath.

Billy said: 'Bridie's right, you know. I reckon he's gunna get better.'

The two little ones, running in, shouted: 'Richard's getting better. Richard's getting better.' Like a refrain from a nursery rhyme.

When Will got back from the hospital, he'd been sad to report to Bridie that there was no change in their son's condition. The child lay as he had done for two days now in the calm state of unconsciousness.

'At least he's not suffering,' he said gently to Bridie. 'He's not in any pain.'

'I know, but all I want is my Richard back.'

196

Will agreed with her, although he couldn't keep the image of the loopy uncle from embedding itself in his mind.

Chapter 26

It was cool the next day. Bridie agreed with Will that they should both go together and visit their son. She was feeling a little stronger, having prayed so hard and earnestly that she felt she could only surrender now to what fate had in store for her. She was pleased that she'd made her brothers and her mother at the farm get down on their knees and pray, though.

All the birds had quietened down, probably hiding from the gloom of the drop in temperature.

Will glanced at the scene in the field below. Gem was grazing under the Casuarina trees. The poddy calves, weaners and horses that Will kept there, were chewing their cuds or dozing next to the tiny creek that served as drinking water for the animals. Peace reigned. The clouded blue of the sky was shot through with the weak rays of the winter sun. He could imagine a higher power having a hand in all of this, if it were not for the fact of his intellect, which told him otherwise.

The sun was a pale ball high in the sky as they set off for the hospital.

Just like in the dream, Bridie thought. That powerful light touching Richard's head from way up in the heavens.

They stopped by Ma and Pa Featherstone's dainty house behind the privet hedge, to give them news and an invitation. 'We're off to visit Richard, if you'd like to come with us,' Will said.

'Yes, we'll follow in our car,' Pa said. 'We'd like to see the young fellow.'

'Don't be shocked by the look of him,' Bridie warned Ma. 'I still can't look at his poor little white face properly yet.'

'There there, dear. We'll all send him some prayers, right there at his bedside.'

The two doctors, Turnbrow and Goldblum, were on duty when they arrived.

They acknowledged the parents, and shook hands with the newcomers. Pa Featherstone and Doctor Turnbrow were old friends from Rotary.

'Many thanks for the care and treatment you have endowed on our young man,' Pa said as he shook hands with the two men.

'We're doing all we can for him,' said Turnbrow. 'It's getting to the critical phase now,' he said. 'The longer he stays in the coma, the more serious we fear his head injury to be.'

'So there has been no change?' Pa asked.

'None at all,' he said, turning to go. 'But we must leave you now to have some time by yourselves with the little fellow.'

'Thank you again from the bottom of our hearts,' said Ma Featherstone as the two men left the room.

'Look, Will,' Bridie whispered, 'his eyes seem to be moving underneath his lids.'

'I think you're imagining it, dear,' said Ma. 'It might be the breeze coming in from the open window.'

Bridie started singing, one of her favourite lullabies that she used to sing to Richard as a baby:

> *Swing low, sweet chariot*
> *Coming for to carry me home,*
> *Swing low, sweet chariot,*
> *Coming for to carry me home.*

She pulled out the homemade birthday cake with the seven multicoloured candles that she'd brought along in a brown paper bag. She lit the candles with matches she'd secreted in her handbag.

Bridie started to sing *Happy Birthday* in a subdued voice. The others joined in.

Will had found chairs for his parents to sit on, while he and Bridie knelt by the bed and searched their son's face for signs of life.

As they watched, Richard's eyes started to open and close rapidly. He seemed to be hearing them. Then he opened his eyes wide and said with a grin: 'Mummy, I'm thirsty. Give me some lemonade, please....'

Bridie kissed him all over his face, his arms, his hands. 'My darling, my little darling...,' she kept saying over and over. 'You've come back to us.'

Will started to cry, big tears dropping down his face and onto the bed where Richard lay.

'You've come back to us, Richard,' Ma and Pa cried almost in unison. 'Our clever boy has come back.'

Will dried his tears away, as he raced out to tell the matron to inform the doctors about what had happened. 'I'm sure they'll want to keep him in for observation,' said Bridie, 'but I want him home with me as soon as possible.'

'Of course, dear,' said Ma, 'but we must follow what the doctors say. There could be some changes, as we've been warned to expect.'

'I don't care,' said Bridie, 'so long as I've got my Richard back, that's all I care about.'

Will attended the hospital every day for the next week. Billy and the Finn brothers took turns to inspect Deep Creek and to report back to Will. He talked to the doctors about what Richard had been like before the accident. Turnbrow wanted to run some tests, and determine if there had been any major damage. During this time, Bridie cleaned the house in preparation for having Richard home; she cooked delicious meals, and warned the little ones to be extra quiet when their brother came home.

'Please, Will, tell the doctors to allow him to come home soon,' she said. 'I can't wait to have him here close to me and in my care once again.'

Bridie got her wish. Richard was to be sent home from hospital after seven days spent convalescing. The fact that he'd been comatose for no more than four days was a good sign, according to the doctors.

'As far as we can see, there has been no change in his intelligence,' Doctor Turnbrow said. 'He told us about his dog, Maggie, that he's had since he was one or two, and about Gem, his Shetland pony that he loves so much.'

'That's good,' said Will. 'I've noticed that he seems to be a little teary, and then excited at times. Is that normal after a fall?'

'Yes, he cried when he met a little patient in irons—a poliomyelitis sufferer, and wanted to visit the isolation ward to console others,' said the doctor.

'Is that a mood change thing?' asked Will. 'Could he have lost his intellectual ability?'

'It's too early to say for sure, as yet, but he seems to be alert, just forgets what happened leading up to the fall and straight after it. He'll need some time to readjust to everything. Keep him home from school until next term. He won't miss much, and will catch up quickly, since his record is so good.'

'Yes, I agree. He needs quiet and rest for some time yet. He's always been an ambitious little fellow,' said Will, 'and we'll have to keep him from wanting to get on Gem and gallop off just yet.'

'Yes, no riding until we're sure his brain has recovered,' said the doctor.

Confused family members, who'd been told Richard was better, stood around his bed as he lay, listening quietly to the wireless in the darkened room.

'He's sensitive to light,' Bridie said, 'and to loud sounds.'

'Hello there, family, I love you,' he whispered, 'and I want to see Gem, real badly.'

Bridie pulled the curtains across, so that the light shone into the room. Richard took one look at Gem grazing in the field, then asked for the curtains and blinds to be closed. 'Too bright, too bright....'

Bridie motioned to the others to leave, and questioned Richard about what he remembered.

'Do you remember falling off Gem?' she asked.

'No, Mummy, but don't worry. I remember when I was asleep. A little child inside me led me by the hand. I dreamt that we stepped over from the left to the right side over a gap, and then back again. It was scary, but we won in the end.'

'Where was it where you went, then?'

'Somewhere, there was a creek we swam in. He held my hand, a little brother, who was me. About two years old. And there was an uncle and a granddad I never met before. But they knew you and everyone, Grandma and Ma and Pa, Daddy and everyone.'

'What were their names?'

'Can't remember.' And Richard turned away from her and faced the wall. He fell quickly into a deep sleep, before Bridie could question him more.

'This is not the same child as before,' Bridie said to Will. 'There's been a brain shift,' she whispered.

'It's too early yet, the doctors say. This could be a temporary reaction to the bump. He needs time to adjust.'

'No, Will, this is not my child anymore. I know him so well.'

'Well, give it a couple of weeks. When he's a lot stronger, we'll take him to a specialist in Sydney. You can ask Doctor Turnbrow for names.'

'Will, I want my boy back. I can't stand seeing him this way, just lying there in the dark. Saying loopy things that I can't understand.'

'Bridie, he's alive. He's going to get better and better. It just takes time.'

'I can tell he's changed. He's not the bright boy from before the accident.'

With that, Bridie went into the kitchen and took the brandy out of the cupboard. She poured herself a tumbler full of the amber coloured, pungent smelling liquid and sat on a hard chair, head in hands at the table. She started to sob, her shoulders shaking. Charlie put his arms around her legs. Livvy, not far behind, came up and said, 'Is Mummy sad?'

'Yes, darling,' said Will, 'You and Charlie go and play in the bedroom. I'll make Mummy better.'

'I can't stand it. The kids seeing me like this. Red eyes from crying. I want to get away from here. Take Richard with me to Sydney. Mumma and your mother can mind the little ones for a while.'

'He's not well enough to travel yet, Bridie. He needs quiet and rest. Away from the noise of the two little ones.' And from you, Bridie, Will thought. 'I'll ask Turnbrow to give you something for your nerves.'

'I feel like it's my fault, Richard's fall.'

'It's no one's fault, just an accident,' said Will. 'In the meantime, I'll make plans for spending some time with him at the Finns' place. They have gardens and orchards, a tennis court, home schooling for kids. It'll be a safe haven far away from the hustle and bustle. We can stay in the servants' quarters, not used anymore, and he can join in family doings, swim in the creek and fish in the river there.'

'He's not well enough to be moved at present,' Bridie said. 'In two weeks' time, perhaps. In the meantime, I'll talk to his teacher about books and things. So that he doesn't miss out on too much school work.'

'That's the least of our worries at the moment, Bridie,' said Will. 'We've got to get our boy back to health first. The Finns' Tumbarumbar might just do the trick.'

Will told her how Bridie and the others could visit as well. He'd help in Tumbarumbar's branding and mustering activities. There'd be kids for Richard to play with. And the Finn brothers would help Will work on his new rugged bush property that he'd started leasing, not too far from Tumba.

He told her he couldn't stand seeing her unhappy, his son wasting away.

Might he be losing Bridie too? This sipping from the brandy bottle was not a good sign. He felt incapable of putting his foot down for the moment. She was too raw. At a dipping point, like dairy cows that had eaten too much clover on the farm. They became bloated and swollen, ready to burst, give up and fall down, never to rise again.

Bridie reaching for the bottle of brandy would be haunting him for a long while. A flight from reality. It was all too horrible to bear. And this sudden urge within himself to escape to Tumbarumbar? Was it because he, Will, had convalesced at Tumbarumbar as a child and got well again? That he felt it might just work for Richard? Or was his thinking all skewwhiff? A knee jerk reaction to shock?

A little time apart might be just what the doctor ordered, for her and for him.

Chapter 27

Bridie sat in a leather chair facing Doctor Turnbrow in his clean fresh surgery. Dressed up in her black and white striped dress pulled in at the waist with a crimson satin sash, she tried to stop from bursting into tears. She looked down at her shiny red shoes and fidgeted with a crumpled handkerchief. Tears rolled slowly down her rouge cheeks as she spoke:

'I'm feeling as if I caused Richard to fall,' she said. 'I loved him so much, that he became spoilt and wouldn't listen to us.' Doctor Turnbrow handed her a clean fresh handkerchief; she met for a moment the kindly eyes of the doctor; saw the concern on his firmly jawed face: 'You know, it's not your fault. I think we'll give you something to calm your nerves, Mrs Featherstone.'

'I just want to leave all this, and go away. Richard is sad and mopey, just lying in the dark all the time. *I'm not me anymore*, he says. He is not the same child as before the accident.'

'Yes, this sometimes happens with brain damage. But it will pass in time. You have to be patient with him. Don't show him you're disappointed.'

That's the trouble, I can't help it. He was my shining star, Doctor. He topped all his tests at school, could read well above for his age. Now I feel all that is gone. It's such a waste of a brilliant brain.'

'Don't give up hope for a full recovery, Mrs Featherstone. These things take time.'

'B-but I can't stand to sit around and wait. I'm not good for him at the moment. Nor for anyone. What can I do?'

'You'll need to talk to your husband about it. He might be able to take over for a while.'

'Yes, he's talking about taking Richard away with him to Tumbarumbar, friends on a cattle station. But I'll fret my heart out for him ... them. Doctor, tell me what I can do.'

'Is there somewhere you can stay for a while?'

'I can go to Sydney and stay with my aunt, who's an ex-nurse. I'd take Richard to a specialist, but Will says it's too early yet. My mother would look after the babies.'

'That wouldn't be a bad idea but ... is there a friend or relative you could travel with? It's not a good idea to go alone by train in the state you're in.'

'My friend Stella could accompany me,' she said.

As he handed Bridie the prescription, the doctor made a mental note that he would *have a word* to Will Featherstone the next time he met him at the hospital, warn him about his wife's nervous condition.

Bridie, leaving the surgery, noted that many of the doctors' homes and surgeries were located in this part of town: manicured lawns running down to the Karrana River, sleek and wide at this point, willow trees lining the banks. She could just make out some of the more modest buildings on the other scraggier side of the town, not far from the road that led to Mistletoe Cottage. Once again she wished that Will had been able to afford a house on the northern side, next to the doctors' and solicitors' homes.

She went to the chemist and had the prescription for the tablets made up, then walked towards the jeep that she'd parked nearby. How remiss she'd been in allowing Richard to jump over logs. *I'm at fault!* she accused herself. And then, almost imperceptibly, her accusations slid sideways in her mind to include Will in their aim. He should have put more emphasis on saving Richard from childish excesses. The words she'd used in the doctor's surgery only targeted herself as failed parent, but deep down, she knew that she was holding on to some inadmissible anger, a need to lay the blame outside herself. *If only Will had been stronger, as the man in the relationship, and insisted on Richard obeying him. If only he had forbidden the boy to show off on Gem.*

Just then she noticed, on a brass plate outside one of the fashionable houses, the name 'Dr Myer Goldblum Physician' at the front of a building not far from the Turnbrows' place.

That lovely doctor, she thought. If only Will could afford to rent a home here, I'd be happy, I know.

Will was keen to get to work at Deep Creek; there was much to be done. Bridie took over seeing to Richard's needs, while their father dropped the two smaller children off at Hilltop. Richard was lying in the dark, needing to shade his eyes from the light outside and, sometimes, inside too. He seemed more perky to Bridie this day, which gave her a little boost. He was a bit too elated, if anything, she thought. And there was still that sense, when he talked, of being spacey or trippy.

'How are you feeling, darling?'

'It's like I'm not me anymore,' he said. She tried to be patient, as the doctor had warned her. 'Daddy just tells me not to talk, to rest my head. But there are words inside me that can't get out.'

'That's not surprising, seeing that you had a nasty bump on the side of your head.'

'Which side was it, Mummy?'

'The left side.' Richard put his hand out and stroked the left side of his head.

'Yes, I can feel the sore bit there.'

'But it's inside where you were more badly hurt.'

'I know. It's like everything's been shook up, the doctor said. Like a milk shake inside my head.'

'You must have patience, my darling. Things will get better with time.'

'I don't think so, Mummy.'

'What do you mean, Richard? Why do you say that?'

'I'm not me, but I'm still me,' he said again, this time raising his voice, as if frustrated at not being able to explain himself. 'I get a funny feeling all the time, the whole world is more real now, but I'm here and not here, like I'm dreaming.'

Bridie looked at the pinched little face trying so hard to get the thoughts out, and felt panic grip at her throat. She thought of her own desperate trials with maths at school, and saw her shining star's scholastic abilities flying out the window on black and white wings. She forced herself to reply calmly, keeping her emotions in check.

'Well, sleep some more now, darling. Daddy's right, you do need to get lots of rest.'

'Thanks for listening, Mummy. The words....'

'Yes, darling. I'm tired now, I'm going to have a nap, too.'

And with that, Bridie went into her bedroom and sank onto the quilted cover, after swallowing down, with a swig of brandy, the little white pills Doctor Turnbrow had prescribed for her. She had a vision, as she slipped down into a deep sleep, that she was Alice falling down the hole into a strange new world, wherein she had very few signposts to guide her.

The sun was starting to fade, and a golden hue had settled over the house and gum trees. Bridie stretched and yawned, stumbled out of bed and went in to Richard's room. He was not in his bed. Through the window she could just make out shapes and movement. Running around through the back door, she passed Will in the kitchen reheating food for teatime.

'Thanks,' she said hurriedly. 'I had to lie down.'

'See what's going on out there,' he said with a sparkle in his voice.

Running around the corner, Bridie almost fell over with shock at the scene that met her eyes. Richard was standing next to Gem, cradling the pony's head and neck, stroking the pert mane, and whispering in the black pointy ears, purring noises that sounded like little declarations and words of love. The pony seemed to understand, in the way that he nuzzled Richard and playfully tossed his head back and forth.

'Richard, you must be feeling better,' Bridie cried out. Charlie was sliding down Gem's rump, and Livvy had just crawled underneath his belly, from one side to get to the other.

'Yeah Mummy. I love this little horsey, so much. The kids want to learn to ride now. I'm going to lead them around first up … maybe tomorrow.'

'We'll see how you're feeling then. If it's not too bright outside.'

'Yeah, head aches….'

'Now that's enough for one day. Time for tea, and off to bed.'

For the first time, Richard tried to sit up at the kitchen table to eat the food his father had laid out. 'How did you coax this fellow out of his bed?' Bridie asked.

'I didn't have to. When he saw the kids playing with Gem just outside his window, he almost bolted out.'

'Richard's better,' Livvy cried. 'He's going to teach us to ride Gem.'

'Yeah,' Charlie said, 'we've got our big brother back.' And everyone clapped and cheered, and looked lovingly at Richard, who beamed despite his ashen face.

'We mustn't tire him out, though,' Will said. 'He won't be able to play rough games with you two for a while yet. And I'm going to take him away for a holiday to Tumbarumbar Station.'

Bridie was pleased as she looked at her firstborn son, at last sitting up and out of bed. 'You might like to read to Livvy and Charlie before they go to sleep?'

She realised, just as the words had slipped out of her mouth, that she might have said the wrong thing. What if he couldn't read yet? What if that part of his brain had seized up? They'd soon see, if he agreed to try it out on one of the kids' picture books.

When Richard opened up *The Shy Little Kitte*n, Livvy's favourite Golden Picture book, he read aloud in a halting way, sounding out some of the words, without intonation. He stumbled and looked embarrassed, frustration clouding his visage.

'I'm too tired, Mummy,' he said, 'and the light's hurting my eyes. 'Sorry, Livvy, Charlie.' He kissed the two little ones, before going into his own bed.

Bridie had seen disappointment cloud Richard's face when he tried to read smoothly and quickly, as he once had.

'It's too early to know yet,' Will said. 'He just might need time to catch up again. Anyway, he's back with us. Isn't that the main thing?'

On the one hand, Bridie agreed with him, but she knew, from talking and listening to Richard, that something had changed inside his head, and that she herself would never be the same person again, either.

A nagging voice kept telling her: *Perhaps if you had a holiday*....

But she wondered if things would ever be the same between them all again.

'Doctor Turnbrow says that a break away would do me … do us … good. The pills he's given me are for my nerves, but they're probably just to make me sleep,' she said.

'I'm worried about you, Bridie,' Will said, as he watched his wife reach up into the cupboard for the bottle of brandy, and slump into the chair with her head in her hands at the kitchen table.

'I'll be alright,' she said. 'Just need a little time to adjust.'

'Well, I've got to get up with the roosters, so I'm off to bed. 'We'll talk about it some more tomorrow.'

Will sank into the double bed. An owl outside made the plaintive mopoke call. He thanked whatever God was out there for the gift of his son's health.

Something deep down in his gut told him that more troubles might be on the horizon yet.

Chapter 28

Bridie's mood had been improving, since starting on the nerve tablets. The family had gone to Hilltop for a roast chicken dinner.

'I'm taking Richard to Tumbarumbar for a couple of weeks,' Will announced to his in-laws. 'To have a break, and to give Bridie a breather, too. I know you'll help out with the kids, Eliza.'

Richard's eyes lit up. 'Can't wait to live in the rain ... forest,' he said.

'I'm going to visit Aunt Annie in Sydney.' Bridie's voice was shrill, her message urgent, abrupt. 'Stella's going with me on the train.'

All four adults turned towards Bridie's pale face. She felt herself shaking inside and out under their glare.

'Bridie, darling?' Will's voice sounded strange to her. Was there a fierce gleam in her own dark pools staring back at him that seemed shocking to Will?

'What a foolhardy damn thing...,' Ned began, but stopped, chastened by a look from Eliza. He thumped his fist on the table, got up and went outside to light up a fag.

'I'll keep an eye on things here, Will,' said Billy, always trying to smooth over rough patches.

'I suppose I'll have to look after these two,' said Eliza, pointing to Livvy and Charlie. She spoke as if short of breath.

Will's face went dark. 'I can't go if you take off, Bridie. I'm unhappy about you going to Sydney. You'd better wait until I get back. Mum and Dad have agreed to help out.'

Bridie was holding onto her throat, as if something, black gall, was caught in there. 'I need to get away from this bloody place,' she shouted.

Everyone went silent. The children's faces were white. They looked pleadingly towards Will.

'Bridie, you can't just take off…. Can't you wait here until I get back? Gordon Turnbrow told me you could count on him at any time if you need help with the children, especially while I'm at work.'

'I need to get away, I tell you … I'm going stark raving mad….' Bridie's voice was shaking now, sobs wracked her body. 'Just leave me alone. I want some peace, away from everyone.'

'Bridie, darling, you're just feeling a bit down,' Will said as he went to comfort her.

She jumped up, knocking over her chair, and ran out past Ned, who was smoking in the yard.

She raced back along the darkened road towards Mistletoe Cottage.

'Let her go, Will,' Eliza said. 'She'll get over it. She's always been highly strung, you know. It's her nerves….'

'I don't wanta stay with Gramma,' squealed Livvy. 'Wanna go with Richard and Daddy.'

'Me too,' cried Charlie.

'How will I find time to work with you lot to look after,' Will said. He'd been hinting to Bridie about starting to build the house on the hill out at Deep Creek, with the help of the Finn boys.

Looking after the whole family hadn't been part of his plans.

Stella was in between boyfriends and came to help Bridie during the week. She liked playing with the children.

'I've booked Livvy in for piano lessons with Dr Turnbrow's wife at their house,' Bridie said. 'Mrs Turnbrow says she's a natural, and has a big future ahead if she chooses to focus. I've told Will, we must buy a piano for her to practise on.'

Stella told of her musical ancestors and of a cousin who had gone to follow a musical career in New York.

'Livvy might be a classical musician one day,' Stella said, 'play in Carnegie Hall in America. Just look at those hands and long fingers, I can see them moving across the keys. Get her taught the violin too, Bridie. She'll take to it, I'm sure.'

Stella talked with nostalgia about a violinist boyfriend, who had left to fight in the War and hadn't returned. He'd met a French woman in Amiens and the rest was history. 'Always a bridesmaid...,' said Stella, without finishing the sardonic comment.

Bridie smoked filter tips one after another on the lounge.

'Will wants to take Richard to Tumbarumbar on Sunday. Leon is taking over the running of the station now, and there's another wedding coming up soon, the younger son and Alice Page.'

'You need to get away, Bridie,' Stella said. 'You're not yourself anymore. Richard's accident has shaken you up more than anyone realised.'

'I know, Aunt Annie says she'll have the lot of us for a month, if we like. But Will wants to take Richard with him to Tumbarumbar. He's been hinting about a site for a new house between here and Tumba.'

'You need a total break away from all of this, I reckon. Will's holding up better than you. I say let him have his way, and leave the kids with your mother. '

'Stella, that nice young doctor that I met when Richard had his accident. You remember the one?'

'Yes, I do. You talked about him last time we met.'

'Well, I keep bumping into him when I take Livvy for lessons. He lives near the Turnbrows' house, and always seems to be coming out or going in when I arrive with Livvy.'

'Do you think it's coincidence?'

'Yes, probably. But my heart lurches in my chest now when I see him.'

'Well, keep it quiet. These flirtations can ruin a marriage. And you've got too much to lose. Three kids, a farm and a loyal mate.'

'I know, Stella, but I can't help it, can I, if he keeps turning up when I'm around? I wouldn't do anything to hurt Will, of course.'

'There's only going to be one person; you can't have it both ways. It's either love or nothing.'

'You're probably right. I'm just flattered by the attention he gives me. What's the word, 'infatuation'? He's got more money than we have, and he's good-looking. Probably moves in higher circles, and he's almost certainly married with a family. I'll be careful.'

'That's my girl. I don't know much about him, as he's come here recently from the big smoke. From what I know, Bridie, it's a pity, but he's Jewish, from Vienna.'

'Oh, Sister Philomena said the Jews killed Jesus,' said Bridie. 'Is that true, do you think?'

'That's crazy, Jesus was a Jew himself. Anyway, this one gets on well with mothers and children. Must have come here just before the Nazis invaded Europe. He might have lost family in the War.'

'Myer's his name, and he is … going to make appointments for me in Sydney for Richard.'

Stella threw a look. 'You're not hiding something from me, are you, Bridie?'

Bridie blushed. 'Just because you've broken up with your latest flame, doesn't mean I'm going to get up to anything,' she stammered. 'Anyway, I hardly know him.'

Stella waggled a warning finger at Bridie, who turned even redder. Then she hugged her friend and said, 'I know, Bridie, you're worried about Richard, and this doctor's holding out a life raft to you. Anyone would take it.'

'You're such a good friend, Stella. Will you come along to act as chaperone?'

'For sure, I'm on Will's side, you know... don't want anyone getting hurt, do we?'

During the afternoon, Stella helped Bridie pack a small port full of clothes for her own trip to Sydney, and another large one full of children's things that they'd need at Hilltop while she was away. 'Now what about Richard and Will's stuff?'

'Will's already done that. They won't need much, anyway. You know what it's like where they're going, rainforests and rivers running through it.'

'Just what the doctor's ordered, as far as Richard goes. I can see him coming back cured.'

The weather was cloudy and overcast. Magpies, currawongs and all native birds were silent. The kangaroos hid in the scrub. Horses and cattle sheltered in the undergrowth from the chilly wind.

Bridie looked out the window and felt greyness descend over her like a shroud. She'd just have time to get the two younger kids dressed and off to the midmorning appointments before Richard woke up. Will was away, trying to catch up with work at Deep Creek.

'Mummy, I'm sick. Wanta go to the hospital like Richard did,' Livvy called, half asleep, as if delirious.

'I've got an appointment for you at the doctor's,' her mother said. 'Come and have breakfast and we'll drive Charlie over to Grandma's place.'

'Want medicine,' Livvy cried out between coughs and sneezes.

They're so independent, both of them, those two, the way they stick together, Bridie thought. They don't need me. Maybe I don't deserve them.

She felt like a bad mother, and she would have to pull them out of bed now to take them to the doctor's.

Everything needed to be done, ready for a getaway. She heated porridge on the stove and placed it in their bowls and drooled treacle over the top of the cereal. They both drank milk, but Livvy hardly touched her porridge. Bridie pulled a clean dress over the girl's head; Charlie dragged himself into the jeep in his dressing gown and slippers.

She dropped Charlie off at Hilltop Farm before the drive to the doctor's surgery. Livvy's face darkened, and her bottom lip trembled, as she watched Eliza lead her brother inside the farmhouse.

'Why are you sad?' Bridie said, as she glanced at Livvy, sitting next to her in the jeep. We won't be long, and I'll buy you and Charlie lemonade and a new book each.'

Livvy's face brightened. She was the reader in the family, now that Richard had abandoned his post. Will had made her a special cubby house, where she sat and read while Charlie played around outside.

She's going to be a true beauty one day, Bridie thought, as she looked at her daughter from out of the corner of her eye. Those blue-green eyes against the red hair. I'll enter her in the *flowergirl* procession for the debutante ball. She's the ugly duckling turning into a lovely swan.

Doctor Turnbrow repeated, almost word for word, Bridie's thoughts about her daughter, when he greeted them and met the girl's green eyes. He admired her pink dress and pearly skin: 'Pretty as a picture,' he said as he looked inside her ears with a light.

'Yes, but she comes from a different country. She only ever turns lobster red and back to white under our cruel sunshine.'

'A rare creature for two dark parents,' he said.

'Yes she's like a twin to her brother, Charlie, at least in nature. They stick together like peas in a pod. He's a little fairer than Will and me, too. Must be a throwback to northern ancestors.'

'She looks to me like she might be hiding her light under a bushel.'

Bridie didn't know what 'bushel' meant, and guessed that it was some kind of a shrub. 'She's just a little shy, Doctor. She doesn't talk a lot, even at home. Her brother and she seem have a secret language that only they understand.'

'Let me see. Stick your tongue out, young lady. And how is young Richard? No worse for wear, I hope.'

'I'm not sure, Doctor. I think I've lost my clever son.'

'You'll get him back, I'm sure. In a little while.'

'No, he says so himself. He's a changed boy.'

'Well, this little one is bright as a button. She'll make up for it, won't you, little lady?'

Livvy poked her tongue out wide, as if in a cheeky response to the doctor's words.

'Thank goodness it's not scarlet fever. There's a bit of it going around. I'll write out a prescription for penicillin for an ear infection. It will clear up anything on the chest, too. She's a little bit rattly there, as well.'

As Bridie was leaving with Livvy in tow, coughing and spluttering, she bumped into Doctor Goldblum.

'How are you, Mrs Featherstone?'

'Very well, thank,' she whispered, feeling tongue tied.

'How is your Richard?'

'Still the same, Doctor.'

'Gordon Turnbrow tells me you're having trouble with the changes in Richard. I'd like to have a talk some time. I've known cases like your son's and might be able to help. Look, I'm leaving for Sydney on Monday, to open up my surgery there, but when I get back....'

'Thank you, so much, Doctor. I'm going to Sydney next week, too.'

'Well, you can ring me there, for the next two weeks. Here,' and he handed her a card with the number of his surgery on it.

Bridie blushed a brilliant ruby colour.

'And what is this young lady's name?'

'Olivia,' she said.

'She's going to be a beauty, I'd say.'

Bridie blushed again. 'Yes, she's turning out that way. And she's going to learn the piano soon.'

'That's excellent. I believe music's the elixir of the soul, without a doubt.'

'Her brother's starting school next year. It's a problem, as they're so close.'

'Olivia. I like that name very much,' he said as his dark eyes met Livvy's green ones.

'Livvy, say hello to Doctor Gold ... bloom.'

Livvy held out her long slim fingers as if she were a queen, and placed her hand in Myer's extended one.

'What a little princess.' And he took her hand and placed a kiss on the top of her palm.

'Goodbye, Doctor,' Bridie said as she led Livvy off towards the jeep.

Chapter 29

'Mummy, I like that doctor's name,' Livvy said.

'Myer?'

'No, Golden … blooms. Sounds like wildflowers, doesn't it?'

'Oh, yes, it does.'

'He has kind eyes, too,' said Livvy.'

'Well, we just might get to see those eyes again before long,' she said. 'He wants to talk to me about Richard's progress.'

'Richard's better,' Livvy said.

On the way home, Bridie noticed flowers of all colours lining the roadside, and spreading in neverending carpets as far as she could see, disappearing well into the brush. She wondered if that was what made Livvy think about the doctor's name. Or was it the gorgeous golden wattles, now sprouting buds and blossoms all along the roads and into the bush. They intermingled with tall eucalypts and scruffy paperbarks.

'Now let's go and pick up Brother Charlie!' Bridie said as she pulled onto the home stretch.

'Pick up Brother Charlie! Pick up Brother Charlie!' Livvy started chanting in a croaky voice, over and over, as they neared Hilltop Farm.

Bridie thought that it made her second son sound like a priest, the way Livvy was shouting out his name.

'You know, Charlie has to go to school next year, Livvy. And you will have to stay at home with me.' Even as she said it, Bridie felt like cutting out her own tongue.

Livvy's face dropped into a stony mask. So sad looking, Bridie thought, as she threw a glance at her daughter.

'No no no no!' Livvy yelled, as she got out of the jeep and ran towards the farmhouse, calling out Charlie's name in a whine, over and over.

Like a bunyip, Bridie thought, running after her. What have I done, setting her off like that?

Livvy's screams had triggered a terrible cacophony of screeches from high up in the canopy of trees overhanging the house.

Parrots, magpies, crows and kookaburras all seemed to join in like a sudden warning.

'Will, I'm going to Sydney on the mail on Sunday night with Stella. We both need a break. You and I do from each other, too. Mumma and Billy will mind the two little ones.'

'Well, I'm leaving for Tumbarumbar with Richard in the morning, Bridie. And I'm thinking of taking them all with me to Tumba.'

'You'd better ask your old friend, Reenie for help. She hasn't got any kids and she'd love to have them.'

'I'll have to cope, that's all,' he said.

She knew he was being bull-headed on purpose, in order to make her feel guilty. But she couldn't let him see it. She could see him bringing them all back to Hilltop, his tail between his legs, like a chastened cattle dog.

The discordant chatter of birds in the trees overhead made her feel gloomy.

The next morning, Bridie stood at the front door of *Mistletoe Cottage* and waved them all off. Unshed tears prickled her eyelids. Richard kept looking back at Gem, who'd just appeared from somewhere and trotted to the end of the paddock. He had his head over the railing of the gate as the vehicle left in a cloud of red dust.

You'd swear that that pony knows they're gone for two weeks, Bridie thought. Sometimes I wish we'd never bought him.

As soon as the vehicle left, Bridie felt waves of anguish rush over her.

I'm such a bad mother, she thought. I love that boy to bits, and yet I'm glad he's gone away for a time. I can't cope with this. What's to become of us?

She went into the kitchen, reached up for the bottle of St Agnes brandy on the top shelf and poured herself a nip in a glass.

'Just the smallest nip of brandy from the top shelf,' she whispered to herself. 'Just to get myself going.'

Then she fell asleep in a heap on the bed.

When she woke up it was dark, and her mother was there, telling her that Will had dropped the two little ones off at Hilltop.

Billy was babysitting and she was fussing over her, making tea and folding clothes.

'I'm worried about you, Bridie,' she said, 'sleeping in the middle of the day like this. You must get up.'

'Will's rushed off and left me,' she whimpered, falling into her *little girl* mode with her mother. 'Mumma, I have to get away, and Stella's going with me. To Sydney. I need to look up a specialist about Richard's problems. I'll stay at Aunt Annie's for a while if you'll arrange it.'

'Well, my girl, you can't expect others to take on your problems, after all, you're a wife and mother now. You have to be sensible, it's your duty.'

'I know, I know, but it's killing me, this thing with Richard, and my life here in this run down farmhouse. Everything looks bleak and dull to me at the moment.'

'I went through hard times, too, you know, with Charles and all. You've just gotta pull your socks up, my girl, and stop the whimpering. This is your life now, here on this farm with Will and the children.'

She was waiting for the cruel words her mother had flung at her once before: *You made your bed, now lie in it!* Thankfully, this time, her mother thought better of it, and became suddenly quiet.

Bridie was quiet too. She'd pack her things ready for the trip down to Sydney. Stella was doing likewise. It would be good for both of them, to get away from the rawness of country life for a while.

The next morning, as she waved to her mother, the haunting sound of a 'powerful owl' sent shivers throughout her body.

Lying outside under the vault of the sky, Will looked at his son's face and the word 'radiant' came to mind. Just like the night sky. Words failed when it came to describing some things.

'I love the stars and the sky,' Richard whispered. 'It's so … peaceful out here.'

They'd taken to camping out as the temperature soared; Will thought it would calm the boy, soothe his wounded brain; washed over by the cool night air, he'd be lulled into sleep to the sounds of the bush.

Will saw the rainforest as a towering cathedral, a structure far better than any that the hand of man could build. Like a bountiful mother.

He pointed out to Richard the constellations above them, 'There's Orion, see, in the shape of an upside-down saucepan. Lots of stars make it up.'

'What are stars, Daddy? Why do they twinkle?' asked Richard.

'Balls of gases, like the sun.'

'Have they got names, like planets, like Mars?'

'Yes, some of them. There's Sirius, the very bright star at the bottom of the saucepan.'

He pointed it out.

'Any fool can build a hut or a church,' he said to Richard, wrapped up in a blanket beside him. 'Just look at the beauty of the trees all around us.'

'Why does Mr Finn cut trees down, Daddy?'

Will now felt a heavy grey cloud envelop him.

'I've needed to chop down a few from time to time, too, Son, to make way for crops and grazing land.'

He felt the loss wash over him at the thought of each magnificent gum tree cut down in its prime; as if each were a precious child.

'I've always planted other young saplings to make up for every tree cut down.' He knew that some of the oldest trees took thousands of years to grow, and could never be replaced by a young sapling.

'I've stopped doing it for good, now.' He felt like he needed to excuse himself to this all seeing child, and that he was guilty as charged.

They heard scampering noises, and bird calls, owls most probably. Will recognised the beautiful, clear piping notes and complex melodies of the pied butcherbird. And then magical, liquid sounds filled the humid air, a crooning followed by a lilting melody.

'I think that's a bower bird,' Will said.

'It's gorgeous.' Richard's eyes widened in wonder.

'Hear that….' Rasping mating calls had filled the humid air. 'That's the riflebird. The male gives that call like a whip being twirled through the air and cracked, followed immediately by the short call of the female.'

'Raah … whiit!' Richard called back, mimicking the male bird, and waited for the response. He continued to play the male part, camouflaged there under the blanket, until another sound caught his attention.

'Daddy, what's that? Sounds like a cat meowing, or a baby crying. You think they could be out here in the rainforest?'

'No, there are no babies or wildcats out here in the wilds. That's a catbird, believe it or not.'

'Leon told me there are lyre birds,' said Richard, 'that mimic sounds, even a violin if they hear it played.'

Richard's eyes widened. 'And they do a dance to attract a mate.'

'Yes, you can watch it sometimes if you're quiet.'

'We'll have to get Livvy to play out here in the forest,' Richard said. 'She's learning the violin and could attract the lyre bird with her music.'

'You know, your mother and I met at a dance before you were born?' asked Will.

Richard was quiet for a long while.

'Dad, why do people kill trees and animals?' The boy had been asking these sorts of questions since they'd come to stay at Tumbarumbar. It was partly this that had prompted Will to reflect on his actions in relation to land clearing.

'I don't know, son. I wish I knew the answer. It's often to do with survival, but not always.' He thought of those men who enjoyed hunting beasts—wild pigs, kangaroos, even brumbies, just for the heck of it.'

'Dad, I feel like I'm finding myself out here in the bush. I want to be a farmer like you.'

'That's good, son. The bush is the best doctor you can have, heals all wounds.' He felt elated, but he wondered what Bridie would think of the boy's plans.

Richard seemed to sense what Will was thinking and asked: 'Are you going to build that house in the bush one day?'

'It all depends on your mother, son.'

Will felt a certain ecstasy, out here in the wilderness with his firstborn, who would take over from him when he was gone. He felt like how a poet must feel. And wished he knew how to express this exuberance. This feeling of oneness with nature. The trees of the rainforest standing in perfect harmony. Nature's lushness, strength and beauty, fertility all around.

He would try to express it to Bridie over the telephone. Explain about the effects it would be having on Richard.

He doesn't have to do anything he doesn't want to here, he'd say. *School of the Air* lessons with the Finn youngsters if he wants. Out of doors work if he feels up to it. He still doesn't like the glare; some nights we can eat with the whole family; other times we cook for ourselves in our cabin.

He wouldn't mention the fact that Reenie had visited once or twice.

Will thought about the first night spent in the homestead, sleeping in the granny flat that had belonged to the elderly matriarch. Richard and Will, in bed together, had been woken up by someone crying. It sounded like a high-pitched female voice, but there was no one there. When he'd mentioned it to Leon the next day, he'd said it was his grandma who died last year, and that she 'wants to stick around for a bit'. As if it was the most natural response and nothing to worry about. Will thought he'd maybe dreamt it after all. He thought of the time he'd seen the ghostly light, while riding back from Tumbarumbar that night after meeting Bridie for the first time.

He thought about their differences that he was only just beginning to understand. Symmetries and patterns in fabrics and textiles caught Bridie's attention; rather than the bounties of nature that enraptured him.

But where would he find the money to support her? Christ, she was talking about a new piano, violins and lessons. And what if Richard needed specialist help down the track? Though there was little wrong with him, as far as he could see, nothing that time wouldn't heal. True, there was a personality change, but one that Richard took in his stride, and he, Will, embraced. Books and learning were not all there was to celebrate. Bridie would surely see that in time.

Richard had slowed down, true, but he'd got in step with the waltz of nature now, in tune with a melody as beautiful and as graceful as any three step dance that he and Bridie had enjoyed in the heyday of their courtship.

The sounds of the breeze through the ghost gums had lulled Richard to sleep; Will found himself falling into a peaceful zone. He was waltzing with Bridie once again.

In the wooden church hall among the tall gum trees.

High up above the river.

In step with the music.

Part Four

Chapter 30

Bridie thought Stella, curled up in the corner of the mail train compartment, her red curls squashed against the leather, looked like a ginger kitten she remembered from childhood. Two women on the opposite bench were drifting off too, lulled into a deep forgetfulness by the rattle of the wheels on iron. Bridie felt herself slipping into a yawning pit, inviting her to surrender.

Snatches of childhood loomed out of the deep ravine into which she was sinking. She was oblivious to the soot and the smoke whooshing past the windows of the train.

There's a pillow fight in full swing. Four brothers and her. On the four poster bed. Duck feathers flying. At first it's fun. Poor Mumma crying out stop! Dirt floor. Mosquitoes on faces. Dadda burning cow dung in buckets to stop the mozzies from biting. Some games are fun. Ned, the Bullens Circus master yelling out orders. She wants to dance on the white pony's back. But no, she's a cat now, scratching at boys' faces. Choking, gasping for air. 'I hate you! I hate you!' Scratching at Ned's face with cat's claws. Then Johnny's. And the fat brother's, eater of charcoal and chook dung. Sitting on her now. Pulling at oily hair: 'Get off me!' Charlie the lion tamer with whip and chair in hand to tame the brute. She is the lion. The fat brother sitting on her back. Laughing and farting into her hair. 'Get away!' Get off me!' She's screaming now: 'Wanta get away!' Sucked into a dark hole. 'Wanta get away.' Someone is putting a frog down her dress.

'Bridie, wake up! What is it?' Stella was leaning over her. Face red and anxious white. 'You were crying out. And you're shaking.'

The other ladies were stirring too: 'Shoosh.'

'Yes, I was back in our first house … with the dirt floor … down near the swamps, mosquitoes, my brothers … the teasing … get away….'

'Like now?' Stella whispered the words.

'Yes, just like now.'

'Well, you don't have to worry, love. You've got a good man to take care of you now.'

'Yeah, and he dumps me in a rundown shack out in the bush. Just like before.'

'You should count yourself lucky that you've got a good man.'

'Stella, when I was in Doctor Turnbrow's waiting room, I could see the old house where we used to live, far off across the river on the opposite bank. I imagined, as I gazed out at the lawns rolling down to the water's edge, that I lived in this solid bungalow on the smart bank of the river. First I felt sorry that I couldn't live in a house like that. My sadness turned to anger at Will for not being able to rent one like that.'

The rhythm of the train speeding through the dark night no longer cast a soporific thrall over Bridie. She wanted to talk. The other ladies in the compartment were stirring and Stella made a shushing gesture to Bridie.

'I'd like to experience living in the city for a while. I love the shops and the excitement of city life.' The words were flying from her mouth in a torrent of whispers.

'Well, you're going to have a nice little holiday in Sydney. A break away from everything.'

'Yes, I'm excited about that, but worried too, for Will and the kids.'

'If I had half the chance, I'd snatch that handsome bloke off you, and go and live in a tent with him.'

'That's what I told him I'd do. It was under the spell of first love, you know?'

'Yes, and things do change. Like a fast flowing river, which seems unchanging, is always moving and never exactly the same elements. You've got to somehow go with it.'

'I'm sick and tired of looking after babies and doing housework. It's dragging me down.'

'You'll feel different about things after this trip. You'll see.'

'I don't know.'

She watched as Stella curled up again like a cat on her half of the seat and yielded to sleep, amid the clatter and jangle of the train on the tracks.

Bridie took out a small flask from her handbag and sipped on it.

Soon she'd be able to fall sleep too.

With the help of the spirits.

This night they'd both fallen into a deep slumber in the bedroom, having spent the day working in the paddocks with Leon and the other Finn men.

Will had a shining dream, as if it were portentous, about the future. Auspicious or ominous, he wasn't sure. He explained it simply to Richard.

'We were living in a grand wooden house. There were six of us now: two boys and two girls. One of the girls was red-headed, Livvy, I think. The other one was dark-skinned, like an Aboriginal child. We were all there together, surrounded by water in an ark. A happy valley, yet high up somehow, as well.'

232

Richard had been in the habit of sharing his dreams on awakening. Will thought it might help the lad, if he shared, too. Not that he always remembered his dreams, as Richard had been doing since his accident. For a long while, his son's dreams had been dark, moody, worrying, verging on nightmares.

'Dad, my dream was a bit scary again,' he said this time. 'I'm in the swimming pool on the riverbank. White things like jelly fish are floating in the water. I've got to get past or around them. But I'm falling into a deep hole. Out on the road that leads to Hilltop, I see Mummy in a white silky dress, lying on the clay next to the road. Then I wake up.'

The train steams into the platform at Central Railway, and screeches to a jangling halt. Sounds like the pink and grey galahs back home, Bridie thinks.

She sees a wiry young man with Aunt Annie. He rushes forward to take their cases. He plonks the bags on the platform and puts out his hand to Bridie, then Stella, to help them down from the train.

Aunt Annie has aged. Grey wisps caress her wise oval face. 'How are you, love?' she says, enveloping Bridie in a warm hug. 'And this must be Stella. So pleased to welcome a friend of Bridie's.' She kisses Stella on the cheek.

'Now this is Rick. He's an intern at the Hospital, one of my favourite helpers on the odd occasion that I go there. Now that I'm well and truly retired.'

Rick winks and smiles at the two women and shakes their hands. 'Annie's exaggerating as usual. The new matron is always calling on her for help. How was the journey?'

'Long and grimy. I was lucky enough to get some sleep,' says Bridie.

Stella stammers: 'G-good to be on dry land at last.' She blushes. She seems tongue-tied, a rare event for her. Bridie wonders if she is just over tired from the ten-hour train trip.

Aunt Annie climbs into the back seat of Rick's car and gestures to Bridie to sit next to her. 'Rick kindly offered to pick you up and drive us in his jalopy. To save me. At least he'll get us there in one piece.'

'I'd be pleased to accompany you two ladies around a bit.'

Stella beams at Rick and nods her head. 'That'd be marvellous. If you've got the time.'

Stella has shaken her curls out and clambered into the front passenger seat. Rick brushes her leg with his hand as he moves the gear stick.

'Rick will find the time,' Aunt Annie says. 'He's a hero at Sydney Hospital, after saving the life of that poor drunk fellow. Everyone else had given up on him. Not our Rick. The poor beggar, battered and bruised, his life ebbing away…. Resuscitated him and followed up afterwards.'

The three women look at Rick, whose face is flushed.

'Oh, it was nothing, Annie. You would've done the same, I'm sure, if you'd been there.'

As they drive through the packed city streets towards the eastern suburbs, Stella tells Rick about her life back in Karrana: 'It's peaceful and quiet, but a bit dull at times for me. I'm so excited being here. So much I want to see and do.' She has found her tongue.

She asks Rick more about his work: 'What do you do as an intern? Are the hours long?'

'We have to be on duty all night. Some of the interns suffer from insomnia and get behind with their studies.'

Stella inhales and says: 'That's awful. But, do you like the work?'

'Yes, helping people ... saving the injured. And you …
what do you do, Stella?'

'I'm a vet's assistant. Learnt stenography at tech, but
don't use it much. Prefer working with animals.'

Aunt Annie is talking to Bridie in the back.

'Your mother says you've been doing it tough. She plans
to mind the kiddies while you're away.'

'Yes, if Will agrees to let her. They're up in the rainforest
at the moment.'

'Sounds like you're doing the right thing, getting away
from it all for a while. You know you can stay here as long as
you like. Stella too.'

'Thanks Aunt Annie. I always know I can count on you.
I'm terribly worried about Will and the kids.'

'Look, love, don't dwell on it. Just try to let it all go. I'm
going to spoil you a little, take you to the shops.'

Bridie's bottom lip feels wobbly. 'I'm so happy to be here
with you. The busyness, streets full of people, the shops. I
love it all.'

'Yes, and I'm going to feed you up, look after you, so that
you'll go back looking sparkling, new and refreshed.'

Rick's driving impresses the young women. He shows
mastery behind the wheel and avoids bumps and holes in the
road with skill. As they near the eastern seaboard, he keeps
up a commentary, pointing out favourite restaurants, bars and
pubs.

'There's the famous Bondi Beach. I live nearby here. Very
popular with young people.'

'Oh, look at those waves,' cries Stella. 'I can't wait to get
down onto that sand and swim in the sea.'

'I'll take you there on the weekend.' He is dodging in and out of cars and trams, impressing the women with his bravado and skills.

'I suppose you'll be a surgeon one day?' says Stella, looking at Rick's hands on the steering wheel.

'Well, actually, I'm interested in paediatrics. A younger brother…born mentally defective, died when he was thirteen.'

'Oh, that's sad,' Stella says.

'So I'm into saving kids, I suppose.'

'See… heroic,' says Annie from the back seat. 'I told you so.'

'Yes, I understand that. I love children, too,' says Stella.

'She's better with my kids than I am myself,' Bridie blurts out. She feels her bottom lip trembling again.

'There, there, dear. You've had a hard time of it,' says Aunt Annie, hugging her.

Aunt Annie's lovely old weatherboard house sparkles white on the edge of Dover Heights in the morning sun. Stella *oohs* and *ahhs* at the sight of it.

Bridie excuses herself and goes to lie down, as soon as she feels it will not offend anyone. She can hear Rick and the two women chatting in the kitchen over tea and biscuits.

The waves pounding the shore down below soothe her spirits. *I'll have to stop the brandy. Aunt Annie'd be shocked if she found out I'm drinking.* She wonders if Will has tried to ring Hilltop and arrange for the kids to stay with Mumma. She'll put a call through as soon as possible to find out how things are going.

Why had she suggested he leave the kids with Reenie? She hadn't meant it, really. It was just a way of saying she wanted him to solve the problem for her. For both of them. She and Will going off at the same time. And not only that, going off separately, and in opposite directions. He to the north, and she further south.

She feels herself being pulled in two, one part relaxing her, the other dragging her down into guilt and worry. She must cleave towards the lighter side. For her own sake and for everyone's.

The attractive wallpaper on the walls of the bedroom make her feel lighter.

Oh, what a dream of a place Aunt Annie has here on the edge of the Pacific Ocean. When will I try to ring Doctor Goldblum?

The thought sings in her mind like the call of the fantailed cuckoo back home, proclaiming the night with its sad melody.

Chapter 31

Bridie's body throbbed with pleasure, as she sat in the tram next to Aunt Annie, thinking of the frocks she would be trying on in the city department stores. She was used to the many stares from men now. *'Such a good sort!'* her brother Johnny used to say before she got married and moved out of home. *'Attract any man, you could, Bridie.'* She preened inwardly at the thought, and tossed her pageboy hair with the roll on top that Aunt Annie had done for her. She felt like one of her favourite Hollywood starlets: like Vivien Leigh, Esther Williams or Merle Oberon; and especially like Joan Crawford, whose rags-to-riches story she had read about in the Women's Weekly magazines.

Aunt Annie touched her on the hand and reminded her to keep a tight hold on her handbag: 'Not everyone is trustworthy in the city, you know?'

Bridie nodded.

Was that handsome young man opposite looking at her, at her lovely brown legs, smooth and shapely, her bust still perky, even today, after having given birth three times?

'I feel so much better now, Aunty,' she whispered, and placed her head for a moment on the older woman's shoulder. 'I love this city.'

'That's good, dear, and you'll soon feel even better.'

Bridie pirouetted on her toes in the change room. She already knew, by lunchtime, which frocks she was going to buy, even if she had to put them on lay-by. The first dress had a chocolate and white checked pattern, a broad belt that pulled her waist in tight and showed off an hourglass figure. She pouted her scarlet lips in front of the mirror and poked out her bust.

'So smart,' Annie said, 'you look like a model. Must have that one.'

The second was a silky white with pink polka dots.

'That's feminine. Will would approve,' her aunt said.

Then a sailor's playsuit in navy and white caught her eye, and she knew that she would have to have that, too. After shoes, stockings and a handbag, all of which Aunt Annie paid for, Bridie wondered what Will would think when he saw the loot.

Husbands didn't have to know everything. Keep a little bit of excitement in the marriage. Will had no idea when it came to fashion.

'Now, we're going to have lunch in David Jones Café on the top floor,' Aunt Annie announced, her face flushed with the pleasure of giving.

'Ooh, that'll be lovely,' Bridie cooed. She was pleased that Stella had gone off sightseeing with Rick, and that she could spend this alone time with her Aunt.

'By the way, Aunty, she said, 'I've got the appointment for later this afternoon with the doctor I told you about. To do with Richard.' She'd got used to telling half lies from living with her narrowminded mother.

'Oh, yes. Where is it?'

'It's in Macquarie Street.'

'Yes, dear. I'll take your things home in a taxi. Will you be able to get back on your own?'

'Yes, of course, Aunt Annie. No trouble at all.'

Bridie was still in the soft silky dress from David Jones, and the delicate strappy shoes with the tiny heels. Aunt Annie walked as far as Sydney Hospital with her. 'You look gorgeous,' she said as she kissed her goodbye. 'You're

239

sparkling once again like in the old days.' Bridie continued on, her aunt's words trilling in her ears, to the address of the clinic Doctor Goldblum had given her. It was on the street level of a grand building with brass name plates and a door knocker. As she stood on the marble steps in front of the door, she felt somersaults inside her stomach, like clusters of small, feathery creatures trying to get out. Don't be silly, she told herself. He's just going to talk about Richard. What is there to be afraid of?

She rang the brass doorbell.

A woman, a receptionist for the building, opened the door, her face a little flurried.

'I have an appointment with Doctor Goldblum,' she informed the woman, both relieved and anxious that he was in.

'He's in the midst of sorting out his affairs,' she said. 'I'll let him know you're here.'

Myer Goldblum appeared in the doorway with a smile as broad as the opening, and came forward with his hand outstretched towards her.

'Mrs Featherstone, so glad you can make it. Come in and witness the terrible state of disorder I am in.'

Bridie responded to the sound of his voice by relaxing, the calm soothing tone, the slight foreign lilt that added charm.

There were cardboard boxes strewn around the room, books and files packed into crates. 'Oh, of course,' Bridie murmured. 'You're moving back to Sydney, bringing your office belongings from Karrana.'

'Yes, the lot will be here by tomorrow. The house contents in a fortnight.'

'Oh, I see....'

'I cannot ask you to sit and talk here among this mess.'

'Oh, it's quite alright,' she said.

'No, I insist. We will be more comfortable in the lounge at the Wentworth Hotel where I am staying. It's not far from here, and we can take a taxi.'

'Well, if that's no bother for you.'

'None at all.' He was already taking his leave of the secretary, before ushering Bridie out into the street where he hailed a taxi.

His movements were sure, confident, as he opened the door of the cab for her to slide in, and went around to the other side to get in himself. How masterful and urbane he seemed.

'My family's preparing to leave the house in Karrana. I'm going to stay on for a week to finalise things here, before returning to help pack up back there.'

The taxi pulled into a circular driveway that led to the main entry of the hotel. Inside, chandeliers threw golden reflections around the foyer. Bridie had never seen such glamour before. Women in evening dress and men in dark suits sat at gilded tables drinking cocktails and smoking cigarettes through thin holders. She felt like a princess, as Myer touched her gently on the elbow to guide her into the lounge.

'What would you like to drink?' he asked as he placed her in a comfortable chair in the corner next to a coffee table.

'I'll have tea, please.'

'They do wonderful Devonshire teas here. I insist on it.'

'What are you having?'

'The tea and scones with cream and jam appeals to me.'

How sophisticated he is, she thought as she watched him walk towards the counter to order. *Were all European men like this?*

After the waiter in the black and white uniform brought the order, Doctor Goldblum and Bridie faced each other across the table. She noted his olive skin with the black curls falling over his forehead and wondered again about differences. When she first met his eyes, dark and mysterious, she couldn't breathe, let alone speak. She saw in his eyes a look … sensed that he was startled … by her face perfected by the layer of makeup…. They stared at one another in silence.

He was the first to speak. 'Look, Mrs Featherstone, what I wanted to tell you is that you are not alone. There is a great deal that one can do these days to improve the life and prognosis of brain injury sufferers.'

She drank in his words, the way he pronounced them, his formality. She trusted him. How accomplished he seemed. The way he'd shown her to her place with a light touch on her back. She imagined dancing with him. He'd guide her around the floor with a gentle but deft grasp, and she'd feel right in his arms. There was no harm in fantasizing like this.

A tear rolled slowly down her cheeks. 'I know you're only trying to help, but the worst of it is how Richard is no longer the boy he was. He was special. Everyone said he was brilliant. A genius.'

Myer placed his hand on hers. The tears started to roll. He gave her a white handkerchief. 'It's good to cry. You mustn't hold it all in.'

She blew her nose hard. Sobbing now. Tears staining her makeup.

'I know, I know. It's just all been too much for me to take in. I placed so much … hope in him.'

'I have some names … of specialists here in Sydney that I can give you. I'll make appointments for you while you're here, if you like.'

'Thank you, Doctor, that would be wonderful. So good to find someone … to talk to … with skills to offer. I've been feeling so … alone … abandoned.'

'I have had children, also, and know the anguish of finding out that something's wrong with an offspring. Of losing someone….'

She looked up at his striking face through her tears and blew her nose again. He showed signs of past cares, a certain sadness, that mingled with an air of quiet dignity that enraptured her. She had never met anyone like him before. And she was flattered by the attention and care he seemed to accord her now.

'How many children have you? And why did you come to Karrana?'

'I married someone … we had close family ties, cousins, in fact. We had two children, one of whom died; the other, a teenager, has mild disablement. It makes you a better person, Bridie, to have to struggle with a damaged child.'

'It's not a fate I wanted for myself.'

'And why did I come to Karrana? It is a long history … but let us say that, after Europe, Karrana was a paradise for us.'

'B-but, you seem so … well educated, with such a lot of experience. Why not Sydney? If I had the chance, this is where I'd be.'

Myer seemed to sigh, and a shadow passed over his handsome features.

She felt a deep compassion for him, wished she could understand his troubles. *And why do people, even my friend, Stella, say it's a shame to be Jewish?*

'It is little more than ten years ago that my family and I had to leave our country and migrate to Switzerland, then to London, to escape the Nazis in Vienna. As an alien doctor it was easier for me to gain registration in Karrana than in Sydney, when we first arrived in Australia.'

His words slid from his tongue like carefully chosen notes, like beautiful chords of melodies played on a piano. She could go on listening to him forever.

'Look, this is just a beginning. We shall meet again. I need to tell you more. I have many things of value to impart to you. But I'm thinking I must get you home to your aunt's place. Let me take you in my car. I insist upon it. Shall we drink a cocktail before we leave?'

He brought her a sparkling champagne like drink in a tall cocktail glass served with two cubes of ice and a twist of lemon peel. There was a hint of brandy, which she recognized from the first sip.

'It's a *Gloria Swanson*,' he told her.

'It's divine,' she murmured, looking up. 'Now tell me this story of yours, please.'

'Well, I led a charmed life in Vienna before the war. Loving parents, lots of cousins and grandparents still living. One of my earliest memories is of a visit to the Hofburg Theatre with my mother to see *Pygmalion*. Even as a four-year-old, I was entranced by the personage of Eliza Doolittle. You remind me of her.'

'I know the songs from the movie. They are some of my favourites.'

'Anyway, my family's lives were thrown into upheaval when Germany annexed Austria on the twelfth of March in 1938. The date sticks in my mind like a thorn. I sensed what was coming. A window of opportunity for getting out of the country opened and I took my family by train to Switzerland.'

'Why not stay there?'

'I had a contact who had gone there. He would have been able to assist in migration procedures. And I could more easily practise Medicine there than elsewhere. But there was persecution, or at least prejudice, even in England, France and elsewhere.'

'I don't understand. Why this dislike of Jewish people?'

'I have often tried to answer that question myself. Fear of difference, perhaps. Jealousy, a useless emotion, is at the basis of much terrible human behaviour. Even in families it exists. I was enticed by Freud's theories and wished to become a psychiatrist. This is what I might have learnt about if I'd studied psychoanalysis.'

'And what prevented you?'

'I needed to engage in more studies, but we had to leave Vienna quickly.'

'What a pity,' Bridie sighed, sipping on her cocktail. 'Were you happy in Sydney?'

'I found myself forced to confront the fact of an unfamiliar culture that both shocked and revitalised me. Once again, I was treated as an alien. I practised in Sydney under the Commonwealth Emergency Medical services, as authorised by the National Security Regulations legislation. *Not registered in New South Wales* had to be displayed on my name plate. The move to the north coast enabled me to gain registration.'

Bridie sniffled and wiped her eyes with the handkerchief he'd given her.

'While in Sydney, I learnt of the deportation and subsequent deaths of my dear mother and father, and several of my aunts, uncles, and cousins who all perished in the Nazi concentration camp of Auschwitz.'

Bridie was weeping once again, but this time for Myer, not for herself.

Chapter 32

The car with Myer at the wheel rounded the corner onto the beachside parade. An orange ball appeared over the cliffs directly opposite them. It loomed lustrous in the dusky light.

Bridie gasped and held her breath for a moment.

'Ooh, look at that ... the full moon ... it's wondrous, isn't it?'

The golden ball sat at the rock ledge next to the brick flats as if tossed there by a giant's hand.

She looked at Myer and saw that he, too, was taken aback by the sudden apparition.

'Ah, yes, it is like a ... celestial appearance, so unexpected.'

Tears of joy and rapture pulsed at the edges of her eyelids. She felt Myer's gaze for an instant. When she turned her face toward him, she knew that he was holding onto something, as if the vision had stirred memories and awakened a thought within.

'We must view it from on high, further up. I know just the place,' he said. He put his foot on the accelerator and sped up the hill towards the lighthouse, shimmering white against the sky. Soon he pulled up at a vantage point in full view of the perfect moon.

They sat in the car near the edge of the cliffs and watched the moon rise higher and higher up into the sky over the Pacific Ocean.

'It's like watching a movie,' Bridie whispered. 'So beautiful.'

'Nothing so lovely in the whole world....' She saw ecstasy on his face. 'I've always loved the moon ... it's like ... a passion.'

'I love the moon too. And to think it's the same moon we see in Karrana every month. Never so beautiful as over the ocean here.'

The surface of the sea shimmered in the shards reflected from the moonlight as it rose above the water.

'I'd like to climb down and sit next to the ocean,' she murmured.

He ushered her out of the passenger seat and together they scrambled like mountain goats down the rough track that led to the grassy verge next to the beach below. The waves splashed and gurgled onto the rocks and pebbles on the edge of the shore.

'Are you warm enough?' he asked as they slithered onto the grass. 'You can have my coat,' and he put his hand on her arm to steady her.

Bridie shivered at his touch.

'Yes, I'm fine.'

She sank down on to the grass and looked up at the moon, now lighter and smaller high up in the sky.

'I'm going to remember this moment forever,' she said.

She looked at his curly dark hair, the slender frame, and those hands—long fingered and sensitive—and yearned to feel his warmth against her. She shivered and started to cry, silently at first, then was no longer able to stifle the sobs that threatened to erupt from within. Her shoulders began to heave and small gurgling sounds joined those coming from the convulsions of the sea.

'What's wrong?' Myer stared at her, then moved in closer to her.

'I don't know. It's all so beautiful and I feel like … I'm part of it, here with you.'

She felt Myer's body touch hers. He put his arm around her shoulders to comfort her. It was the most natural thing in the world, the most normal pull, like gravity; their bodies met; they found one another's lips and kissed. And this coming together of their two souls, when their lips met, was perfection itself.

They kissed for a long while.

'Oh, I'm sorry,' Myer gasped, when he became aware of the situation. 'I'm so sorry.'

'No, not sorry,' she murmured. 'Please, don't be sorry. I wanted this just as much as you did.' She could tell from the way he'd looked at her. 'No one need know. Please love me. Make me feel safe now.'

Then they were kissing again. She tasted him—his tongue against hers. She tasted his breath, like the salt from the sea carried on the wind. She drank him in, his teeth against hers, his saliva, and his lips tasting like nothing she'd ever tasted before. It was magic. And she knew that this moment would never die, that she'd come back to it over and over again. She didn't care, at this moment, if it broke up a family or two. She regretted nothing, cared nothing about the consequences of these actions. The moment was all that she cared about. This precious golden moment. She wanted him despite any future strife.

Be careful what you wish for came to mind and she spurned it.

He kissed her face, nuzzled her nipples, making her cry out as if in pain. She pulled his face down into her breasts for more. She felt her nipples harden and reached for his lips again.

Then he was pulling away from her. Gently resisting her advances and trying to speak.

'Look, I'm so sorry—I'll tell you what. Let's leave this until tomorrow night. I'll take you out to dinner. We can dance, talk, listen to music, whatever you want. Then we'll decide what we want to do about this … umm … attraction.'

'Oh, yes, you're right. I'm sorry too. Not about what happened. Just about my thoughtless ... you know … I can't bear to think this might be the end....'

Myer too was shaken. 'I'll take you home now, and you decide what you want. I know that I don't want this to end here, either.'

'I know, I know. You've got a family, and I have too. But I can't help myself. I find you very attractive.'

'And I you.'

On the way home, she kept stealing glances at his beautiful profile. Being alone with a man in nature had been, for once in her life, a turn on. The throbbing in her belly was for him. She ached to hold him in her arms, nothing more, at that moment.

The ocean, the sky, the moonlight, it all made her ache. She wanted to sing out loud. She wanted to dance with him on the edge of the sand. But she knew that he was right, and that they should go home.

The moon had risen over the ocean. A still bright perfect round ball, it threw shadows across the dark waters below. Bridie was pleased that Aunt Annie was already in bed, and that she wouldn't have to share with anyone what had just happened. She tiptoed out onto the verandah to check out the moon.

Stella, only her red hair showing, was wrapped into the shape of a chrysalis on the swing chair with Rick.

Bridie stopped short.

Stella popped her head up, her eyes seeking those of her friend. 'If I didn't know any better, I'd say you were hiding something from us.'

'What?'

'Your face is aglow,' Stella cried as she pulled herself out of the cocoon. 'Your aunt said you had an appointment?'

'Yes.'

Bridie felt herself blushing.

'It wasn't, was it?' Stella dropped her jaw, her eyes shining wide.

'Yes, but it's alright. We didn't need a chaperone.'

Rick sat up. 'What's all this about?' he said.

'It's a doctor who's moving here from Karrana, who's possibly going to lead Bridie astray, or the other way round,' chortled Stella, her face glowing with mischief in the moonlight.

'Don't be silly, Stella. Rick will get the wrong idea about him. He's helping me with advice about my son, who's suffered a brain injury.'

'Oh, that's terrible,' he said. 'I know what you're going through.'

'And so does her doctor,' said Stella, snuggling up to Rick, who was seated at the end of the chair now.

His warm eyes rested on Bridie for a moment. 'Look, I'm sure your doctor is an honourable man.'

'And he's married with children, and so am I,' said Bridie.

'Yes, but that doesn't mean a thing,' said Rick. 'My father took a mistress after my younger brother was born. Couldn't cope with the idea of a damaged son.'

Bridie felt like Rick could see through into her soul. Like she was a goldfish inside a glass bowl. Yet he was kind and open, and she felt that, too.

'Well,' she said, looking up into the night sky, 'I can see that the stars and planets are aligned for you two this evening, that's for sure.' And she threw a longing glance towards their bodies, leaning into one another on the swing chair.

'Yes,' said Stella, her starry eyes looking into those of her newfound friend, 'but this handsome young doctor and I are separated by hundreds of miles. Not to mention that he's younger than me by two years.'

'And shorter,' Rick said, showing his teeth in a wide grin.

'No matter,' Stella giggled. 'I can wear flatties all the time.'

'I can perhaps change places, swap with your doctor, Bridie,' said Rick, with a half serious look on his face.

'I can't see why not, if you want to practise in the country when you finish your internship. But, if I were Stella, I'd consider coming to Sydney for good.'

'So you don't like country life?'

'Not at the moment. But I know I'm going to miss my children terribly before too long,' she said, and stifled a sob.

The little faces of Charlie and Livvy flickered into view for a moment, competing with the view of the night sky.

'Well, just take care, that's all,' warned Rick. 'I've seen too many relationships come to croppers through infidelity.'

'Thanks for your concern, Rick. Anyway, I'm not going to sit around and mope. Myer is taking me out tomorrow night. And we're going to have some fun on the town. So there.'

'Not sure how I'm going to explain it to Aunt Annie, though,' she thought aloud, as she went off to bed.

She'd started to forget what *Richard-before-the-accident* looked like exactly, the white face against the white sheets in hospital, only too invasive and clear in her mind. She tried to conjure up Richard's true features as she was falling asleep. Plenty of time for thinking about Will, once she'd understood her real reasons for coming to Sydney. She didn't even know, as yet, what they were *for goodness sake*…. She'd need to discover the mystery beneath the magnetism that had brought the two of them, Myer and herself, together.

Chapter 33

Will leant his brawny trunk against the Tumbarumbar branding yards. He placed the red-hot iron with the 'V8' symbol on the steer's rump. The beast bellowed, showing the whites of its eyes, as its singed flank sizzled, and the smell of burning hair filled the air.

Reenie, her brown skin relishing the rough and tumble of station life, was there in tight fitting jodhpurs.

Will climbed up and sat on the top railing of the yards to chat with Richard, who'd been watching the mustering and branding from a safe perch.

'Does it hurt them, the branding iron?' he asked.

'No, just gives them a bit of a fright. Their hides as thick as leather, you know? It's what shoes are made from.'

'I'd like to muster cattle one day, ride behind a mob, sleep out under the stars.'

'There's nothing better on God's earth, young Richard, than a life on the land.'

'That's what Reenie says, too.'

Just then she climbed up and joined them. She tousled Richard's hair, and told him she'd have to take his dad away for a while. Will told him to go up to the homestead for his bath and tea. They'd help the Finn men driving the cattle from the yards.

Reenie mounted her horse and cantered after the herd. With hoots and whistles, dogs barking and snapping at heels, they got the herd moving.

Will and his darkly hazel eyes followed after her. If only Bridie liked country life as did his old flame, he'd be as happy as a king. They all had their crosses to bear, Reenie still waiting for her husband to return.

The phone call he'd made to Annie's house had unsettled him. Bridie's mood had lightened, but she seemed even farther away than the miles that separated them. Sure, she'd asked after Richard, but her mind was on the shopping spree with Annie to David Jones and the beauty of the Pacific Ocean beating at their back doorstep.

As they rode along behind the bellowing mob, Reenie tried to get him to unburden himself.

'Will, are you going to fetch Bridie back from Sydney? Aren't you worried she mightn't come back if you don't?'

'Ahh, Reenie, she's got a mind of her own, my girl, and I feel like it might push her right away, if I don't tread careful-like.'

'Well, you've got to put your foot down at some stage.'

'You don't know my Bridie. I fear I'll lose her unless I let her have free rein for a bit. Richard's fall near shook the life out of her.'

'You're a saint, is all I can say, Will Featherstone, an' that girl better realise it one of these days.' She cantered off in pursuit of a couple of strays.

Will was left with his thoughts.

Even in mid childhood, he'd felt a dark form shadowing him, taunting him for his sensitivities. It was not right that he should take after his mother's nervy side and not Henry's tougher one. She'd tried to protect Will, her favourite child, from bullying in the school playground. Now he was expected to rein in an unbroken filly, the spoilt only daughter of a widowed mother.

Will dug his heels into the horse's belly and galloped off to catch up with Reenie, his mane of tawny dark hair flying, his feelings windswept, too.

Not once did he consider that he might have made a mistake in choosing his bride. She was all he'd ever wanted, and would ever desire.

His natural outlook made him believe that things would get better between them.

The Finns were placing kerosene lamps on posts all around the outside of the garden. There would be dancing well into the night. Richard thought it was magical.

The closest Anglican church was too far away for guests to travel back and forth, so the family had hired a cleric friend to come to the family home and conduct the service.

Will had helped set everything up for Carl Finn's garden wedding. He'd also assisted in building a new house on the flats nearby for the young couple to live in after the wedding.

'There's another block waiting for you to build on, Will, whenever you and Bridie are ready,' said Stan.

Will knew that fate would not allow him to take up the offer straight away, if at all. How could he tell them that Bridie despised the idea of living so far away from the hub of civilization? Nor would he partake of the offer, without contributing savings to the project.

Richard had attached pink and white crepe paper roses onto the parachute material covering the frame erected for the reception. The family had planned everything for the outside, rain or no rain.

A feast had been prepared fit for kings. For weeks the men had been choosing the best beef carcasses, whole pigs and lambs for the spit, and chickens and ducks to be roasted for the banquet. They'd long had their own slaughter yards on the farm. The leftovers would be cut and cured and kept in the homestead freezers on the two thousand acre property.

Will thought how perfect the weekend would be if only Bridie were here. News of his wife came to him in erratic bursts. Eliza O'Toole had taken on the role of looking after Charlie and Livvy, the two youngest Featherstone children, and getting them off to school.

And today, Pa Featherstone and his wife had collected the two excited grandchildren from Treetop Farm and driven up in their large cream Ford to attend the ceremony. Silver-haired Henry, in a dark suit and a white shirt, black bowtie and a starched collar, led Alice Page on his arm along the flower bordered path toward the makeshift altar.

Mendelssohn's *Wedding March* floated out over the balmy afternoon air from the musicians on the homestead verandah.

Carl Finn waited with a nervous grin for his bride. Alice, a puffy veil covering her face, primped along the aisle in an ivory satin dress with lace overlay that had been worn by her mother. Two bridesmaids in pink tulle followed closely behind, accompanied by the groom's brothers, Leon and Stanley Finn. Little Charlie, dressed as a page boy in black and white like his grandfather, and flower girl Livvy in pink organdie, brought up the rear.

The whole scene reminded Will of the wedding cake that he'd glimpsed on passing through the kitchen, frothy white and pink cream all over it, and figurines of a bride and groom on the top. He was used to Bridie's simpler taste, but he was pleased for the couple.

As Carl placed the antique ring on his wife's finger, tears welled up in Will's eyelids. If only Bridie could be there to see them, he thought.

If only... if only....

As he watched the little ones, his eyes sparkled anew, moistness signalling joy and pride in his children.

'When will the new house be ready for the young couple?' asked Pa Featherstone at the high table after speeches had finished.

'It's all done and dusted, Henry,' said the Finn patriarch with a clap of leathery palms together. Out of his sunburnt face, his teeth and eyes gleamed with satisfaction.

'Yeah, an' your good son's leant a hand for which we're in debt,' added Leon. 'We'll all of us pitch in when this bloke's lovely wife and he are ready to build.'

'Ye-es,' said his wife, seated next to him. 'I could do with some more female company out here.'

'I cannot understand how she can go off and leave the little ones like that,' Margaret Featherstone could be heard whispering in her hostess's ear, 'not to mention my son and Richard.'

'But the child's thriving, Margaret,' said Mabel, 'such a lovely, happy boy since he's been here.'

'You know his brain has been affected, don't you? He'll be nowhere near the top of the class from now on,' said Margaret with a sideways glance at her friend.

Mabel Finn's kindly powder-puff face smiled back, 'Yes, but I haven't noticed anything out of the ordinary. Coming here seems to have done him a world of good.'

'Now there, Mum,' said Will, 'you mustn't make things out to be worse than they really are.' He placed a large arm around his mother's shoulder.

'Yeah, we'll have young Richard back on a horse before he can count to a hundred,' said Leon with a grin. 'That one's got a future on the land like his dad.'

'It's a mug's game unless you have a family inheritance passed on to you,' said Henry, his silver head entering the conversation. 'I wanted Will to go to university and study pharmacy.'

'No offence, Henry,' said Stan, 'but I can't see this old cowboy here in a white coat mixing up minerals or potions, you know?'

'Well, he'll be on his own, I'm afraid, when it comes to building his house.' Henry steeled himself against the kindness of the Finns' words and offers.

'Look, Henry,' said Stan, laying a parched hand on his friend's arm, 'we're keeping a nice sized block of land ready for Will whenever he wants to build on it. We're in his debt, you know?'

'Well, he's going to have to stay put and save some money. My motto is never a lender nor a borrower be.'

'Can you see Bridie settling down here, like you, Mabel,' added Margaret, 'on a beef cattle station far from town?'

After the ceremony and banquet, the children raced around the gardens and into the orchard, happy to play hide-and-seek, while the adult guests danced or chatted at the tables.

Will went outside with Richard and kept watch over the small children as they played.

Should he warn the young couple that nothing, not even love, assured them of a smooth ride into the future?

He wasn't one to fantasize or over stretch the truth, but there was always Fate, the haggle-toothed witch riding high on her broomstick to test young couples like them.

God, why did he let it happen with Richard? He envied those, like the Finns and their clergyman, and all those who believed in an old man sitting up on a cloud in the sky ruling over things, good and bad.

For him, the land was paradise and the bush with its gumtree forests his cathedral. He was living out his natural destiny underneath the canopy of the eucalyptus trees.

Only his one true love was missing from the scene.

Chapter 34

It was already spring. The hours and days since she left Karrana had slipped by without her noticing. Bridie dreamt that she was living on the north bank of the Karrana River with Myer. She was one of the in-crowd with a modern house agleam on a sunlit shore. Yet there was something missing in the golden dream. It was a bit of a conundrum. Where were her children?

'When are we going to meet this doctor friend of yours, Bridie?' her aunt said that morning over breakfast on the verandah. 'Are his intentions honourable?'

The question was said with an ironic smile. If only she knew, Bridie thought.

'Yes, Annie, but I'm afraid mine aren't,' she said, smiling back at her aunt. 'You don't have to worry. He's just a friend. And he's going to be living in Sydney soon, with his family in tow.'

'That's good to hear, but I haven't heard about any appointments with specialists, dear. I was just wondering…?'

'Well, Myer's set up an appointment for the best man in Sydney to see Richard, but it's unfortunately far in the future … I may have to come back.'

'I see.'

'Remember that I have three little ones back home waiting for me, so I can't really go off with a lover, can I?'

'That's true. I just hope you know what you're doing, that's all.'

'We're meeting this evening, so please don't wait up for me. And if Mama rings tell her I'm fine. I'll be home before too long.'

They met in the foyer of the Hotel Australia. She inhaled silently when she saw Myer. He looked so…European, dressed in a smart jacket and tie, his curly hair smoothed down a little.

'You look … nice,' she said, her eyes feeling moist.

'Beautiful…,' he murmured, staring at her.

Was that a tear, like the one she felt in her own eye, glistening at the edges of his dark brown lashes?

They moved towards one another, almost touching.

'Let's get out of here,' he said. She felt an ache inside.

'Yes, but where?' Bridie touched him and felt him start beneath her fingers.

'The house in Sydney has become available today. It is on a bay, and there is a boat included.'

'It sounds lovely.'

Bridie saw that the bayside house was lit up by a half moon, shimmering its magic effects across the watery landscape at the back.

All her senses were alive. Beauty radiated from her face. He stared at her in rapture, took her face in his hands and kissed her long and slow there on the edge of the bay.

A timber sloop with 'Nefertiti' in black on its bow stood, waiting for them at the private jetty. Their first lovemaking was to be on the water, not inside a strange house that she would never live in.

Myer had that look that was pure want, and Bridie recognised the same feeling within herself; she was in total consent.

It seemed the most natural thing in the world that they would come together in this way. He had barely steered the yacht out into the water before he pulled her down gently on top of him, and they sank onto the bunk.

The boat rocked in the bay, back and forth, back and forth, as they found one another. Their bodies joined together in rhythm with the movement of the vessel and they became one with the wind and the waves. He explored every part of her, like a musician playing a dance tune, with perfect mastery.

After a long while, when they had tasted of one another, they lay back satiated. He recited the words of a poem by an old-fashioned English poet, a little twinkle in his eye.

> *Had we but world enough, and time,*
> *This coyness, Lady, were no crime.*
> *We would sit down, and think which way*
> *To walk, and pass our long love's day...*

She didn't understand the exact meaning of the words that he'd learnt by heart. She loved the sounds as they tumbled from his lips and guessed it was about love and fate. She wondered about the word 'crime'.

He told of his amusement over the fact that there had been no shyness, not on his part, nor on hers. It had all happened naturally and graciously, as if it were meant to happen, just like this.

'I couldn't bear to think of not expressing how I felt,' she said, 'even with so many rocky … hazards in our way.'

'I wish I could carry you off to another country, somewhere far away,' he said, nuzzling her neck. 'On the banks of a foreign sea, a land that would take us in.'

Afterwards, they walked out onto the sand dunes and made love there under the softening moon. Idyllic, feeling one with nature, both of them.

It was late when she returned to Dover Heights. There would be time tomorrow to seek answers to the questions Annie would throw at her.

As Bridie drifted off, she listened to the Pacific pounding on the rocks below.

She wondered what her dreams would bring this night.

She knew only that Myer would feature in them.

The next evening, they met with Stella and Rick at the house in Dover Heights. Annie had cooked a lamb roast for them; they drank red wine and laughed and joked.

'Isn't it funny, Stella, how you came to Sydney to act chaperone for me and I have hardly seen you since our arrival in Sydney?'

'Yes, I'm sorry, Bridie. We've been having too much fun, Rick taking me to Luna Park and all over the city.'

She smirked at the two lovebirds nestling in to one another on the opposite side of the table, Stella's red locks against Rick's black hair, a lovely contrast.

'Will you invite us to your wedding?' Bridie's speech was a little slurred.

Wine had loosened Bridie's tongue, making her unaware of the aptness of her speech. Myer pulled away perceptively.

'You're moving a bit fast, there,' smiled Rick. '

'Yes, wait until we're engaged at least, my Bridie,' laughed Stella.

'So I was right, wasn't I?' giggled Bridie, looking for Myer's approval.

'Rick's driving me back home,' said Stella, 'just so you know. We'll probably be leaving for Karrana the day after tomorrow.'

'Stella has invited me back to Karrana to meet her parents,' added Rick.

'Myer, what are your plans for your practice?' asked Aunt Annie, choosing her words.

Bridie saw into her aunt's mind, it was plain to see: Annie *knew*.

'I plan to close my surgery in Karrana and move here to Sydney. I already have a rental house and rooms arranged. My family will follow shortly.'

'You are used to city life, coming from Vienna?'

'Yes, more than the quiet of the country, in fact.'

'Myer knows about Mozart and concerts,' Bridie exclaimed, staring bright-eyed up at him, 'he plays the piano and the cello.'

Her tone was high-pitched now, and she was aware of the wine making her talkative.

'It must have been rather dull for you at first in Karrana, Myer,' said Annie.

'I was kept busy by my work there with my patients, especially young children.'

'My niece has told me of your kindness towards her and Richard.'

Bridie blushed at her aunt's words; waves of shame flowed over her.

'I must ring Mumma and see how the children are,' she said, three little faces peering up at her out of the vapour of guilt.

'Do so now, if you wish,' said Annie.

Bridie felt all eyes on her as she left the room. From the furthest reaches of the semi she picked up the receiver and dialled the number. Through the pings and noises coming down the line, she heard Stella and Myer picking out notes on the piano.

Bridie and Annie sat on the verandah in the morning sun.

'I must ask you, dear, what is going on between you and Myer?'

Bridie looked down at her fingers, newly painted.

She stammered: 'Nothing, Aunty, what do you mean?'

'I'm not your mother, Bridie, you can confide in me. You know that.'

Tears brimmed up in Bridie's eyes. She sniffled and wiped away the salty overflow.

'Oh, Annie, it's just that something is missing in my marriage to Will. I've been feeling it for some time now.'

'And you have fallen in love with your doctor friend?'

'Yes, Aunt. I'm afraid so. But I'm so confused, Annie.'

'How are things in the bedroom with you and Will?'

'Not so good lately. I'm not in love with him anymore. I've got all the things I wanted, a family, a good husband, a house, but I feel I should be happier.'

'You say you still love Will?'

'Yes, but I've lost my *desire* for him. Even his smell … I've turned against. I'm just not *attracted* to him anymore. I don't even want Will to touch me now.'

'That's normal after six or seven years of marriage, Bridie. It will pass.'

Oh, Annie, is there something wrong with me, or is it Will's fault? His lovemaking, perhaps? I feel so guilty.'

'I don't know, child, all I know is that you were shining last night in Myer's presence. And that you're in a dangerous situation. You know you're playing with fire, don't you?'

'Oh, yes, yes, but I can't help it.' Bridie was crying now, tears streaming down her red cheeks. 'He makes me feel alive, Annie. He's awakened me from the dead.'

Aunt Annie was opening and closing her fingers now, then clinging them together.

'I don't know myself anymore. I wish someone would just tell me what to do,' Bridie said. She'd started praying at night to a God she hardly believed in. But it gave her comfort, a sense that things might turn out right in the end.

Annie sighed, 'Oh, dearie, I only ever loved one man, lost him before it all began. I'm the last one to hand out guidance. All I advise is that you keep it secret from the world, this love affair.'

She wrung her hands together again.

'But you might have to confide in Will eventually. He's such a good man, and he deserves to know the truth.'

'I know, I know, and I don't deserve him.'

'The point is, dear, that you risk losing the children. Men have more rights when it comes to divorce. And you'll be called a bad mother.'

'Oh, Aunty, I couldn't bear that. But what if I've found my soul mate and I throw it away?'

'You know that Italian actress, Anna Magnani and her love affair with Roberto Rossellini? She's married and people are calling her a 'she-wolf', even though she thought she'd found her soul mate in that womaniser.'

'Oh, how terrible. Myer is not like that at all. What will I do if this gets out?'

'Darling, only time will tell what is the best thing for you and the children. I think it is time for you to return home now, much as I love having you here and I know I shall miss you terribly.'

Bridie knew her aunt was right. 'Oh, Aunty…,' she whispered.

Chapter 35

Several days passed before Myer could find time from work to talk to Bridie face to face. She had been going over and over their predicament in her mind. She was torn. Her children's faces with tears streaming down; Myer's beautiful face ever more radiant as the time of her departure drew nearer.... These few days of separation had only made her more desirous of seeing him. It was obvious that they shared the same feelings.

He parked the car on a hill overlooking the ocean. Shoreward blowing winds kept them inside the car, warm and protected. White seahorses played on the waves down below, as they rolled towards the golden sands. There were many such places around the area. Salty waters had replaced the Karrana River for Bridie, so much a part of her background.

He pulled her towards him. 'I can't let you go, now that I have found you.'

He clung to her as if his life depended on it. 'I love you, Bridie.'

'And I, you, also. But, Myer, my children....'

He, never having been able, to keep his hands off her for long, was in a pontificating mood. He moved a little away and looked into her eyes. He'd obviously been ruminating on their dilemma, just as Bridie herself had.

'Our daughter, being born a cripple, we felt as if we were being punished by a vengeful God for something we hadn't done.'

Bridie gasped at this admission. But she was only too pleased to listen to his polished words, so European sounding, so pleasurable to her ears. She felt safe within their cadence. Listening to him made her feel as if he would surely come up with a solution to their quandary. She certainly couldn't.

'I, like many of my countrymen at the time,' he continued, 'had inter married. In my case, it was to a second cousin. There were many others like us, cleaving together for protection, as political machinations produced the ugly fangs of anti-Semitism to threaten, nay devour, us. We married in haste and produced a child. This child and our union needed protection. We fled Austria in a hurry before the talons of fascism reached out to take us. We ended up here in this country with a similar sounding name but worlds away from ugly politics. Others were not so lucky.'

His face fell at this moment and took on a grey pallor. Bridie, too, sank into sadness.

Myer's face brightened quickly again.

'Now I feel the pull of your being, like that of metal to gravity, to magnet, I mean, as if I have never known sensual ecstasy before. It is as if this love is a first and innocent one for me.'

He took her hands and looked into her eyes with deep longing. 'The balm to soothe all the foregoing pain and sacrifices of my life.'

He pulled her towards him. He repeated words from the Book of Job, wherein the morning stars sang together and all the sons and daughters of God shouted for joy.

During the night, poetic words had called on Bridie, too. They were snippets from a nun's classroom recitation: 'Children's voices should be dear, call once more to a mother's ear, children's voices wild with pain, surely she will come again, call her once and come away. Margaret! Margaret!'

She'd tossed and called out, in her sleep, sensing ghosts in the room. She'd called out *Go to the light*, waking her aunt, whose darkened figure was standing over her bed, a shadow like an avenging angel, only half recognized by the dreamer.

In the morning, she knew that she was stuck. There was no one to appeal to for help. Not a soul, not her aunt, nor a priest. No one. How could she make the decision to run away with Myer? How could he abandon his wife and child for her?

All she knew was that they might lose all if they acted on their passion.

The easiest thing, and they would both come to know it in the end, would be to do nothing. Duty called, and they were both used to the sound, the scent and the look of its greyness by now.

It was like the little grey church on the hill in Matthew Arnold's poem. They had both tasted ecstasy, and it was time now to return to reality. Only madness lay on the other side.

'Let's forget all of that for the moment…,' he beseeched her, pulling her tightly towards him.

'Is this little bit of time together all we have left, my darling?' she whispered into his ear. 'I trust you to keep me safe, as you have been doing, from an unwanted pregnancy….'

Myer sits amid the boxes in his empty house on the Bay. His wife and daughter will be arriving before very long.

How can he tell his Esther the truth? How can he not? He has never been one to keep secrets. Back in their courting days, when they were students together in Vienna, their decision to wed was pragmatic rather than romantic. She was older than he and desirous of having children. Yet he was

271

worried about the world into which they would be bringing this child.

He'd had a sixth sense, though, about when to flee the country. The right moment to leave presented itself; he acted on it and they fled their beloved Austria for good; they left via Switzerland and England; and found themselves far from home *down under*, in Australia.

The joy of introducing his young lover to the theatre intrudes suddenly. There is *The New Theatre* in Sydney, certainly. Or the exciting experimental theatres starting up in Melbourne.

Now he's holding his head in his hands, like Rodin's thinker. The full weight of guilt, shame too, a darkly grey cloud presses down on him.

How could he have allowed this to happen? He, the elder one, is entirely responsible. For everything. What would Herr Doktor Freud have to say about his guilt and shame? *An excessive degree of superego, perhaps?*

The pain is like the weight of gravity pinning his forehead to the ground. Bridie is putting off the decision to return to her family back in Karrana, all because of him. Each day she rebuts calls from home; the children ailing; her mother not coping with childcare duties.

It is *Eine Liebesfalle*, a love trap. That is what it is, and he is the one who must break them free of it.

'Reedy River', showing at the left wing *New Theatre* in the city, would be the first choice for himself. It's an Australian musical about a shearers' strike, with colonial songs, such as *Click Go the Shears*. But he realizes that Bridie would probably prefer something different, an American movie, perhaps *A Star is Born*, starring Judy Garland and James Mason. Everyone is talking about it. Much easier to get seats for, showing in cinemas everywhere.

Then he discovers a French film by *Rene Clair*, about life in Paris, showing at the University of Sydney. Something that she won't be able to see, once she is back in Karrana.

Perhaps just one last little folly before she must depart?

He makes the booking for the following evening, a Saturday.

Arriving at the courtyard in the grounds of the University of Sydney, Myer straightens up at a private thought. Ancient buildings far exceeding in architectural merit and expansiveness these ones, inhabit his thoughts.

He reaches out for her, seeing Bridie gasp and place her hands together at her chest, rapture light up her face. *The grand beauty of the place*, she might be thinking: *This is where I could have come, if only someone in the family had known about the importance of learning.*

The nuns had told her mother that she was clever.

He tells her how the architecture is styled after similar buildings in England, and that he attended, as a student, just such a glorious building in his home town of Vienna. He leads her through the alleyways between darker buildings towards the Teachers College where the film is being shown. He is talking all the while, filling her in on the movie they are about to see.

It's a frivolous story about a young woman, Paula, choosing between three lovers in a suburb of Paris. The story, he tells her, is sentimental, not to be taken seriously, but the views of cobbled streets and rooftops in Paris, are to die for.

Would she like to visit Melbourne, he asks, to experience the drive-in theatre there where you can have a meal and watch a movie in the privacy of your car?

They sit close together, enraptured by the quaint urban landscapes in black and white on the screen, by the exotic characters, who go about their strange antics, almost without dialogue. She is learning about French culture, where *concierges* mind dark apartment buildings, street singers, beggars and gangsters share the streets and the cafes, and where life appears to be joyous and full of passion.

Afterwards, as he drives her home, his face is shining, mirroring hers, their eyes damp with moistness that speaks of love and hope.

He is already thinking about another rendezvous, another French film, perhaps, before their final separation.

How strange love is, so fickle and able to replace sane thoughts and the memory of duties in an instant.

Bridie invites him in for a warm drink. The house is in darkness. Annie will be sound asleep in readiness for the following day's call to duty. She is always on call. They creep in and sit on the swing chair and watch the lights starting to fade over the city.

She feels like they are a couple now. How could she let him go? She would never ever tire of Myer's attentions. Life would be one continuing arc of discovery. Learning about music, European culture and books....

They sit quietly. They sip the hot chocolate from chunky mugs. They don't need to talk.

There is just enough light on the balcony for her to see his face. A serious face now. Serious and handsome. If only she could press a button and make this moment stop forever. But those other high-pitched voices and noises would be there in the background for all eternity. It wouldn't do.

A feeling of dread has descended on her, invisible as the breeze across the cool night air. Is she tired? Ready to sink into sleep, perchance to dream? She needs to be alone now with her thoughts….

Myer is getting up. He gives her the sweetest of pecks on the cheek. *Stay, stay,* he seems to be saying. Then he is gone.

She falls onto her bed without getting undressed. Dread has wedded her to the mattress. Her shoulders begin to shake uncontrollably. She is taken away on a dreadful shudder and begins to sob. She is crying quietly into the bedclothes so as not to wake up her aunt.

The sobs subside a little as she is slipping into oblivion. Sleep is like an attentive lover who will bring comfort to her.

The guttural sounds issuing from deep within her throat relate, she knows, to a sense of loss, profound sadness, not for Myer this time, and not for her husband or her children back in Karrana.

She is weeping for herself.

Chapter 36

Early the next morning, there was a phone call from Hilltop.

'Mumma's had a heart attack, she's in the hospital,' said Ned. 'Mrs Featherstone's got the children at her place.'

'Poor Mumma,' gasped Bridie. 'We'll have to rally around. She'll need help. Where's Will?'

'He's coming back today, to help with the little ones.'

'I'm about to leave, Ned,' she cried into the receiver. 'To come back home.'

Bridie felt torn: Excited to be seeing her two little ones again, yet dreading the parting from Myer.

She telephoned Myer and told him about her mother's heart attack. 'Just as well you're going back, then,' he mumbled.

'Yes, and Will's arriving home for the two little ones, leaving Richard in the meantime with the Finns at Tumbarumbar.'

'You know, your boy will be better off in a special school, if he has a chance of improving at reading. It must be awful for him, not being able to perform at his past level.'

'Will seems to think the *School of the Air* is best for him.'

'There's nothing much in Karrana for him, that's for sure.'

'I'm so excited about seeing the kiddies and darling Richard again. I can at least think about him now, without, you know, wanting to die.'

'That's good news, my darling,' he said with compassion. 'You're going to be alright, now, no matter what happens.'

'Yes, I need to get back to see them all.'

'Oh, darling...,' he whispered into the receiver.

Bridie got on the phone and made a booking. She'd catch the overnight mail train back to Karrana this evening.

'If only you could stay in Karrana, and we could meet secretly,' Bridie whispered in Myer's ear when she told him of her plans to return home. They were sitting in his car outside the house by the bay.

'It would be harder there than here,' he whispered. 'People would crucify us in Karrana.'

'I know, I know… at least here we can be swallowed up by the city.' Bridie put her hands to her forehead, then let her head fall onto Myer's shoulder.

'And we would live with such terrible guilt for breaking up two families,' he added.

'Oh, Myer, what are we going to do? I don't think I can live without you now.'

'Nor can you live with me either, is that it?' He tried to look at her.

She pulled herself away and sighed, 'It might be easier just to say goodbye now.'

'Don't, darling,' he said with a shudder, 'Let's not think about it for the moment.'

'Love can be so cruel, like dying, the thought of leaving you,' Bridie sobbed.

'We must make the most of these last hours together,' Myer said, taking her hand in his and kissing it. 'Who knows what the future holds?'

'You're so much better than me. I haven't got your strength, your wisdom.'

'To me you are perfection itself. I think about you all the time, dream about you.'

'It's so unfair. There's Stella and Rick falling in love and no obstacles in their way. How I envy them.'

'Yes, but there's no guarantee, is there, that the fairy story will continue?'

'They'll get married and live happily ever after, wherever they decide,' answered Bridie.

'It would be possible for me to run off with you,' said Myer, a little saddened. 'My wife and I are cousins and have long outgrown one another. But there's our daughter to think about.'

'I see.'

'What about you? Would you ever leave Will?'

'Perhaps, but only if I could keep the children, and he wouldn't hear of that. What is more important, I wonder, duty or love?'

'I suppose there are many different kinds of love,' Myer said. 'Compassionate love, romantic love, erotic love. Divine love is different again, as is love for one's children and family.'

'You are so wise. I sometimes feel like a child next to you.'

'I have had a thought,' he said, 'I'll drive you back to Karrana tomorrow. That way, we'd get to spend two whole days ... before you must return to your children.'

'Oh, Myer, that would be lovely, but I don't think that's a good idea. I'm all packed and ready to go.'

Myer's face dropped.

'But we still have some time, some hours left together,' she murmured, only half believing it.

Bridie snatched sideways glances at Myer's handsome profile and hands on the wheel of the car, as he drove her towards the city, noting his olive skin and dark hair. A regal face, really. It was what had first captured her attention, the exotic look and those kind eyes staring down at her the day of Richard's fall.

She never tired of watching him now, and listening to his voice—the lovely sounds the words coming from his mouth made, as, she imagined, notes from a cello.

She thought of the differences between him and Will, her husband, whose body was what had first impressed itself on her, the height of the man and the width of his shoulders.

She thought of the words at the marriage ceremony when she'd promised to keep him in sickness and in health. A small tear pricked at her eyelids.

After a little while, Myer pulled the car off the road and drove into an area of foreshore land. A sign said 'National Park'.

'This will do just nicely,' he said and took Bridie in his arms for a long goodbye kiss. He laid a rug out on the ground beneath a tree, with the sound of the waves somewhere in the background. Late sunlight threw golden reflections through the leaves of the trees onto the grassy bank where they lay as they made love.

Bridie had never before felt her body respond so completely. Myer knew how to play it like a musical instrument. Her skin tingled, every cell and nerve whirred with electrical impulses as he touched her all over with those beautiful hands. They became as one; the duet continued; it gained in rapidity and reached a crescendo; the release was as exquisite as the prelude.

Lying on their backs, they looked up at the darkening sky and the clouds. The sun was going down over the water and they felt warmed by the lovemaking. Like two small children, they ran towards the gurgling sound, Myer chasing after Bridie, who was too fleet of foot for him to catch up. There was no one around. They threw their clothes off and jumped into the sea. 'I can't swim,' Myer said, 'but I don't care, even if I drown.'

'I will save you,' Bridie sang.

Somehow, they managed to make love in the water, couldn't help themselves.

They ate the mock chicken sandwiches Annie had made for the train trip. They made love once again, this time in a hikers hut alongside the beach with, they felt sure, possums, bats and other small creatures in the roof. They didn't care.

'My dear, the time has come....' He put out his hand to pick up her suitcase, standing on the platform between them. 'I shall take you up the steps into the carriage.' He gestured towards the train.

Bridie took her case from him. 'No,' she whispered. 'It's okay.'

The train had whistled its warning cry. She thought of the sound of a powerful owl, *Woo hoo*.

'Au revoir, my darling,' he whispered in her ear.

She pecked him quickly on the cheek and whispered, 'Au revoir.'

Myer was turning on his heel as she climbed the steps up into the carriage.

The train pulled out of the station in a cloud of smoke. Gone was the romantic courtesan who had wooed and risked all for her a few moments before.

He'd turned his back and walked away as the train pulled out of the station. Would he, like Lott's wife, look back, as the train was chugging off into the distance?

She'd stood at the door of the carriage and looked back towards his already invisible form. Tears that had been welling up for half an hour poured forth as the train got up speed.

It was pitch black when the train reached the outskirts of the city.

Tired after the afternoon's lovemaking, she at last sank into the leather bench inside the compartment.

City life with its meandering tributaries was far more frightening to her at this moment than the thought of the bush she was heading back to.

She reached Karrana late the next morning. The taxi drove her straight to Mistletoe Cottage. There was no sign of a vehicle in the yard. Bridie wondered where Will's jeep was.

Children's voices were coming along the road out the front. A deep man's voice too, one that she recognised. And then they were there, the three of them: Will, Charlie and Livvy.

She looked at the great bear of a man standing in the doorway and felt a frisson of something like fear and also *déjà vu*. It was as if she were seeing, for the very first time, beneath the skin of the man she'd married.

There was a glow shining from his core. She sensed that his heart, beating like a drum for her, was emitting this strange light that radiated soul and goodness.

She wondered how she had missed seeing this deepest quality of the man she'd chosen as her spouse nearly seven years ago. Perhaps she could spend a few more years with him, after all. How she'd come to take him for granted. This good man deserved better.

'Mummy, Mummy,' screamed Charlie as he rushed to throw himself into his mother's arms. 'I missed you, Mummy.'

Bridie bent down to hug both children, noting that Livvy had tears flowing freely. 'I'm home to stay, darlings,' she cried, 'I love you both so much.'

Will joined in, and they were hugging and kissing one another, and holding the kids between them, and Bridie was making little snuffling sounds: wanting to show him that maybe she'd been wrong to run away like that.

'Darling, Bridie, I've missed you so much,' he almost groaned into her ear. 'Look, I know I haven't always been able to give you what you wanted, but....'

'Shh, darling,' Bridie whispered in his ear. 'You've given me these darlings, so what more could I want?'

'No, I feel like I've been unfair to you. Haven't given you what you deserve.'

'Darling, I'm fine. You don't have to....'

Now he was shooshing her: 'I've got a surprise for you. How would you like a modern house? High up on a hill overlooking the Karrana River? I'm working on it, darling, and with the Finn boys' help, it won't take too long to build. You'll have the dream home of your choice...get to decorate it with pretty things and anything you like.'

'Oh, Will, but where is it? I can't really think about it at the moment. I just want all of us to be healthy and happy. So long as I can help Richard with his reading and school work, I'll be happy as a .....' She was on the point of using Will's own expression 'a pig in mud' when she thought better of it. 'I've realised some things, too.'

'Bridie, I can see that this trip to Sydney has been good for you. We might make it a habit for you from time to time...to have a little break, you know?'

'Oh, Will' was all Bridie could say.

Chapter 37

The two children clung to Bridie, once she'd returned from visiting her mother in hospital. Standing there in the kitchen, in front of the hot wood stove, she thought how much she'd changed. She'd have shooed them away in older times. Now, she didn't want them out of her sight.

'How about cooking dinner fit for a king?' she cried.

'King Daddy,' shouted Livvy, clapping her hands together.

'Can I help?' begged Charlie, his face alight.

Will was now standing in the doorway watching, eyes glistening.

'Will, dear, we'll have a meal ready by the time you get back from visiting your parents.' News of his mother-in-law's ill health had sent waves of regret throughout his being. He needed to see his own mother and father, to know that they were all right.

'I'll be back in time to sample this amazing feast you're cooking up for me,' he said and maybe,' whispering into Bridie's ear, 'some alone time to catch up where we left off from, eh?'

'I'd like to visit Mumma in hospital again, but thankfully she's doing well,' Bridie smiled up at his twinkling eyes and nodded. *All in good time*, she thought.

'Will, I'm so sorry that you had to come back early because of my mother's heart attack.' She felt the same old whoosh of guilt spread upwards through her body.

'It runs in *my* family, this heart business, too,' he said. 'Luckily I don't take after that side of the tree.'

'Yes, you're like a bullock with that chest of yours and that energy,' she said, moving in close to him, placing her hands at the level of his heart, her eyes closed. She wanted to feel the blood pumping organ beating, to breathe in some of its spirit.

Will enclosed her body within his arms and planted a kiss on her crown.

'I'll tell Mum how your mother's getting on, and that we'll pass her blessing on to her in hospital.'

The next day, after the children were fed and safely in bed, she lit candles and listened to him talk about the Finns' wedding. And about how Richard was coming on.

'You know, I've really missed him,' she said, 'I'm so pleased to hear you say he's happy.'

'He's aware that his brain has changed, you know, Bridie. Gets a bit frustrated when he tries to do sums in his head, and he's reading like a beginner now. But he's okay with it, I think. I know it sounds funny, but it's as if he's using a different part of his brain, to balance out what he's lost. He's got in touch now with what I can only call instinct. Or something like that. Intuition, maybe. It's weird, he seems to know what I'm thinking sometimes. He knew that you were coming home. Don't know how.'

'You seem to be closer to him now than before,' she said. 'As if the part of his brain that's gone was the one keeping him away from you.'

'Yes, strange, isn't it? I like him more now than before. He's become my little mate.'

'Why didn't you bring him home with you?'

'Thought it better for him not to be around, with the news of your Mum's heart attack and all.'

'You're wise,' she said, 'but I'm dying to see him again.'

'Well, all in good time. The kids are in bed, so what about us, now?'

Bridie smiled up at him, as she took him by the hand and led him towards the bedroom. They were both laughing like two small children, *both mad*, she thought, as they tore off their clothes, threw themselves on to the quilt and turned towards one another.

She felt a stab of guilt and regret, but pushed them away like old drab coats, fit only for the rubbish dump.

'I love you, Will,' she whispered into his ear, and really meant it.

'Oh, Bridie,' he groaned, as he nestled into her hair. 'I thought the day would never come....'

'Sh ... I'm back for good now.'

She realised with a shock that it was she, Bridie Featherstone, who was leading the way in this bedroom pleasure romp now.

Something had changed in her, deep inside her core, was it inside her soul? She was a woman of the future now. The past was the past. She would look toward the new half century now with glee. Life was good. Luckily, her husband had no idea where her renewed sense of confidence and sensuality had come from. She hoped that he would never have to find out. Some secrets were meant to remain just that. After all, she'd learnt a lot about love as a by-product of her escapade. No sense in ignoring the benefits to their own relationship, was there?

She took to stoking the fire of Will's male sensuality once again. Feeling the ripples of pleasure erupting over them both like a tidal wave.

Flesh on flesh, they became as one, just as it had been in those early days.

When they lay back after the romp, she thought again about married life.

285

Yes, it was a prison, this union with Will, but it was a prison of love, and one to which she would happily surrender herself forever, if only … the guilt and the longing … would stay at bay.

There were always two sides to her, she thought once again, for the umpteenth time. And she'd just have to live with it.

On Saturday morning, Bridie clapped her hands and did a little jig around the clothesline in the backyard where she was hanging out washing.

'Let's all go pick Richard up from Tumbarumbar,' she said to Will. 'I'd like to catch up with Mabel Finn, such a warm hearted soul. And see what you men have been doing while I was away.'

Will had a smile as wide as a watermelon slice. He checked the landrover for the drive to the edge of the rainforest.

Bridie packed some offerings to take to the Finns' cattle station. She knew it would offend them if she packed a hamper for lunch.

The two children joined hands and spun around, falling on the grass in the sun and yelping like puppies:

'Gunna see Brother Richard again,' shouted Charlie.

'Hurrah,' sang Livvy.

'Yes, we're going to bring your brother back home where he belongs.' Bridie's words were blocked out by the children's voices. 'Gunna go to Tummba-rumbar, gunna go to Tummba-rumbar.'

She would teach her firstborn how to read once again.

'Can I drive part of the way?' she said as they set out. 'I must learn to handle this vehicle if I'm to drive the kids to school.'

'Yes, once we're out on the main road,' Will replied, pleased by the increased confidence and zeal he saw in his wife's demeanour. He felt proud of his part in it. He'd given her her freedom, like a little trapped bird set free, and she'd come back to him, renewed.

Bridie at the wheel slowed down as they neared the bridge at Halfway Creek. Will told her once again about the strange light he'd seen all those years ago, not long after the dance where they'd first met.

'I remember hearing on the news something about flying saucer viewings in the area,' she said. 'Did you actually see anything, apart from light?'

'No, but just because we can't see things, doesn't mean that they don't exist,' Will replied. 'I felt something was ghosting, following me, at the time.'

'I don't know,' she said. 'I like to have proof of things before I can believe in them.'

'I think that everything capable of being imagined is at least possible,' Will said. 'Take love for example. I can't see it, but I can feel it and I know it's there.'

This talk of love sent Bridie's mind into a spin. Into a place it didn't want to go. How could she ever keep the secret to herself? Of a love that now seemed to her to have taken place outside of time and space. A love that could never be spoken of to anyone.

As they turned into the road leading up to the homestead at Tumbarumbar, Bridie knew that Richard would be waiting for them. And he was. He came running towards the car, a look of pure joy lighting up his face as he ran along the side of the tree lined avenue, waving his arms around and whooping like a Red Indian. Bridie turned the engine off, got out of the car and left it to Will to park. She ran toward her son, arms outstretched.

'Oh, how I've missed you,' she whispered.

'I love you, Mummy,' he cried into her hair.

'I'll never leave you again, darling,' she whispered back, 'I promise.'

The other two children were racing towards them, screaming and crying out to their brother to look at them. 'Hey, you two,' he said, 'I missed you too.'

'Come in, come in,' shouted Stan Finn from the verandah. 'We've got a lunch fit for royalty here.'

And I've brought three offerings to add to the table,' said Bridie, holding out her gifts of eggs, cream and loquats from Hilltop Farm.

'Oh,' said Mabel, coming up from behind, 'just like the Three Magi. And are you celebrating the birth of a new wee one?' she said, looking down at Bridie's stomach.

'No, nothing like that,' Bridie said. 'But we're taking back a longed-for son.'

After lunch and conversation, followed by a trip to the citrus and macadamia orchards, and lastly a Devonshire afternoon tea, they were ready to set off for home, their family complete.

Bridie cuddled Richard in the back seat. On the way, they stopped at Reenie's place to say hello and to ask for news of Len.

Dogs ran out barking. Reenie, red-nosed and grinning, appeared in the doorway.

'Come round the back,' she cried. 'I've got a new foal and a baby joey to show the children.'

The palomino foal ran up to Richard and put out its nose to smell his outstretched hand.

'He knows you like animals,' Reenie said. 'When he's big enough, you can come and ride him.'

'Aunty Reenie, Aunty Reenie,' the little ones shouted. 'Show us the joey.'

'Their mother was shot,' she said, 'so I'm raising it by hand. Some cow cockies are shooting them to save the grass for feeding their stock. Nothing new under the sun.'

'So many baby animals here,' said Richard as he cuddled the tiny kangaroo and showed it to his sister and brother. 'I'd like to have a baby animal farm at our place.'

'All in good time,' said his father with a loving smile.

Chapter 38

Contentment was making her euphoric. She stood on the parapet of the new house, and looked out over fields to the west. Little did her husband know how close he might have come to losing her. But then, the fecundity of Nature, if nourished by natural laws, would always win out in the end.

She thought of her four gorgeous babies tucked up in beds in the new house that had become their castle. Ma Featherstone was only too pleased to stay at Deep Creek now from time to time. She had become chief babysitter, second only to Stella who wasn't always free. Ma liked the idea of having a second home here in the lushness of nature, where she could apply her well-schooled nurturing skills, and develop the bigness of her heart. It was never too late for that sort of expansion.

They'd moved in to the new house during the school holidays. Bridie knew that schooling would be a problem out here in the bush. She might have to drive them to school in Karrana, or consider home schooling, with the help of her husband for maths. Life was never plain sailing. There were always two sides to everything.

It was the middle of spring when she'd first realised her situation. Excited creatures, birds and mammals, were cosying up to mates in readiness for spring births. She'd wait until she was showing before she told her husband the news. Will was hand feeding the newborn calf with the white patch on its face around the time. The calf had tumbled out of its mother onto the soft verge near the creek bed the previous day. Will had looked at Bridie's enraptured face, and noticed how full-blown she was becoming, how blooming she looked; he was even more desirous of her.

'Bridie, that trip to Sydney was good for you,' he said, 'but not so good for me. I don't know that I could bear to part with you again ever....'

'Don't be silly, darling. Of course you could. But you won't have to.'

'Not for so long,' he added, 'at least.'

Within little more than one month after her return, Bridie had begun to feel the well-known signs of morning sickness, of another little being forming inside her body. She had waited before breaking the news to her husband.

Oh, no, she thought. This one certainly won't have been planned. What if it's Myer's and not Will's child?

It couldn't be. She remembered how careful Myer had been to keep her 'safe'. But she knew, too, that she was as fertile as the lush fields all about them. She fell pregnant only too easily, like the other creatures of the bush surrounding. The miracle of conception was the most natural, no supernatural, thing in this world, and could spring some surprises.

What if the baby came out looking Jewish? Was there even such a look? she wondered. Would Myer say '*Masel Tov*' to her if he saw that she was pregnant, that she was going to have another baby?

If it had those gorgeous black curls and darkly Semitic features, would anyone think anything of it?

There had been a couple of times when the phone had rung and there was no one there on the line when she answered.

Could it have been Myer, trying to say hello, to say goodbye, that he was still thinking about her?

She imagined him now in the house on the bay with his family. If she thought too much and too deeply about it, all the longing and the hunger would come rushing back in.

She realised that Myer had been right: there were many kinds of love, and they had experienced one unique sort, not offered to everyone. It was a love that reached out over time and space. She knew that he would carry this with him forever, as he had carried his love for the relatives he'd lost during the holocaust.

An infinite love that didn't need contact to exist.

She didn't want to go there just now.

But maybe, just maybe....

The end of the year was approaching. Will took Bridie along to the site of the new house for the first time. He would surprise her. She was about to surprise him with her news. Her figure was already filling out.

Mr Finn and his two sons had worked on the building alongside Will during the time she'd been away. 'We'd wanted you to build out our way, of course, Will,' they'd said. 'Still, it's good for Bridie to be near her mother and friends. This'll be like a palace up here on the rise.'

'Yes, Bridie'd fret away from her family and Karrana, I think,' Will had said.

She'd always talked about her love of Spanish style houses, of being drawn towards them. Photos in magazines, sparkling white homes she'd admired on the banks of the Karrana on the north side. But nothing like this....

She stood in front of it now and held her two hands together at her throat. Will watched her every facial movement. She had to hide her shock from him.

He was seeing her as a princess living in a castle surrounded by a moat. It was not how she saw herself.

The dwelling, situated halfway between Karrana and Tumbarumbar, stood about a mile from the Karrana River. It commanded a beautiful view of undulating cattle country, running down to fertile river flats, with the *Mounttain Ranges* as a background, surrounded by beef cattle country. The access roads had recently been improved, negating the necessity of punts to get there.

Will had lost no time in stocking the pastures with his favourite beasts. His herd of white faced Hereford cattle with their bright tan coats were populating the fields already. Profits had started pouring in, once he'd set his heart and will on the job.

She saw in her mind's eye, horses and ponies for the children to ride. She could see a dam for water for the animals and for the children to catch yabbies in. Later on, orchards of fruit trees and nuts could be grown.

There was a future here to look forward to for all of them.

But the house…

The Finn brothers had come and worked as if the wind was in their sails. Where they'd found the sandstone blocks, she had no idea, but find them they had. And bits of leftover *red gold* cedar timber for stairs and trimmings had appeared out of nowhere and were populating the plans for the building.

Will had leafed through Bridie's *Home Beautiful* magazines and found photographs and pictures of houses that she'd admired, which she'd marked with a biro, ages ago. He'd noted her likes and wishes and incorporated them into his grandiose plans.

He'd envisaged a charming and magical place, like royal homes and parks in the northern hemisphere, only lifted into an Aussie bushland setting.

It was going to be a castle fit for a queen.

'Oh, Will…,' she whispered, not taking her eyes off the shining structure that had risen up in the sunlight of a summer's day

In no way could she reveal her surprise and disappointment that he'd not allowed her in on the scheme.

She could imagine chandeliers, an Italianate fountain and stone lions to guard the front steps at some time in the future. Still, it was not what she'd imagined for herself, at all.

'I can't believe I'm going to have a gas stove and all the mod cons that I've been dreaming about from the *Women's Weekly* magazines,' she said.

'You're going to have the time of your life decorating this place,' Will told her.

She banished negative thoughts from her mind.

'It's beautiful, Will,' she said. 'If I can't be happy here, where can I be?'

She pushed thoughts of her stay in Sydney down, even as they struggled to come up like bunyips out of a billabong.

Just the knowledge that Myer was still in the world, was enough for her now.

Perhaps, one day in the future, she might be able to visit Sydney and stay at Aunt Annie's. Maybe with one or other of the children in tow? Richard, and the baby? Who knows?

As they stood now on the front balcony of their new home, Bridie was no longer the innocent farm maid who'd had to get married in a hurry. She knew what life expected of her as a wife and a mother now.

She looked back towards the Karrana River and thought:

That's the north-east.

That's where the sun rises.

That's where I wanted to live.

She would make something of her new life here, join the Karrana Library and read books. She'd have a library in her home. She'd invite friends and relatives to stay, have a dance floor and lots of music. She'd make her life bright in the country.

Modern ways were important to improving life,

But there was a dangerous side, too, to everything.

Perhaps this would be the best of both worlds.

Her fecundity, like that of Nature itself, was the *mother lode,* she'd been meant to explore and exploit. The multiple pregnancies that had occurred so quickly had pushed her to greater and greater catastrophes, but also to greater and greater heights.

There'd been a few bumps along the way, but they were all here together now, her family, heading away from war towards a new century.

From the tower they could see in all directions, north, south, east and west. They saw views over river and land. Will, standing beside her, looked like a ruler overseeing his bounties.

She knew she was a queen, at least in his eyes.

Was Fate the big unknown until it happened?

Or could you make inroads into your own destiny?

One day in the future, who knows....

Chapter 39

The War had long since finished, and peace was in the air. It was the first day of spring in this part of the world. They were well into the second half of the century.

Reenie had heard from the War Office that her husband's remains had been found and would be shipped back by boat, before the end of the year. She was sad, but the hours and days, weeks, months, years of hoping were coming to an end. She could, at least, now get on with her life.

Stella was in-between love affairs once again.

Bridie was already planning, in her mind, the huge housewarming party she would organise in their new home once they moved in. Hopefully, it would be large enough to put on a dance, organise music and all. She might even be able to hold a sort of ball for the extended family and friends.

And Bridie was relieved at the look of sheer joy on the face of her husband when he looked at the bonny baby in her arms.

The fourth Featherstone child had been born at the Camelot Hospital on May Day.

It's spring in the northern hemisphere and, I've given birth to a darling bud of May!

Dr Turnbrow, who had operated on Richard, had delivered the baby girl.

This child had slipped out easily from Bridie's practised womb. The baby girl didn't even cry. Just looked up through half-opened eyelids, blinking while seeking the light. Bridie had a sense that this one wanted to be here.

'She's a little beauty,' the doctor crowed, handing her into her mother's arms.'

'Oh,' she murmured … an olive-skinned angel's face, fringed with dark curls.

The name 'Esther' came to her as if from a hidden source.

Bridie ogled the baby, before kissing her still wet mop of a head, noting once again her olive skin and black curly hair. She kissed her on the forehead, letting her lips linger there. A little bump where the baby had probably pushed against her pubic bones.

'That's commonly called a 'stork bite' or 'angel kiss', Turnbrow said, indicating the faint pink blot on the baby's forehead, 'that will fade in time.'

'Oh…,' said Bridie, feeling a strange surge of pleasure.

'They're considered a blessing,' Turnbrow was saying, 'nothing that won't heal in time'.

'Thank you, Doctor, I'm so happy. She'll complete our family perfectly.'

'By the way, how is Richard? Myer Goldblum was asking about him recently. He was in town for a few days. I can pass on your good news.'

Bridie almost gasped, as she looked up into the doctor's features to see if she could read anything into his words.

'Richard is doing well, thank you, Doctor,' was all she could manage at first.

Then she added:

'Doctor Goldblum was an angel of mercy, the way he helped me with contacts and plans for Richard's recovery.'

'Yes, he's had to learn how to help his own poor child. So you went to the right person. As I said, I'll pass on your good news.

Will arrived full of joy from having heard the good news.

'Two boys and two girls' he crowed, 'a happy balance'.

There'd been a letter from Dr Myer Goldblum on the mantelpiece when Bridie had returned home from Sydney. It had been sent before her trip. It stated the name of the specialist he'd recommended for Richard to see. He'd made an appointment for them to meet, with him one year in advance.

It would be Will, this time, or both of them together, taking the whole family to Sydney for Richard's appointment. Henry Featherstone would just have to come good with financial assistance this time. Will would insist this time.

She opened her eyes when directed. There on the highest hill, overlooking the flats at Deep Creek, was the completed façade of a rustic building, dominated by a high tower. She was staring at a sandstone building shimmering in the sun with a space for a central garden and pond. It wasn't a house at all. It was a castle.

Bridie recognised in it a Moorish sort of design.

Will had envisioned the castle with Moroccan influences as the answer to Bridie's dreams. Stone and rubble had been quarried on the Finn cattle station, and leftover timber from the local bush had been brought to the site.

The building of a tower twenty feet high had been planned to the smallest details. There would be a drawing room for entertaining, a dining room of generous proportions with a high ceiling; an inner courtyard large enough for fish ponds and lush gardens.

They stood together in the completed castle at dusk, and looked out onto darkened fields to the west. Lights winked and twinkled at them from the far-off fields. The children, looked after by Ma Featherstone, were safe in bed downstairs.

She felt like one half of a whole once more. The river would not be there separating them anymore. It was off in the distance, far enough away to enjoy, but no longer a dividing line between them and now what was causing the display far off in the fields, fireflies, the tiny carnivorous beetles and their maggot-like larvae called glow worms. But what were they hiding? What was the truth? Where was it to be found?

She wasn't sure what she was musing about. One day she might be able to study. Improve her brain capacity. But for the moment she was contented with her lot, if not happy as a pig in mud.

Suddenly the whole bush was lit up with dancing lights.

There is the answer, she thought, right out there.

But there was no answer.

Everyone went over to The Castle to meet the new baby. It would be a sort of housewarming party, too. But not as grand as the one she had in mind for later on. They each commented on who the girl baby looked like, what she weighed and how clever she would be. Knowing who in the family she resembled was paramount. *They were all so interested in genetics*!

Grandma O'Toole, well again after her heart attack stint in hospital, was there. Even Stella, without her doctor, who'd not been able to relocate to Karrana, was there.

Perhaps she'd invite Rick and Annie to the grand ball she was preparing in her mind. And, of course, all the Finns and Reenie…. Only one person would have to be absent, she thought. Or would he? He'd always be present in her mind somewhere, that was for certain.

'I'm sure it was nine months to the day from when you returned,' Will whispered in Bridie's ear, 'that we conceived this little one.'

'Yes, I've got to give it to you, Will,' said Ned, as virile as that bull out there in the paddock.'

'A bullock of a man, and with a heart to match,' whispered Bridie in his ear.

Everyone *oohed* and *ahhed* at how beautiful the new baby was.

'Look at that dark hair!' said Billy. 'Like yours, Bridie.'

'Yes, she looks just like you, Bridie,' said Grandma O'Toole. 'You had real dark hair when you were born.'

'Yes, I did have that sort of hair … I remember … from photos,' Bridie mumbled, 'but not so curly.'

'Well, then, maybe that's where the olive skin and dark looks come from,' said Ma Featherstone, 'it's certainly not from our side of the family. Charming, nonetheless.'

'May I nurse the baby?' asked Pa.

'At least she isn't red-headed,' said Johnny. And then, after a pause, 'Could pass for a little picaninny.'

The three children sat on the settee and took turns at nursing her.

'There, you see, plenty of babysitters this time, Bridie,' laughed Billy, who wanted a nurse of the baby in his turn.

She was passed around to Stella and Reenie, who was no longer waiting to hear news of her husband, since his remains had been repatriated.

'Born into love, this little one,' from Johnny, the black sheep of the family, 'no doubt about it.'

'And you know who's going to be the best minder of all,' said Bridie proudly, pointing to Richard, who was stroking the baby's forehead at this moment.

'I've loved her since she was a tiny speck in Mummy's tummy,' said Richard. 'I don't care who she looks like. She's my littlest sister and I love her.'

Beer was brought out to celebrate.

A kookaburra laughed outside in a tree.

And at that moment, the whole bush seemed to laugh.

It's gonna be alright, Bridie said to herself, slipping back into her old ways of speaking, *and I've loved honestly and truthfully without hurting anyone. So long as Will doesn't find out...*

'You're right, Richard,' someone called out. 'It's all about love, not war...'

'Let's put some dance music on,' said Johnny. 'I've got itchy feet from sittin' around looking at this little one.'

'Yes,' called out Stella, jumping to her feet and turning on the gramophone, while pulling Johnny along after her. 'This place is ideal for a dance, even a ball.'

The adults and children jumped to their feet as the strains of Johnny Rae's and The Four Lads' modern music lit up the house with its rollicking modern sounds.

Other songs that were played this afternoon were *Three Coins in a Fountain, Till the End of Time, Oh My Papa, and Stanger in Paradise,* sung by popular crooners Perry Como and Eddie Fisher. At a certain moment, the whole party was on its feet, dancing and singing in tune to the nostalgic lyrics and rousing melodies.

Bridie, who was dancing with Will, drowned out the voice of the current crooner as she shouted: 'Let's have some female singers for a change!' She pulled gently away from her husband and put on some tunes sung by Rosemary Clooney and Doris Day. At a later point in time, she found the Vera Lynn recording of *We'll Meet Again,* and there were tears in everyone's eyes as they got up and waltzed to this.

She picked up her crying infant and sat this one out as she listened to the dusky voice, holding her baby girl in her arms and feeding her.

No one noticed the tears trickling down Bridie's cheeks, and if they did, they never doubted that these were tears of happiness and of joy.

About the Author

Anne Skyvington is one of five siblings born into a country family in rural New South Wales, Australia. After leaving her rural origins, she qualified as a teacher and spent some years in Paris, France, before returning to Sydney. Much of her writing today is informed by the bushland setting of her childhood. She holds two Master Degree qualifications, one in French language and literature, and another in creative writing. Anne lives near the beach with her husband in the Eastern Suburbs of Sydney.

www.ingramcontent.com/pod-product-compliance
Lightning Source LLC
Chambersburg PA
CBHW071251170626
46809CB00001B/165